First Printing: 2018

ISBN 978-1-9993471-0-9 (eBook)

ISBN 978-1-9993471-1-6 (Paperback)

ISBN 978-1-9993471-2-3 (Hardback)

Offworld Publishing

www.offworldpublishing.com

This novel's story and characters are fictitious. Certain long-standing institutions, agencies, and public offices are mentioned, but the characters involved are wholly imaginary.

CONTENTS

1   The Battle of O'Hara's Bar

It was just a low hum at first. Then it started to wobble and get louder. More and more noises and tones got involved. He started to recognize some of the sounds and the sensation in his body started to return. He suddenly felt himself running and running fast. He was out of breath and exhausted and, just as he thought he couldn't run any further, the black void ahead of him started to warp. It stretched and popped and ripped open and birthed him into this new scene at full tilt. Lasers were firing off all round him, ripping shit and hellfire out of everything. Everything was on fire. There was a car. Swallow dive behind that car right now. Alternatively, trip over something large, feel the sting of it on his foot, then feel the sting of landing on other large metal things behind the old burnt out car. Either way, safe. The lasers were focused on the car now. Pieces were starting to melt off it but it was holding.

Jesus, wasn't he just in a car park somewhere?

He wasn't surprised to be dumped into a place he couldn't explain but this was pushing it. His descent without ropes into this bizarre state of existence over the last couple of months was clearly continuing and in some style. The descent without ropes into the bourbon bottle probably wasn't helping.

What on God's green Earth had he been shat into this time? It didn't feel like a dream and the VR games he played were good but nothing like this good.

Every corner he turned or blink he took could morph into something and somewhere else but his mind was always on the single most important thing he'd ever have to do, the thing that dropped him into the bottle in the first place and he still didn't have the answer. It was the only thing that was ever consistent in his mind.

Other than that, just flash memories of his life mixed with memories of these jumps to other places, like this street, jumps to other times, sometimes jumps into other creatures, once there was a jump into something a lot smaller than an ant, talking to an ant called Pete.

He'd long since passed the WTF stage but it was becoming more difficult to tell where any particular memory came from, a movie? A dream? A game, a real memory of his real life or one of these spacetime jumps? What was real and what wasn't? What was this street he was in now?

Right now though, here he was, nothing he could do about it, dumped into this chaos, looking like its sole target. Wondering why would have to wait. His head was throbbing. It felt like the morning after a fat session in the bar, with Tony probably. He couldn't remember being in a bar with Tony last night but then again he couldn't remember anything about last night.

It felt worse than a hangover. It was like someone with little else to do was sitting on his shoulders, dropping a big hammer on his head every few seconds, pulsing shudders all through him, possibly whispering something about dogs.

In any other situation, ideally a situation where he was watching it in a movie from a nice soft couch with a beer and tortilla chips rather than dropped here in the middle of it, he'd have been mourning the steady demise of this beautiful old car protecting him, but right now he needed to simply accept he was here and get with the programme. It looked like anytime soon these lasers would make their way to the fuel tank or directly into him. And either way that was him fucked. This was no way for your average computer programmer to spend the afternoon but there was no time to attempt any mulling over of things, just get the flock out of here.

The street and it's bars and alleys were torn into illogical piles. Salvador got a sharp twinge when something was illogical. It shouldn't be happening. It was a kind of enema, invasion by unnatural forces.

The scraping metallic noise and smell of everything burning conspired to paralyse him. He was now becoming slowly joined to the car. The heat and smoke had started to overwhelm his breathable air and shrapnel and molten metal flew around him, bouncing off other cars and walls.

He checked over himself. It looked like he had all his arms and legs and he could always see the blurred tip of his damn silly nose pretty much everywhere his eyes went, like the virtual gun in a video game. He seemed to be the same lump of human he should be.

Then a fracture in the chaos appeared and suggested the potential for some strategic thought. Salvador stole a slitted peek under the car and started to unwrap himself to consider escape.

He was bedraggled and desperate but critically he had no gun or laser or anything. The only thing left to him was chucking rocks and maybe a little shit like a chimp. He thought for a split second, if this was a dream, could he think about having a laser and one would appear for him? So he did. But it didn't. Not that kind of dream.

The people shooting at him had to be getting closer. He couldn't see any comrades, if he'd ever had any. His plan had to start and finish with retreat and escape. Maybe soon he'd materialise somewhere a little softer, like a nice quiet bar.

Salvador sensed the urge to drift into thoughts of the bar and its chatter and chuckles, chunky glass, one cube of ice and three fingers of God's own tipple in his hand, but he was swayed back to licking his lips in the here and now. 'Stop drifting you bonehead. Concentrate,' he said.

Who were these people coming after him? Government? Terrorists? Was he the terrorist in this scene? Maybe they were freedom fighters. Why were they pissed off at him?

Maybe this lot were a different kind of freedom fighter, as much freedom fighters as Butch and Sundance, freedom fighters that freed money from kidnap victim's parents and liquor stores, no more a cause than a dirty weekend, inventive enough way to commit suicide.

But right now it didn't matter who they were. It was clear they would throw this fire down until there was nothing but vaporised matter and the fire itself left. Salvador needed to find a sanctuary and a safe route to it.

He scanned around through the smoke. There. An alleyway thirty yards away. If they were in there too, he'd already have been taking fire from it. It could be a dead end or could lead him to at least a chance to escape and anyway what else was there?

There was an upturned bus about ten yards in front of him. The direction of fire from behind would nail him all the way to it but the ten yards he had to the bus was better than trying the straight thirty to the alley.

His watch said 6pm. He had no idea what day 6pm but it looked like it'd be dark inside an hour. Maybe he could get to the bus and hold out till it was but then what? An hour seemed an awful long time right now.

It was an inconvenient time for it to happen but out of the corner of his eye he noticed something unusual. There was a blurred semi transparent figure hovering along the far side of the street against what used to be the shop fronts. It stopped long enough to know he was here and he felt it scan him but then vanished and instantly reappeared five yards further on.

Salvador rubbed his eyes but it was still there, glistening.

Was this his grim reaper, courier for his trip to the hereafter? As soon as the thought stuck, the apparition vanished again and this time stayed gone. It seemed to have no physical form but it was definitely there. This apparition suggested this place might not be real. Was it that sort of dream?

Suddenly laser fire exited three feet from him through the driver's door. His cover was disintegrating. He tried to vocalise his terror but his dry throat managed only a series of squawks, like a ventriloquist's first karaoke. 'Fine,' he thought. He didn't like a long debate anyway. He stared into mid nowhere, emptying his mind of everything but his goal.

'3... 2...'

He took what might have been one of his last breaths and launched himself towards the school bus, his mind buzzing like a wasp round an open fridge.

He put his best dancing shoes on and he was into the salamander swing, weaving side to side, changing angles, trying to make sure he was no still target for them behind him.

With the sweat pouring over his eyebrows stinging into his eyes, he expected the crackle and agony of his back tearing apart at any moment. He'd heard about getting hit by a regular snipers from his buddies. One guy said he'd never forget it, nor would the medics who had to sew it back on. But this laser stuff was another level.

Every yard Salvador was closer to safety, six to go and his hair was parted by a laser and another beam dismantled a wing mirror just behind him, four to go and two beams merged to take a slice out of another car. It was time for a headlong dive to the end zone. The buzzing in his head subsided with a jolt as he landed hard and slid on his belly to the safety of the bus.

The incoming fire was now hitting some three yards away from him through a lot more metal than the old car he'd left behind, which was now in flames and kicking off thick black smoke.

Stage one complete, now the twenty yard straight dash of death to the alleyway. Salvador decided thinking was surrender, instinct ruled this. He got his head down and took off over fallen masonry, car parts and all sorts of burning things. He even noticed a tiny pair of kids shoes peeking out from under a car and had to wonder if their little owner could possibly be OK. He was weaving and jumping, crouching and sliding and before he knew it, he smashed into the far wall of the alley, and hit the floor between its walls. The diverted incoming fire was slow to anticipate it but now created an angry flaming frame of the alley entrance like the start of a magic show before some sparkly suit in a wig minces in.

There was no time to celebrate. He took himself down the alley and just followed where it took him, a right, a quick left then up some stone steps, over a four foot railing and then a lot more steps but these steps looked like they led to trees, cover, maybe a way out.

The sense of home, a different scene, anything but this, sent him up those steps like an athlete. His heart and legs brought him out onto a flat roof, and beyond that, what looked like a decent sized gap to a cliff face with a toupee of trees. Even before he got close enough to know the size of the gap, he knew this was his only route. There were no options left or right. He couldn't stop now. He was hearing angry voices close behind him.

Twenty yards from the edge he figured it was at least a five yard long jump and two yards up in the bargain. His grab-on area was a chalk edge and there would be plenty of barney rubble.

Either he made it or he'd die in the fall or he'd die when they caught up to him, teetering at the mercy of their every desire. They'd smile and look forward to later ales, seeing which bits they could slice off without making him fall, then slice off that final bit that sends him down.

Six paces from the edge he knew he'd take off on his left, he summoned all his demons for the final planting on the roof edge and hit it sweetly.

Just as he was about to hit the rock face, he prepared for a painful touchdown but he didn't grip onto solid rock and barney rubble, he grabbed onto a large circular table. The idea was the same, do not let go but this table went over on top of him as he fell back. A healthy collection of beers and glasses and all sorts of breakables hit the floor and the six or seven people sitting round the table.

This wasn't what he was expecting but what ever was? The six or seven people sitting around the table were his old buddies from college. It was a relief not to have another battle start here. He even had his UCLA jacket on. His buddies hit the floor laughing and spilled almost as much beer as he just did. Their buddy, this Salvador, had surely taken the prize for being the most wasted, some several hours before winners were even meant to be announced.

Salvador got up, confused. Not a sound came out of him. His heart rate slowed from battlefield to bar but he had to check behind him and make sure there wasn't any more of that laser fire about to spray the whole place. He still smelt the orange burn of the firestorm in the town he'd just escaped. He was pleasantly surprised that his idle fancy of jumping to a bar had become just that, or had he been asleep and dreamed it all? Not possible. If he'd dropped off with this lot, things would been done to him. He checked. Things hadn't been done to him.

It took his buddies several seconds to collect themselves. Sammy Jahania recounted to him what he couldn't recount himself. There they all were, they'd been there all day, several ales later, and suddenly, flying in at full tilt from the back, came this great Salvador. He'd launched with a gorgeous and committed swallow dive at the table, grabbing on for dear life, not releasing his fierce control of it until it was on top of him. Sammy was on the chair opposite Salvador when it happened. Sammy saw Salvador grab on, open his eyes wide in shock and horror and sink below his line of sight as everything collapsed onto him. Sammy lost it again and just prolonged their agony for several more seconds.

This was their favorite bar when Salvador was at UCLA, O'Hara's on Gayley Avenue, but this wasn't a reunion drink, this was back then while he was still at college. He hadn't seen these guys for years. Sammy and John Ardle died in Afghanistan a few years after he left UCLA but here they were again. Sammy and John were surprised at the sudden ferocious hugs and some poorly hidden tears they got from Salvador and poured some more beer over him.

Salvador remembered them like it was yesterday. Sammy and John had their transport dismantled in a landmine and mortar attack combo and one or two of the other guys told him, sure they got back, but what happened to them after they came back wasn't easy.

They introduced him to the concept of post conflict life, how these boys couldn't deal with humans who weren't trying to kill them or kill with them. They'd be hanging in there with their wives and kids and Sundays and ice cream but they wouldn't make it easy to be loved.

They'd try and re-absorb themselves into the thing they were fighting for but it was the new enemy, an enemy that didn't fight back, just loved them. They couldn't deal with it but they had to deal with it or they'd end up like that old guy selling flags at the bus stop.

All they could see, when not in places like Salvador had just come from, were their wives and babies and their only dream was to get to know them again.

Many of them had contracted out of the Marines years ago and went for the short sharp shock, private contracts, a shed full of rapid cash and early retirement with the family. They didn't figure on the several small wars or how much they'd love it. They also didn't figure on how much they were having transferred into their accounts every week.

Pete Suarez had been in that hummer when the attack came in and pulled everyone out but it was too late for Sammy. John hung on for a few seconds longer but, with his injuries, the only thing Pete could do was take him in his arms and talk to him as he drifted off. Pete said he'd never forget the last words to come out of John before he went. John was already in a different place. Who knows, maybe it's prophetic, maybe it's just the brain dying.

John grabbed a handful of sand and his breathing calmed as he watched it trickle through his fingers.

'This is the coolest beach I've ever been to, Pop,' he said. 'Look at that awesome car. Can I have an ice cream?' and he was gone.

Pete was quiet for a while. It wasn't a moment you get anywhere near interrupting. It would have the same effect on Pete as long as he lived. Pete reckoned John was a kid again on some beach with his folks, what a lovely way to go out, living in the best day of your life. Maybe that's why people who don't quite die think there's a heaven.

Here, back in O'Hara's all those years ago, Salvador just enjoyed the moments he'd never have with them again, a different take on the same day. They all looked so happy over there, trouble free. Later, whether it was in the marines or whatever the other guys ended up doing, Mitch went into banking, Danny designed houses, every last one of them shared in the one thing Salvador didn't have, kids. It all seemed so simple for them, here they were younger, wasted and just happy. Compared to them, there was a big fat lump missing from Salvador's life and pretty much most of the time he was entertaining the blackest thoughts of losing the one person put on this Earth to be with him.

He had no idea why he was here in O'Hara's any more than why he'd been in that battle before or anywhere else. Whatever was happening to him wasn't helping his situation and his own mission, the only thing he had to do. It still didn't feel like a dream but it sure was behaving like one.

As the buzz of the guys mellowed, Salvador took a subtle few seconds to run his hands over himself to feel for any damage, expecting at least some sudden pain but he was fine.

He was exhausted, the adrenalin from his last scene and the beers from this one combined to remind him what sleep might be like. He wasn't sure he remembered the last time he slept.

Pretty soon he couldn't help yawning and closing his eyes in the process, anticipating the ridicule to come at him, but this scene had already been replaced.

 That's not my Dog

This time it was more normal, more like where Salvador was supposed to be, this might be real life if such a thing exists. He did know this place though. It looked like he was back to the here and now. He was standing on the corner of El Camino and Verdugo street. It felt like he still had a filthy hangover. He started to scan around his surroundings to make sure he was where he thought and check for any signs of pixelation, things vanishing, anything that didn't sit right, but life simmered on as usual.

As happens in the early stages of the worst hangovers, there was an onset of the deepest embarrassment, that cold shudder up the spine that closes your eyes and starts to tell you what you did wrong last night. You start formulating plans for the apologies you'll need to make. You may even have to return someone's front door.

He remembered waking up naked in his car, looking around it for his keys. They weren't anywhere in the car but finally he saw they were over there, ten yards away on the floor of the mall car park. It was pointless to wonder how. A quick sprint to retrieve the keys wasn't quick enough to avoid being seen by a woman and her very young daughter, preparing to deposit groceries in their car.

They were suddenly glued to the spot as his bare dick flapped past them and then his bare arse got back in his car and fucked off. Hopefully the daughter wasn't too indelibly affected. Salvador quickly checked he was still wearing clothes. Normal clothes. Good. Right now let's see how normal the rest of the day is.

He shook out the recollection of that apparition skimming along the other side of the street watching him, moving in and out of dimensions but not able to stick in this one for whatever it needed to do.

It was like the moments before seeing a spider. He hated spiders. To him they were ambitious alien invaders hell bent on enslaving and generally sitting on mankind. You know you've seen it out of the corner of your eye, you know what it is but you don't know where it's gone.

When he was in the mood to see spiders, everything looked like a spider, a piece of mud off his boots, a dropped mushroom from lunch. String tended to gang up on him to form the finest replicas but whatever it was, he was not at ease.

He knew being afraid of spiders was irrational. He'd started his relationship with them in awe of their place in the world, sitting outside Larry Gomez's place while his parents argued inside. He saw a spider appear in the bushes growing round the top of the gazebo, it approached, analysed and then wrapped up an errant moth trapped in its web.

It spun the moth up like fresh candy floss, injected its digestive fluid into the poor thing and nonchalantly fucked off to consider something else. It returned later for a fine supper courtesy of the melted insides of the moth. An efficient way to feed, if a little cold, and only if it's confident an even bigger nasty thing wasn't about to come and do nasty things to it as well.

Larry and Salvador wondered what it would feel like to be encased, stuck fast and then have something drill through your coffin into you and inject oomska to dissolve you from the inside. Having that oomska, mixed with you and sucked back out again at feeding time would not be your problem.

Salvador eased his oncoming sweat and then remembered O'Hara's. So that's where the hangover came from but it couldn't be. He thought the battle was a dream when he was in O'Hara's but now he's here was O'Hara's a dream? It was the past when he was at college, years ago. How could a dream of getting wasted years ago give him a hangover today and what was he doing naked in a car?

If it was a dream, how come he was now standing on the corner of El Camino and Verdugo this sunny morning and not in bed where dreams are supposed to kick you out. Maybe he slept standing up right here like a drunk horse. Maybe it's still a dream, level three. Salvador thought of his bed, that soft cool, cosy bed. He knew he had a bed. He knew where he lived.

He was dirty and exhausted and luckily of no interest to anyone else. He reminded himself never to expect anything to be as it seemed. There could be cops seeking his bare arse for a variety of reasons but, so far, all was well and calm here.

He hadn't got any sort of handle on why all this suddenly started happening to him. He never knew how long he had in wherever it was until he was dumped somewhere else.

The whole idea was chaotic. Who knows where he might suddenly emerge, maybe with a beard and some injuries? Maybe it was like narcolepsy, he falls asleep with his face in spaghetti and trips off to some place, returning at a time not of his making. It removed any notion of free will.

He thought about talking to doctors about it but what was the point? The first thing they would do is fumble for the panic button under their desk, possibly insert something into him and then the white van would turn up with two calmly spoken guys telling him everything was going to be alright.

He had no idea which day this was but maybe he could resume his life and resume his quest for the answer to his problem.

'Fuck,' he said loudly enough to check he wasn't heard.

Being seen shouting at himself in the street wouldn't help. Things kept piling up, slowing him down but there was only one way through it. Keep trying. Keep fighting wherever he gets jumped. He needed to try and figure out when jumps were about to happen. Maybe then he could figure out how to stop them.

The booze had become a bit of a problem. The longer he didn't find the answer, the more the booze helped. Booze numbed the gut pain of every new day. It was his epidural. The thing is it sometimes did help address the problem but also landed him in a fair bit of trouble, a tedious irony. And with this who-knows-where-the-fuck-I-am situation, perhaps the booze needed to back off, or not.

He'd had friendly words and some very loving support from the folks round here but, as the months wore on and the bottles piled up, this waned, became more covert whispers, he was drunk again, tragic, scruffy, damaged and angry.

Today he was definitely a mess. He felt like he'd carried through the sweat and dirt and beer from where he'd been before. He looked like someone who should smell bad, might well swear at you for no reason and in fairness, some people deserve and ultimately benefit from being called an asshole for no reason.

Today though he felt feeble, atrophied and hunched up like an old rag tag Fagin battling the cold of a London January, like influenza if it took human form.

On the days he didn't turn to the bottle, he scrubbed up just fine. That was the Salvador this town knew and loved. They always said they could see his smile coming from round the corner. It was infectious. That was the Salvador they could nurse through this horrible time, this Salvador was harder.

Salvador had skills, computer programming skills. He wasn't some teenage prodigy or super rich tech maestro but he was solid and adaptable and even more curious. He was just a good coder and innovative. He was a smart hippy, about six two, unusual good looks even with his big nose, the sort of look girls liked.

Smart girls look a little deeper. Sure, physical attraction is important and Salvador's floppy dark hair and blue eyes just about cleared that hurdle but it's more a confidence and demeanour thing for smart girls. They want love and naughtiness like the rest of us but they also want a mate capable of knocking up some decent kids and a certain outlook on life, an intuition to match their own, that special something. Salvador was lucky enough to have a bit of that.

Salvador and his team designed and built VR stuff. The company he worked for, Net Nano, was kicked into this world due to two speculative but inspired ideas. Why couldn't you bounce light off water droplets in the air to see millions of miles round corners? As it turned out, you could, and they did.

The other idea was the cleaning project. Nanobots fly around inside you and clear away cholesterol and other gooey shit in your arteries, eventually reducing it to newborn levels. The bots latch onto the nasty gooey shit and each one chews off a tiny amount. When they're full, they exit via a magnetic outlet point and on it goes. A few sessions over a few months and you could be permanently de-coked. Early on, the extraction side of it hit problems and the bots ended up staying in the bloodstream and making a lot of problems. But the extraction theory was basically sound and here we are with a serious company, now in San Juan over on Great Heights.

Net Nano was one of those places people liked to talk about. The grey, tinted window high security building had to be aliens or some other flavour of conspiracy. Apparently they had military contracts and these people used to say *what they did* wasn't software development.'

It kind of was though, give or take this and that, and like it said on the tin, they dabbled in the very tiny. It'd been suggested that Net Nano created tiny artificial intelligent viruses capable of many thousands of miles wind deployment, LA to Hanoi or Kabul to New York.

Salvador was prohibited under penalty of all sorts of horrors to make further comment on it, apparently nipples and frontal lobes were at risk. That was the thing about government contracts, once you were in, you were in, deep down in. He got the impression from the stooges suddenly materialising onto him from behind doors to check up on him that once they were done he could easily be flushed, loose ends and all that. They just had to keep them dangling with the next idea. Run out of ideas and hold your nose.

The company also more than dabbled in the production of virtual reality environments and that's where Salvador earned his crust. It was all he ever wanted to do since he first heard about VR. With his current situation, it brought him the chance to design worlds when his own brought no such design.

VR had come a long long way from the massive glove, walk on the moon sized head gear and an orange cube limping around a big lump of monitor. Today's VR can take you anywhere, murder on the Orient Express or, as one magazine reviewed it. 'Piss wet through from ancient Egyptian pussy in Cleopatra's bedchamber' or you could indeed 'attack ships on fire off the shoulder of Orion.'

Sometimes there would be a few glitches, shadows, pixelation, some distortion, the occasional mini freeze frame, a bit like that apparition in the street before. Laser fire would freeze and the soldiers would wobble a bit, no way to conduct a serious battle.

It was annoying enough when your PC started dicking about, those days when everything on it needed updating just when you needed it and eventually you forget why you sat down in front of the damn thing in the first place.

But when you're immersed in a VR programme, any interruption is a deeper interruption. It raises the fury, extracts you from paradise and deposits you in the mundane. Take the controller off any twelve-year-old and see that same fury.

Kids who'd been in VR and then came out of it couldn't hide their emotions and they were immediately disappointed re-entering the real world. Their little faces all full of para-chuting into a volcano to surf on lava were suddenly on the way to school on a Monday morning.

He knew some players lingered in VR space for a short time even when they were out of the programme, only shaking it off some time after they rejoined the real world. That pixelated creature in that laser street can happen, he thought, things could easily vanish and reappear standing in a different spot.

The Net Nano 'Neuronet' interactive VR system was next level. It was a system that could make you physically feel your virtual environment. It sent electrical impulses into specific areas of your brain and the brain was fooled into producing the required physical feelings. If you got a jab in the ribs you felt it. If you stubbed your toe you felt it. You could feel a warm sun, a cool breeze and as that same maga-zine put it. 'You could definitely feel a blowjob.' Not only that, it recorded your brain activity when you experienced something and stored it. You could access and re-experience a file of your own emotions. You couldn't get better than literally controlling your own emotions not to mention controlling the emotions of others, hence the DOD being around.

VR coders like Salvador raced to create lucrative new signals to make the user feel different things. Naturally most of this early work focused on orgasms enhanced to a frightening and messy degree, mostly for women.

As with most things, a few idiots always came along and had to spoil it. There had been plenty of hacks. Unfortunate players had experienced first the snakebite, which prevented you from using the controls, lost and spinning in virtual space, and then, once you were suitably VR roofied, came the hit. This was what they really wanted you to sit through. In one case the hit was a ten hour acid trip in a coffin instead of 'Monica comes round for Breakfast.' It was indicative of the Neuronet's real power that players failed to simply abort by removing their headgear. To them there was no headgear, where they were was real.

Coca Cola even sponsored the design of some of their VR headsets and added the strapline 'if you think you're buzzed now, have a coke.'

Net Nano had been good enough to give Salvador an extended leave of absence to get himself together after it happened. He would have been pointless to them anyway, just moping around, ruining the energy. Once he'd picked up the bottle, they were super glad they did.

Was it all a VR trip? The idea he was dreaming had been shot down because he'd be aware he's in a dream. Dreams don't work like that, but VR can. He looked around the edges of his field of vision. He knew the street. Was anything different?

He thought his mind was jumping into the body of himself or whichever creature it might be, jumping into whichever time or place it decided to drop him, the body of Salvador at the time but with today's head on him, a game character thrown into another level but who's playing the game? In O'Hara's, he wasn't reliving a scene from the past, following a preset, he was adding to it, creating something that didn't happen at the time, part of a whole new scene, like an overlay of how it might have happened in another dimension. The battle? Who knows. Maybe that was his future?

Back in this sunny street scene, he continued to make some quick moves to try and uncover if all this was VR, but there was still no obvious controller and there had to be a way to control it, and if it was VR, how the hell could they get this place so real? If it was VR, there was a next level company out there designing it. He thought about government conspiracies and new drugs designed to trap people in controlled VR environments. Surely not.

So, what of him in this street right now? He needed at least one more notch cut in his belt. His jeans made him look like some rapper, crotch hung so low to suggest a fictional cock and balls of epic proportion, the majesty of an elephant cock transplanted into 501s.

His shirt smelled like his old dog's bed and he oozed out onto the open space of the sidewalk and tried to convince himself he was ready for the day. His head was still hurting and still numb, which was a concern. The bright sunlight troubled him and he reached for the shades in his back pocket, concealers of excess, the stalker's friend. He took a breath and absorbed what appeared to him.

Galvanised though he may have been by his anonymity, he was still unsure of these new surroundings, like a duckling approaching the water's edge for the first time, small flappy advances and retreats until splashdown. He knew where he was but when was it and could some giant reptilian suddenly emerge and start taking bites out of the buildings?

His primary near term goal right now was avoid people. He needed sleep, he knew that. Maybe it was another dimension when he jumped, a place like this but down the rabbit hole. Anyway, the jumps and then trying to analyse the jumps and handling his real life situation ganged up on him and a cool bed was what he wanted.

After it happened and his main problem started, he had to face the very big questions that went through his mind, the realities of life and death. He thought, in the end, what have we got to leave behind for our descendants or any other being that may be here at the time? Would history still be recorded? Surely they'd know we were once apes, then men with big sticks, then hunter gatherers with tools, then farmers with proper tools, and finally men with no tools just little annoying machines, wondering how little they can possibly get away with putting into a big box.

By and large, men were the hunters and women were the gatherers but you can imagine some poor sod, terrified all the time, perhaps more in tune than most with the shit box era he'd ended up in, trying to avoid the dangerous stuff. He might have joined the girls for a bit of gathering. Maybe it was better for a man to be a hunter than a gatherer, far more sexy, but if you become the peer, the ear and the friend of a gatherer you stay in tune with all of humanity and you might get a bit of saucy cheekiness from time to time in the bargain. And who knows one day, the gatherers may call the shots.

But what would we leave behind? Salvador was a mug for the shows about aliens and space and weird stuff on the discovery channel and one of them covered it. The show reckoned it depends what had happened to us. We store huge amounts of data in deep cooled storage areas but that relies on cooling and maintenance. If that starts to perish over time, whoever stumbles upon our once beautiful world might find only evidence of reality TV shows and consider us a fairly futile waste of air.

They may well giggle at our departing truth, we'd flitted from place to place finding new places to infect and we'd finally shat on ourselves and gone the way of the dinosaurs, coming up a mere hundred and sixty five million years shy of their record. Makes you wonder if anything is really worth it or should we just be concentrating on our next plane of existence. It's not clear if these temporal worlds are meant for us humans. Maybe they were meant for the dinosaurs.

It was a quiet early morning here on El Camino. The bright warm sunshine hovered over the street and sent the willows lining it to graffiti the colorful shops alongside.

The first place on the right just over from him was Brannigans, the town bakery and cafe. Joe Brannigan had the honour of running the only commercial enterprise to border and be allowed to place tables in the Town Square. He was a cantankerous old relic but he was also a canny operator and he knew some forty years ago that there was only one place to deposit a bakery and cafe here in San Juan, CA.

There were purveyors of various beads and braids, hats and hammocks and the like, owners perhaps formerly of San Francisco. How did they have the patience every day to painstakingly move it all outside, put it up on display and then take it all back inside a few hours later? He wondered if they've considered holograms.

You could lay your hands on a damn fine coffee, pancakes, gun accessories, sweet smelling flowers and a general store complete with its very own aproned Nels Oleson.

All was well, the American dream in its own magazine, picturesque perfect, only $3.99 little San Juan, a Southern California jewel.

People behaved themselves here. Respect. Charity and Credit.

There was just one small note of abstract dissent occupying most of town notice board on the Ortega Road side of the square. In bold red paint the words 'that's not my dog' sat effortlessly over the messages beneath. Another Che was alive and well but possibly abusing substances. Its simplicity and confidence with itself was beautiful, majestic. 'Publish that fucker,' he thought.

Odds are it was one the town's smarter high schoolers, little swines, squelching around the place crackling and being generally happy, terrorists. This one was calmly and slowly subduing his prey by base confusion. Delicious, impeccable panache.

'This could become very watchable,' he said to himself.

But right now the town worthies, bound like marines by the black arts of gardening, fishing and shooting something, were happy and collected in various locations around town doing their thing, the majority of them over there at Brannigans.

The sun unfurled flora and fauna to the new day. A few people were gathered across the street at Brannigans, a pre-work breakfast. An older lady slipped over the road with the mobility of a far younger woman and dropped a letter in the box and many flavours of birds fevered around the willows.

And then something entered the scene that immediately diverted him from anything else, something that slowed time and demanded his attention. He was seeing everything else fine but suddenly there was pixelation, a kind of flickering just before the signal drops. There was something over there appearing, or trying to appear from the mini-market next to Brannigans. What this again? It looked like a girl? It was a girl. She flickered in and out and vanished only to reappear instantly further in her stride and then, after someone banged the top of the TV, there she was in full vision. She'd crackled and faded into the scene like the apparition did in that battle street. The case for being in a VR game strengthened.

She was about his age, hoodie and leggings of a curious green hue, tall, slim and delicious with shoulder length blonde hair. She's the reason 'girl' sounds like it does. He was sure he knew her from somewhere but couldn't quite place her.

She was struggling to keep her little black dog tethered while she opened her car door to insert supplies. She was stunning and understated, graceful, elegant, at ease with herself, at ease with those around her and emitting this addictive power. The way her hair fell and a little piece of ear would stick out like an elf, the way she skipped rather than stepped off the curb, hugely important, the way even her untied shoelace could taunt a man. This was a girl that captured you and drew you to wherever you were in her scene. And then he got it.

'Camille,' said Salvador again louder than he'd hoped. 'Oh my fucking God.' He hadn't seen her since they were about thirteen. It was Camille. 'Scrunchie.' She liked to wear scrunchies, long since out of fashion, no reason other than that, few quips from the other girls but trends were of no interest to someone that looked like Camille.

Camille was awesome and so pretty, not fluffy cheerleader in-your-face, actually-kinda-not that-pretty-close-up pretty, Camille was another level. She was grounded, kind, sweet, never had a bad word for anyone. The thing was, she was lonely. The girls couldn't compete with any aspect of her. She had symmetry and a smouldering intellect and that frightened the boys away too. They wouldn't go near her. But Salvador did, like he'd known her forever. Jesus, with the sun beating down on him in this street, he closed his eyes and he was there. It was the last time she'd sit on her own in recess.

'Can I sit here?'

'Possibly, how do you feel about that, Floyd?'

'Good, confident actually, definitely sat down earlier, kinda do it a lot, reckon I got it.'

'Then be seated.'

'Nice hat.'

'Its not a hat, its a scrunchie.'

'Looks like a hat.'

And that was that. Camille was Salvador's best friend and soon became a friend who kissed him a fair bit and then he fell in love with her, his first love, well perhaps apart from Cindy Hawkins, who also showed him her pants when he was eight. He hadn't seen her since then. Jesus, so she's back in San Juan and there she was the other side of the street to him now.

Back then, suddenly one day she wasn't there any more. Salvador waited all day to see her at school but she didn't come back. He asked the teachers but they couldn't tell him anything. He even cycled round to her house loads of times but there was never anyone there. His mom and dad had no idea either but the long and short of it was his first love had broken his heart. She'd gone awol and never come back, abandoned him. He was sad for a very long time. So where did she go and why couldn't she say goodbye? And what's with all that flickering and fading in and out?

He wanted to go say hello but he really wasn't in any fit state and what would he say? Another time maybe. Her vanishing still hurt his teenage soul a little.

Instead he just stayed where he was, half in and half out of a doorway, watching her. It was nice to look at her on a warm sunny morning.

Fumbling for the keys in her pocket, Camille succumbed to that rigid cold feeling, when we're in the slow motion throes of dropping something irretrievably. Her eyes closed, braced for defeat. Her supplies teetered in her unassisted hand and finally passed the point of no return.

The brown paper bag first yielded a surprised tomato, peeking over the edge of the bag telling the apples and oranges it was on and soon there was an emancipated glorious grocery charge over the hill. Camille's attempt to prevent this only served to release her grip on the mutt, who without further ado escaped towards Brannigans. There was bacon.

The scene reminded Salvador of something he and Camille used to suffocate themselves cracking up over back then. It was the story of Sammy 'El Gunto' Chavez, boxing promoter turned nightclub singer, overall 'connected' guy, now a hermit Zen Buddhist and estranged son of this parish of San Juan. Sammy once said 'Juggling to avoid failure in one hand usually leads to failure in both.'

Fair enough, the moral was clear and Camille had just proved this perfectly but it was all about why Sammy was called 'El Gunto.'

Rumors persisted, mainly from Sammy, about his taming of a fierce beastie of some order in his younger, more hallucinogenic days, an act of such courage and fortitude that he proudly took the name of the vanquished.

Back in the real world, to everyone else it was simply an unsympathetic reference to his extraordinary tragic waistline.

The question of 'belt under or over the belly' had long since plagued your average man of a certain scaffold. Sammy, with a bizarre and acute abandonment of awareness tended to pull his pants up to his chest just below his nipples and thereby reveal, on a daily basis and without shame, a cameltoe of such proportion so as to terrify. They had a photo of him on the wall in Brannigans of all places displaying a fine example of that very cameltoe as Sammy smiled and shook old Joe Brannigan's hand. Salvador and Camille would grab a coffee after school and try and look at the photo without losing their shit. Then they'd leave pulling their pants up as high as they could and totally lose their shit.

Salvador couldn't help but grin from this side of the street as Camille admirably accepted the comedy of her fail. She stood calm, still and quiet against only the sound of the willows swishing in the slow breeze and a jar of olives coming to rest against her back wheel.

Camille let it all settle in the breeze while those outside Brannigans also looked on and failed to assist, some of them planning to do horrific things to the wife when they got home.

Camille's eyes opened wide. 'Shit, the dog,' she said.

With fleet of mind and nimble hand, this Camille was back in the game, she opened the door, deftly re-enslaved her shopping and lobbed it on the passenger seat.

She spied her happy little dog with its dangling leash trailing it like it had a tiny owner. By virtue of the sneakiest and briefest of glances towards her mommy, this mut knew the game was almost up. She turned up the heat on old Bill Jenkins and his bacon sandwich outside Brannigans. Jenkins would undoubtedly yield but perchance not soon enough.

Camille used to have exactly the same little mutt at school, remembered Salvador. That one was called Pepper. Camille said it was the the only name she could ever be called. Pour out a pot of freshly ground black peppercorns onto a worktop, form it into the shape of a little puppy and you had little Pepper, the illustrious and fabulous 'Miss Pepperpot.'

Coupled with that, apart from compounding her comedy by deciding to spend her life with one ear up and one ear down, she tended to sneeze rather a lot when she was a tiny pup. It was the cutest thing on YouTube for at least eight minutes when a surprise sneeze toppled her over, her little pink belly and pink paw pads in the air wiggling to right herself. She wasn't nearly embarrassed enough in truth and wiggled off to chew a curtain, nothing to see here.

This new Pepper prepared the move dogs do so well, the seamless transfer of total affection from one asset to another, timed to perfection, a lesson in animal to us humans, a species so in need.

Her time was up, bacon on hold, Camille was upon her.

'Hey Mommy, oh my God you shoulda seen this bacon and there was a mouse under the green thing over there and it's really good to see you... what's that?... and can we have bacon?'

Salvador was more than happy to let his memories of a softer time play out thanks to the appearance of Camille. He had known the old Pepper quite well and loved that silly little pooch.

The little pencil tail attached to this new Pepper looked like the stick you put in the first rubber band motor you made. The way this little dog generated so much super wag rate made her even more lovely.

Camille loved this little animal to bits just like she loved version one. Who wouldn't? She picked her up and their eyes met. After a brief game of 'who can nibble ears first,' which Pepper nailed before Camille was even out of her tracksuit, Camille gave her a nose to nose rub and stirred the pooch to the next level. This type of act can never just mean a nose to nose to a little dog. It means super lickies and lots of them plain and simple. Camille absorbed a face full of furious licking before she could move the little thing, still licking thin air but now out of lick's way.

They enjoyed a brief cuddle and Camille offered some calm but admonishing words relating to new Pepper's cheeky escape, she was a wicked little puppy and wicked little puppies get less tickles, all suitably ignored by this tiny mut, who knew tickles were always on tap.

Camille opened the back door of the car and deposited the mut. Flicking her hair back and carefully shutting the door as a little fuzzy face pressed, tongue staining the window, she paused. Salvador sensed it would happen before it did.

Without warning, Camille looked right over at him and straight into his eyes. He was still transfixed on the goings on and literally about to think 'for fuck's sake don't look over here.'

At that moment the fifteen odd years since the last time he saw her just faded away. This was the first time since then he'd seen her face even if it was from across the street. He remembered the slight raising of her left eyebrow when she looked at him. She did it every time, like she was constantly analysing. The only difference this time is she had just a little hint of sadness in those eyes.

But Salvador saw his friend again. When she looked over and nailed him right between the eyes, memories came flooding back into him. He was wearing his shades so maybe she didn't know who he was, to her this was no more than another pervy hobo gawking at her.

Wrong, he was busted. Camille threw a lingering smile over at him, a smile he knew so well, cotton wool and vodka and all things that smelled nice. Mortals would fall right where they stood, the birds hit the trees like it was the last elevator and there was submission all around. The universe drooled just a little.

Salvador was locked in the past and hypnotised in the here and now, unable to match Camille's tenure of the day but at least he managed to offer a little low wave. He wasn't sure if he smiled. So she did recognise him.

He'd missed her so much when she left all those years ago. He had to go and say hello. But no sooner had he decided what he should have decided right away, than Camille quickly slipped into her car and this little blue buggy took its contents shrinking up El Camino. A tiny fuzzy face looked back out of the window and seemed sorry not to meet him. They turned left up the hill and past the Police station and they were gone.

Salvador was angry with himself for not doing that. 'Just go say hi, idiot.' He hoped he would run into his friend again, find out what happened to her back then. There were probably more questions coming to mind than this first reunion chat would have allowed anyway.

So, back to the idea of sleep. No. First he gathered himself and decided to brave humans and secure food at Brannigans. Maybe a bacon stack and hot coffee outside in the sun, a nightcap. He was in no fit state to resume his mission right now anyway. He wasn't having the killer ideas he needed. He was stuck, needed to regenerate, sleep and a shower and then coffee and get back into it, as long as he doesn't just disappear somewhere else.

He scanned over the street to the Brannigans set to make sure no-one was familiar to him. It was a simple truth of his current existence that meeting people he knew usually started with an apology. He preferred to avoid that this morning.

Confident and undaunted, he crossed El Camino and the sun hit him, slowing him in allegiance. He entered Brannigans territory from the square behind a line of palms to minimise human contact, spotted a nice table and headed over to sit quietly and thumb the menu.

But of course at once he was undone by a chair, a heavy metal chair pulled back across the stone slabs and releasing a nasty metal fingernail on chalkboard noise. Not the recommended start and guaranteed to draw attention.

He sat back and absorbed the low hum of social interaction, the porcelain chinking of coffee cups into their saucers and the continuing buzz of the birds' morning task list. A short but athletic waitress with dark hair and ever such a faint moustache came over with a nice 'Hey how y'all doing? What can I get you?'

She was an accomplished smiler, her notepad was primed

and ready and any eye contact was avoided, she wasn't messing about, it was busy and he'd better step up or she was gone. Seconds add up in the overall scheme of a busy cafe morning. Her plastic name badge said 'Marianna' and so she was. 'Bacon stack, black coffee please,' said Salvador, pausing slightly for what followed, given the fledgling hour. 'And a bourbon, one cube, straight,' encouraging a tiny yet detectable nose twitch from Marianne.

He couldn't remember the last time he ate anything. In fact his memories of life before today amounted to a single defining track, his mission, and flashes from just about anywhere. The smells of Brannigans reminded him how hungry he was. He thought of asking how long it would be before he could get stuck into it but he did want to ask Marianna something else. He'd seen her and others here watch Camille's comedy just now.

'Excuse me. Sorry,' he said. 'That girl.'

'Girl?' she said, having heard countless cute customers ask her about one of her countless cute colleagues. Perhaps just once someone could ask about her.

'Yeh, the blond girl with the dog,' he continued. 'You know, over there out front just now, dropping her bag?'

Marianna's raised eyebrow, tilted head and an essence of tumbleweed blowing through the place suggested no she hadn't seen any pesky blond girl but he continued.

'She dropped her shopping and then went to get her dog. You couldn't miss her, little blue car?'

'I'm sorry sir, I didn't see any girl drop her shopping or any dog, sorry.'

There followed a short interlude of quiet in the air between Salvador and Marianna, which led to nothing further possible to say. She was confident she had fulfilled her role both as waitress and contestant. She repeated 'stack and black coming right up,' offering a slightly confused eye contact. 'about ten minutes' she said, and turned triumphantly into somewhere else.

How many times did Marianna have to say 'stack and black' in the average day? 'Stack and black.' It was a popular combo but did she say it to everyone who ordered it? Was it her catchphrase or Brannigans? Did the old fart insist staff said it regularly? The tyranny.

Salvador tended to imagine things, they'd call it ADHD these days but in essence it was chronic wandering mind. He was continually releasing his mind to the wind, collecting stories and theories about any random thing at any moment, does anything eat wasps? Every time he blinks, does the universe disappear? What if you ran a feedback loop on an orgasm moment in VR? There was a movie about that. The simple task of pouring wine in a restaurant became a moment tiny bugs were waiting for as they surfed down into the glass. What their plan was after that was unknown. So if this shit was going to happen to anyone, he was an enlightened choice of test subject, o great controller of his life. Among his battles to focus on his mission, this rambling brain had been a constant so he was probably halfway to crazy anyway, never mind adding the booze and these relentless jumps.

He saw exactly what went on with Camille out front and this Marianna was front and center and even offered a smile on it. Either she had an affliction similar to his own or she was covering up. His hunger and its craving for bacon took a temporary back seat as he scanned around the cafe for likely targets so he could acquire a second opinion. He knew what he saw and that was that.

There was an elderly couple having coffee at a table right at the front, almost on the sidewalk. They were so close, surely they'd seen the demise of poor Camille's groceries as well. The old chap would have thought about getting up to help, he was that sort of age, but Salvador imagined speed and agility were a couple of clubs left at home. But he had to ask.

'Excuse me,' he said. 'I'm sorry to interrupt but I was keen to know if you saw that girl in the blue car, the girl who dropped her shopping just now.'

Straight to the point, he thought, don't give them time to collaborate with Marianne and fabricate the truth. The lady assumed the table's response.

'Blue car?' she said. 'Shopping?'

'Just a few moments ago, you were watching her.'

'Oh I'm sorry I didn't see any blue car,' she said, starting a nervous feeling in Salvador like he'd just coughed on them and asked them for spare change.

'Did you see the girl though? Pretty blonde girl?' persisted Salvador, confident by now this lady had not.

'No I'm sorry we've been here for about half an hour. Leonard had to get some hemorrhoid cream,' which raised a shifting sub growl from Leonard. 'It's such a lovely day don't you know, we thought a coffee in the sun would be lovely.'

'It is a lovely day and thanks. Sorry to have bothered you, do enjoy your coffee,' ended Salvador, and with a courteous farewell, returned to his seat.

This was clearly a cafe wide conspiracy or perhaps he'd had the misfortune to poll a busy waitress with her thoughts elsewhere and a sweet couple of old duffers with their thoughts long since lost at sea. He hoped Leonard's piles improved and had to enjoy a secret smile at the calm but incisive words Leonard might be having with his wife at this moment.

To the calm coffee drinkers of Brannigans this morning there had been no Camille, no little black dog, no shopping, dropped or otherwise and no little blue car. He resigned himself to feeling hungry again.

Very few seconds later, here was his order. Impressive time, Brannigans, well played. After this, he will get himself into the shower, get himself out of the shower and the bourbon will get him gently to sleep.

All elements of life removed themselves in favor of this bacon stack. Marianna was a distant memory, Brannigans was elsewhere. He took at least a third of it in one bite and sat back ensuring air was getting through his nose. It was lean and stacked into a fresh toasted French stick and mildly drizzled in maple. Add a twist of black pepper and a whisper of lemon juice. It was, in the words of one renowned ex-vegan of this parish. 'Fucking Nirvana.'

Eventually, he re-opened communication with the day. His blank stare had been directed across the square and as his mind returned to him from a place he couldn't remember, what he was looking at was the town noticeboard. Why not check out this abused noticeboard for himself, thirty odd yards across the square then back to the car.

He was looking forward to this subversion. He was keen to see what the wicked and covert in this town had to offer. Since he'd lived here, he couldn't ever remember a similar attack on the American dream. 'Please make it hilarious,' he thought to himself as he approached the noticeboard.

Normally afloat with sewing clubs, cake making and the occasional cheeky escort, the board had been overhauled by brash but heartfelt bright yellow graffiti.

'That's not my dog.'

'Awesome, why not?,' thought Salvador. There were too many guesses to be had. What dog? Some hacker that crossed the line? Something on a TV show?

He could make out some of the original fare underneath. Something about burning something and plenty of job offers for the shops here. A San Juan Times headline about some guy being shot in the head. Harsh.

And there was a partly obscured A4 poster. On it, most of a little girl listed as missing, *can anyone help?*

'Holy mother's bicycle,' he thought, remembering Father William, the priest who taught him God likes to have fun too.

'The parents' he thought, what do you do? Do you sleep, do you eat, how do you breathe? You've seen them paraded on TV with the detectives. They sit akimbo, leaning, drawn, not taking it all in, desperate and zombified, repeating their lines. They know they've got to do it but for the love of baby Jesus get them home to a nice hot bath and a cup of tea and may every moment guide their babies home.

This little girl went missing three months ago. What do they say about be first forty eight? If there's no progress with a case inside the first forty eight hours, chances of success are cut in half. He imagined if he found her and saved her? He'd either be locked up right there or carried on shoulders through the streets, streamers flowing over him, picture in all the papers.

3 Letter

After a stroll across the square back to his car, just off Montgo street, his old '65 Mustang, temperamental green-house gas factory though it was and not even close to the restoration he'd promised when he bought it. He could smell the ripped red leather before he got close to the door. After almost sixty years, it was an old musty leather smell like the chair in grandad's shed. It had curves and the promise of noise and smoke. Once she opened her eyes and got going, she shivered right through his feet and plugged into his spine.

When he started her up, on days he was permitted to do that, she whined and complained, crackled and popped and set herself. This lady deserved patience and she'd let you know when she was ready. She was warm and safe like your dog dreaming and snoring at the same time.

He hit the road for home and sleep, ideally sleep without dreams or any other funny business. DUI pace was engaged. Salvador wasn't drunk but this felt like a doozy of a hangover, the aftershock of a hell of a night, it felt like the infant son of the guy you crashed with slowly battering your couch sleeping head with a plastic bat, finding it high pitched hilarious.

So it was far from impossible in his new strange world for his blood alcohol level to be of frightening proportions. There was no hurry and the slower he went, the more deep rumble grumble he felt from this old girl. After sleep, he'd get back into his mission, fresh and inspired.

Tony was stopped one night. The cop got him out of the

car. Tony was a buddy way back to high school and Tony had plenty of tales about most things. He's what you call a fire-starter, trouble always follows and it tends to get all of you. If you want to spend a peaceful time of an evening do not hit Tony up. But the thing was about Tony, it doesn't matter what state he's in, he's there for you, all the time, big wrap up and hug. He looks after you. He'd give you half of his last biscuit. That's Tony. Salvador loved Tony. He had nothing apart from his van and the occasional transportation gig for some iffy local, no family, no-one to love him but Salvador did. He was a gentle giant of a man, always smiling with this wiry frizzy hair that looked like it should have bits in it. He wasn't one to abide by the rules of any road or any particular civilisation. He was the wild man to Salvador's sad angry wild man, partners in wet shouting, never an effective calming and comedy central to everyone he knew.

Once he was out of the car, Tony couldn't help his internal smile reaching his face. For the first time since he used to shit into his mother's hands, he hadn't had a drink or smoked any weed. Two days now. Bring it, he thought, and shall we also bring a little fun?

After the line walk, this fun took shape. He looked the cop up and down, cross eyed and mentioned a thing or two about chickens really being cunning little feathery aliens colonising mankind by ingestion. He then leaned back on his car and watched the confusion.

The cop rested his hand on his gun, his eyes rotated a full three sixty and reappeared none the wiser, his mouth twitched and Tony thought he may even have released wind.

The breathalyzer was introduced quick smart. Tony gave it a force ten of a blow and smiled to see green... green... green... The cop let him go. Even if he'd taken him for a drugs test, probably ok as well. "But play carefully," he used to say. "Its a pro's game."

Salvador was driving as slowly as a car can go until legally defined as reversing. Just as he was starting to zone out and switch to autopilot the rest of the way home, he heard a strange grumbling, like a distant spitfire. Grand old Edna Voller-Nagel, seasoned librarian and former San Juan crown green bowling legend, ninety three years old, thundered up behind him in her old black smoking '57 Bel Air and eased past at a gorgeous ten mph. It was a fine sight, two old relics casting off their zimmers and damn well having a go.

Edna really enjoyed it on her way past, willing her smokey friend on, perhaps the last charge for both. She knew she had the mustang but suddenly pulled tight in front of it and almost clipped his front wing. Dear old Edna was oblivious, proven the victor and bunkum to anything else. She would now power ahead into the distance to the adulation of the fans. Here in the twilight of her winter was a shout at a world that didn't listen to her anymore, she was taking something head on, without due cause, just for the hell of it. Salvador smiled through the smoke and thought if only she'd given him the finger, it would've been perfect.

As Edna polluted Ortega all the way to the mountains, Salvador made his way off left and up the hill onto Rancho Viejo, ten minutes of his own gurgling through the countryside.

Although he could probably have slept standing up in a fire, he was starting to become wary of being alone with his thoughts. This tended to be a slippery place.

As soon as you think of a situation you tend to find yourself dropped in it. Was that a clue to what was doing this, his own imagination? Jesus, Camille. Fifteen years. That first kiss, oh, God, and then the second kiss on the beach. The shoulder charge game, most of the time sending one of them clattering into a load of pot plants or almost tipping over an ice cream cart.

One time, as the streets got narrower to a point where you can't even get two people side by side in the doorway at the end, there was no room left for charges so they raced to be first through the gap and caught it in sync, wedging themselves facing each other. They cracked up laughing and feeling each other cracking up laughing just made them crack up even more and when they were done, Camille grabbed Salvador by the hair and pulled him towards her. She dropped the softest kiss on his mouth, held there for a second or two and then pulled away and smiled. This was at the very same time their first kiss and the moment Salvador would never think of anyone but Camille. Its wasn't the first time he'd felt urges and he'd thought about her quite a lot when he did, but this was the first time he'd felt it specifically for a human person while wedged in a tight gap with her. He knew she'll soon know what's pressing into her belly and she'll be amused or recoil in disgust. Camille raised an eyebrow and smiled.

All the secret kisses they had and then that day, the first day they touched each other. And here she was all grown up. Jesus, she looked so lovely. Thoughts came flooding into his mind, his teenage love transferring to today's Camille. What would it have been like when they got older, together. What would she be like. What would fucking her be like...?'

'Jesus stop, what the fuck? What's the matter with you?' he yelled as hard as he could into the car. Among the peaceful pines of Rancho Viejo, Salvador felt no peace. He'd seen Camille for a few minutes and she already had his cock in her mouth? Asshole.

It wasn't sitting well with him at all and he found himself preparing to dialogue his inner self, a place where logic lurks imprisoned and demons sit on each shoulder, whispering shit in his ears.

'How's it all going then?' said one demon emerging from

his left ear. 'Seems someone's got plenty of time for stalking blonde tarts, eh?'

'She's not a tart, Fuck off.'

'Oh, hello, bit special is she? Something you wanna get off your chest?'

The demon pulled the hair by Salvador's ear.

'You need to do a whole shit ton better than that, bozo, if you're gonna save her.'

'I know, fuck off.'

'Here's something. What of you can't save her?'

His whole body froze as he considered the thing that mustn't be considered.

'Never, never, now fuck off.'

'You can't escape it, Salvador. You have to think about it. What of they're right? What if you're wrong, nothing works?'

Too late. He was already thinking about it. He was driving into the shade of the woods almost at the top of the hill when he felt it coming. He put the radio on to confuse his enemy with noise. Four stations of advertising later, he found 'a crazy little thing called love.'

'Love do indeed be crazy,' he thought, straight away knowing his fate was sealed. As a tactic to avoid contemplation, the radio idea was a fail. He'd pretty much pressed the 'contemplate now' button by finding this song. The music drew him into the inevitable connection with himself. If you're troubled, this moment of connection is far from fun and Salvador was indeed troubled.

He arranged his breathing, shuffled in his seat, and tried to recover his center but it was too late, inevitable. Here were his troubles, here was his problem.

She was his Jemma. When moon landings are mentioned you think of Neil or Buzz or maybe an alien or two, when cartoons crop up, you think of Bugs or Daffy and with women you think of Jemma. And he'd thought about his dick in another girl's mouth, plain and simple.

He thought maybe these jumps had been sent to distract him from it, keep him sane, but at the same time risk disabling his plan. He couldn't tell if they were friend or foe. But right now, the fears were upon him. All the ghosts he'd been running from were gathering around him again, out of the glove box, under the seats and through the windows and the air intakes, emerging from everywhere and into him. There was even a smell of hospital in the car, overwhelming his memory of her own essence like evil had him bound and gagged and was sticking its vile self up his stupid useless nose.

His face contorted. He was once again presented with the depth of his sadness. He felt dizzy. He thought now would be a really useful time to jump him somewhere else. This was a dark place, the blackest place and his demon was still there, reminding him of the grey reality of his life.

'What's the point?' said the demon. 'Wake up. Smell the coffee. What's the matter with you? Get with it.'

'Look, just fuck off already,' yelled Salvador, punching the dash. 'It's not going to happen and I don't need it in my face every time I'm alone, just fuck off and let me try.'

Jemma was the love of his life and she always will be, the one you design in dreams, the one who leaves you with just a feeling on your skin, the one.

When he first met her deliciousness, she was eighteen, a freshman at UCLA when he was there on a post-grad. The first day he saw her, he was sitting on the steps of the California Nanosystems building, mulling something.

She appeared at the end of the driveway dressed in tight slim jeans, cons and a top combo of two layers, a lightly collared white button up blouse with a frilly collar, covered by a slim fitting baby blue V-neck, a well considered combo, maintaining body temperature and more importantly, so very pretty. This combo wrapped itself around a human female of impeccable quality.

Her hair had that lopsided thing going on. Her right side, shoulder length, a soft light blush red with bits of blonde streaked through it in just the right places, tucked behind her ear. On the left side, shaved just over her ear but keeping the top layer, some straight, some with a little wave, it all gave the sweetest tickle to the back of her neck and this interaction sprung up the most divine smell.

Jemma was new and a little nervous and this only added to her. There was a hint of wicked naughty abandon waiting to be released, savaged, but maybe that was just Salvador at twenty two. She spotted him on the steps and instantly smiled and headed towards him at a focused clippety pace. It was like she already knew him. Clearly his telepathy was fully functional. He was her sanctuary to help pretend she wasn't alone.

Washing over him was the air Jemma had accumulated on her way over, freshly mown grass, something of that old V8 that passed her, her bubblegum peel me off sweater and her own unique wonderful smell, lavender and sunshine.

'Hey,' she said.

'Hey.'

A joined smile offered her a seat and she took it next to him. She sat with him on that step for at least an hour. They covered just about the first three months of a relationship while pretending they weren't going to be in a relationship. All Jemma wanted to do was teach tiny people to be happy tiny people and one day have her own tiny people in her own class. She said she wasn't afraid to say it defined her. It was her life mission.

'There's an angel in every tiny person,' she said.

'Probably Lucifer,' said Salvador. It was fifteen odd

minutes into them knowing each other but Jemma already wanted to tweak him or punch him, more a desire to touch him, but not yet, too soon.

'Don't be mean, they're the goodness in the world before it starts leaking out. I want to keep it from leaking out as long as possible.'

It was about the time cars were arriving and leaving with students. The cars contained all sorts, parents of course, little brothers and sisters, dragged along, bored and pissed off, what's wrong with taking the bike to the sandpits? Most of them filed slowly past the California Nanosystems building in slow procession, a pilgrimage to a great love in the making.

'Kids kinda see it in me,' said Jemma.

'Sounds like magic, m'lady.'

'That's exactly what it is. Its like a magic connection. Do you think some people just get lucky enough to do exactly what they were put here for?'

Before Salvador could tell her yes he did think that, they were both drawn to the back window of a beautiful old car easing slowly past the steps. There was a boy, half hanging out of the window. He was about five, maybe six. He had Jemma in his eyes and now he had both of them in his eyes. His timing was solid. Just as the car was turning right for the main drive, the kid raised a middle finger and held their gaze all the way down that driveway. When the car finally disappeared into the LA afternoon, there were a few seconds of quiet here on the steps.

'Well, obviously not that one,' said Jemma and Salvador and her lost it right here on these steps.

When your eyes hook up and stay there dissolved while you're both blue with laughter, there's no finer feeling on God's green earth. You're home, never leave it, never risk it, and never take it for granted. From that moment, Salvador could never imagine either of them being alone.

So how do you know when she's the one? What are the signs, the intel, what is it? Is it a glance or a laugh or the way she stands, the way she holds her glass? Is it the potential of pure porn she brings? Is it the fact that she wants you to help her steal the Dean's antique desk on Saturday night? It was a few weeks after they met on the steps. They'd already done dinner, done getting drunk and done something safe and unusual, in this case, a Jai Alai game. They'd already kissed with a passion that told them only time separated them from the inevitable and they both very much looked forward to the inevitable. And now, Jemma thought it was time for their first felony.

'Why some heavy old desk we can't even lift?' said Salvador.

'Fear not, I've got it all planned.'

And she had. She'd borrowed the key to the Dean's office from his secretary's desk and quickly had a spanking shiny copy of her own. The trick was the lifters couldn't know. It was Salvador's task to locate four large and oblivious guys and load the desk into the flower truck Jemma would have waiting. They'd be delivering flowers to various parts of the building, not least to make the Dean's Sunday a fragrant one, albeit one without a desk.

'So what do we do with the desk?'

'We give it back to its rightful owner.'

'Who is?'

Jemma pulled out a little notebook. 'Sebastian le Zaro, 2416 Parade street, San Diego, great grandson of Emilio le Zaro. It was Emilio's desk before Emilio and his family had to head south as the US swallowed up California.'

'So, the Dean's desk is a stolen desk, wrestled from innocents during a tyranny.'

'Indeed it is.'

'Then this is a mission to right a terrible wrong.'

'Correct.'

'Delicious. Scandal. I'm in.'

The Dean and his wife were out at a dinner party and the plan went without a hitch. Jemma's arrangement of the flowers left behind in that deskless office was a thing of beauty.

So, how do you know when she's the one? I'm going to go right ahead and say it, you smell 'the one,' it's more than a smell, an essence, a blended mix of all she's seen and everywhere she's been, where she goes swimming in the morning, the feel of her feet on the carpet when she gets up. When you know her essence it's not possible to forget it, something in nature demands its permanent retention.

By the end of her first semester they were living together. Jemma had never thought going to college would so completely define her life quite so quickly. Day one, she meets this gorgeous guy with a silly nose, he's cool and kind, passionate, ambitious and inventive and just so darn cute with his uncontrollable fringe and those eyes. She knew he was the one at pretty much the exact time he knew she was the one, the steps of the California Nanosystems building.

They were instantly two halves of the same human pod and for pretty much the whole four years Jemma was at UCLA. They ended up renting a really cool place in Ocean Park, a walk from the beach but still just private enough for some peace and quiet, sometimes. Dinner on a warm Santa Monica pier at that awesome Mexican joint, swimming in the morning, making love in the afternoon and drinking in the evening, the finest of times.

The first time you start seeing minor flaws in the one you love is the first time you truly realise how much you love them and lucky you are. One sleepy evening in front of the loud, game show shiny, mindless applause of the television, Jemma sneezed and at the same time farted and peed herself just a little, the holy trinity, a universal abandonment of valve control. He couldn't believe what he'd just witnessed and eyed her, demanding comment. When she removed her face from her hands and guiltily turned to look at him, her face pinkening rapidly, realising things would never be the same again, the short silence in the room was overturned as they lost their grip on couches and their faculty and hit the floor laughing. Jemma pleaded 'don't make me laugh, please,' she couldn't promise more valve failures but it was too late.

When Salvador got a call from his boss and buddy, Yuki, about relocating Net Nano to San Juan, it was back to Salvador's roots, the place he grew up, and it was Salvador and Jemma's next chapter. Yuki could find VCs under every chair and he knew how to make them listen and they had, the VR thing was funded.

Jemma had graduated with all she needed to do what she always wanted to do, teach. She had a load of part time jobs in schools while they were in Ocean Park and conversation spread to ankle biters not that long after they met. When you know you know, you realise you could never ever meet anyone else. Your whole future is written for you and it all becomes so easy.

There was a little school in San Juan, San Juan Elementary, they were looking for a grad for the early grades. The students' former favorite, twenty four year old Miss Jenkins, long chastised by the faculty for her thigh length skirts and over the knee black leather boots and consequently long hailed by more than half of her third grade class as 'the one,' had left under a cloud with some petty cash and the genial Mr Spector, a man of science for the higher grades. This had to be carefully revealed to the third grade or there might be revolt.

Net Nano's VR project got seriously funded thanks to Yuki and the company took a building in the Great Heights business park in San Juan. Jemma's new job at San Juan elementary was everything she wanted, she fitted in perfectly and adored everyone there, she could make little people happier people here, she could see her own kids at each stage of their young life and she was ready.

The day the letter arrived they'd been in San Juan for about three years. They both woke up in the night with a jolt at the same time for no apparent reason and with a mutually reassuring cuddle, sleep was soon reclaimed.

The whole place felt different that morning, like there was someone else there, hiding, waiting to jump out at him, it just didn't sit the same. He got the coffee brewing and knew Jem would be down in about ten minutes. Just as he heard her feet come down the stairs he spotted the letter partially inserted under the front door on the mat. Without much thought, he went over to pick it up and froze solid right where he stood, the symbol on the letter was Mission Hospital. OK so today was the day. They'd been trying to put it out of their minds and done pretty well for this to be almost a surprise but they did know it was coming and waking in the night was its sign.

Since their early conversations about kids, they'd let nature take its course for a year or so but nothing happened. They didn't let it affect them, they just inserted some science into it. The booze took a back seat, ovulation time had to be good for them simply because they spent most of this bizarre upside down ritual pissing themselves laughing, surrounded by an abundance of large cushions and incense. This became their party night.

But it wasn't happening and he could see this start to drain his little Jemma. This is a primal fear for your average female, facing the prospect of no issue. It affects men too but men always have the fallback of salvo theory, apply volume to the problem and one day you'll knock someone up.

But a woman can either be knocked up or not. For Jemma, her reason to be was under threat and somewhere deep in her mind she would be sharpening claws for the battle ahead. IVF was a no-brainer and re-injected some life force back into the room but it did leave Salvador with the feeling that they were a very tiny and useless minority considering all the species in this universe who reproduce with such little effort, give or take the occasional dose of post-coital cannibalism. They get knocked up even if its fifty below zero and three metres under the ice in Antarctica, they multiply on comets in the bleak vacuum of space. Conception could never again be taken for granted.

During the various tests, the consultants spotted something in Jemma's brain. Salvador's initial reaction was 'why the fuck are you looking in her brain, we're doing IVF' but the fear of being childless was replaced with the fear of losing her altogether. He couldn't imagine what she was going through but wished he could take it off her, she was quiet and more inclined to comfort him than him comfort her, stroking a cat to ease herself.

Salvador's perfectly mapped out future of forty or fifty years, completely in love for every single second with this lady and fussing over their grandkids, this had all been tabled, eyebrows had been raised. You can take just about anything if it's told to you straight but waiting just doesn't work. Waiting forces you to consider too many directly opposing possibilities. Your brain doesn't like it at all. Your brain presents you with confused analysis and awkward logic in response, it transplants you into a chrysalis, writhing, dark and claustrophobic and in pain, waiting until you can either fly or remain sealed in to wither and die.

The discussions to come about buying cars, insisting on

college, teaching them to fight and longing for that day you're asked something about girls, these were now the lives of their future, Salvador and his Jemma, and they were now filed away pending further investigation and more tests.

What they found was a growth near her amygdala, the area responsible for emotional responses. They did their tests and Salvador and Jemma would hear in a week or so. The consultant's office was so cold that day, a dull day that cast a dull light through the dull window. There was a spy movie texture to the room which made it feel like a dangerous day in post war Berlin and also made it all feel very serious in San Juan. A deadline of one week had been implanted, a week to face your most horrible demons.

They'd made a silent and mutual pact that the week was to be some of the most fun they've had. It was unbothered by this alien thing growing in her. They went dancing, drove all over the place to new restaurants and bars, new countryside to walk through. They went to a comedy gig for the first time in years and during that week Salvador felt closer to his Jemma that ever, like they'd just met all over again.

Back in this morning kitchen, Salvador moved over to the coffee and put the letter on the table for her on the way past. He poured her some coffee and sat next to her at the end of the table. He felt like he was getting seriously high, like this coffee was drugged, his eye movements were tracing, speeding up and slowing down and there was just this dull low hum in his ears, the few seconds after you get a whack to the head.

Jemma stared at the letter and ran her thumb over the slightly embossed Mission Hospital logo. Her mind was not on the logo, the letter or the tumor.

Every breath and heartbeat in the room could be heard. Their muted moment was joined only by a fly fumbling around up in the high front hall ceiling by the windows, bouncing off them in some martyred belief that there was salvation on the other side. Salvador knew how it felt.

Jemma was focused with every fibre of her wonderful being on IVF and her children. IVF had to be suspended now because of this 'fuck you' lump and without kids did she really give a shit about what this letter said? There certainly wouldn't be any better mother on this rock of ours and it hurt just that little bit more than it already did, like having vinegar poured on an open wound or the woman you love telling you 'I've been seeing someone.'

He could imagine seeing her with their sprog, smiling and gurgling at each-other, flushed with primal joy. This moment puts you at one with the universe, when this little pooper looks you right in the eyes and cracks into a big drooly smile, you need never more look back in anger.

The word 'terminal' is just about the most terrifying word humans can utter, it oozes evil, green foul smelling evil, it smashes you in the face and breaks your back at the same time. It creeps up on you in the dark, it's that last bus heaving off over the hill as you run behind, the people in the back window flipping you the middle finger as they go.

'Terminal' raises the fury and fuels the rebellion, your hairs rise up and your mind switches to furious red sweat attack. Salvador laid down his curse on Jemma's multi-celled invaders. They know them now, they know where they are, they know what they look like and they will fucking end them. Salvador imagined them cowering in their dark, cold evil place, shivering with the discomfort they love, craven and covert, in total fear of this onslaught. 'Fear it well,' he said just under his breath. 'It's coming.'

He looked at his Jemma and his Jemma looked right back at him. She was calm, more in control than she'd ever been, at some kind of new level. The letter was no longer needed, it had been digested and discarded. She stood and looked down at him, time had the good grace to slow for him to analyse outcomes, her face was moving in slow motion, something was going to happen, was it to be silent resignation, hysterical tears, breaking things? And then she laughed.

'You look like one of those little Marmoset Monkeys ogling for a peanut,' she said.

How effortlessly she'd released this fog from the house, even that fly seemed to have escaped somewhere. Salvador pulled her onto his lap. She was warm, she wriggled herself into a cosy spot and started teasing his fringe with her fingertips. That baby blue nail varnish and how light she was and just the smell of her, freshly laundered and honey, gazing into him like it was the last time, same as the first time, what sort of angel was this woman?

She was an angel that had just started to lick his earlobe. This is the only thing required to have sex with your husband, note it well, breathe deeply, caress and give yourself to the ear.

She shifted her position on his lap ever so slightly allowing him access to her back. He made his way under the back of her T-shirt and gently massaged her spine with his fingertips. She was wearing just a short white T-shirt and white lacy panties. As she sat on his lap, these panties became more evident as his back massage shifted the gravity of her T-shirt. Her panties bordered the smoothest tanned skin of her thighs and she very slightly opened her legs.

He gave her a little tickle on the knee, it still made her giggle, he created a soft circular motion with his fingers up her thigh to the warmth that lay nearby. It seemed he'd be heading for the panties but instead he stopped, slowly retreated and continued to caress her thigh, snakes and ladders and he smiled at her warm frustration. This drew a breathy lobe lick from her, which was designed to and succeeded in summoning him to greater heights.

The panties were breached. Jemma opened her legs to allow him to gently cue the pantie edge with his left thumb and feel her with his middle finger and she writhed on his lap as he stroked deeper and deeper. She signalled the panties were redundant and he timed the raising of her bottom with his slipping down the legs of the panties and over her toes. As he pushed the panties over those little toes, one or two of those little toes would gang up and wrestle the panties from him.

They kissed again so soft and warm. He felt a tension in his belt. Within seconds she'd released the belt and was into the stud button. The button was open and she ran her hand down under his shorts and started stroking him. He was pretty much instantly next door's big dog trapped in a tiny little puppy house and with another wicked smile, she freed him, licking him and playing with him. He shifted to rid himself of apparel and she moved on top of him, arching her back to uncoil and devour him and he was inside her.

As she smiled down at him and he returned only a kind of drooling look, she started pulling her little T-shirt off. She looked him right in the eye until the shirt obscured her face. Sometimes he'd take advantage of her temporary blindness, hold her shirt tight over her face and tickle her but today he didn't. He was presented with the finest upper body known to mankind, pert, erect and quivering with what next, put there by God himself to show us he loves us.

She rode him slowly from side to side and he pulled her to him and enveloped her chest. They kissed and he lifted her up and took her to the lounge, he wanted to turn her round against the wall but he had to face her.

She didn't diminish her ferocious devouring of his ear as she was placed on her back on the couch. He departed his chest from hers and reared like a hydra shoring himself up on the armrest. She spread her arms above her head and he ever so softly started to move her toward orgasm.

He saw the swaying trees outside, again he was inside this unbelievable entity, the most beautiful female form ever to have roamed this fair planet of ours. She started to elevate her response and looked at him again. The ones that love you always look at you when they come, that is unless they're facing the wrong way, then mirrors are useful.

At no point during their shared orgasm were they not locked in this gaze, they rolled over and fell off the couch and rolled some more. They came to rest still in the gaze and finally collapsed back onto the soft couch giggling, still joined but physically separated.

Jemma wrapped herself around him and here they would sleep on this couch. If you're in Nirvana right here what use is the afterlife? Through all this and forever she was his protector, his guardian angel, she stopped his nightmares and made him feel worthwhile. As they lay together on the couch, she curled up a little and fell asleep on his shoulder. He pulled a blanket off the back of the couch and covered them both, tucking it into the top of her shoulders and under each little tiny toe.

Salvador took Jemma into Mission Hospital about 11am.

She'd lost consciousness about five minutes earlier and would go into a coma at 2pm that afternoon.

He couldn't process it. He was on autopilot, getting things done. He wouldn't remember getting her into the car and smashing it down the lanes to Ortega and on to the hospital. He wouldn't remember carrying her inside, yelling for help. He wouldn't remember many of these blackest minutes of his life.

Jemma was taken in and made comfortable. Salvador took a few minutes to stroll around and try and clear his head. He was bouncing off walls and his first minutes out of emergency mode had not sat well on him. He couldn't piece anything together. He was abandoned in a snowstorm.

In the most desperate of places, you appeal to anything available. Salvador had never been sure the Man upstairs was permanently resident, flitted in and out or even existed at all. Until the reality of today had sunk in and created only a hatred of him, he had a word with that Man upstairs in the beep-crazy room they put her in.

He said they didn't really know each-other and he was really sorry about that and all the shitty things he'd done but if ever He could listen please listen now. Take the house, take his freedom, his mind, he didn't care. Send him to hell but bring her back. The Man upstairs was not immediately responsive but immediacy is rarely His way.

Staying with her unblinking for two days and watching for any sign she was on her way back, a twitch, a different breath, a new beep, this wasn't achieving anything but he cared not. If the world thought him a terrorist and he could bring his Jemma back before being taken apart and left in messy bits around six counties, bring it on.

Jemma's nurse, Angel had seen her share of people hanging over a bedside. One quiet midnight, Angel came in and told him softly to go away and sleep, she spoke to him like a mother licks her cub. It was a simple message. But how do you leave someone for the first time, what pulls your gaze away from her, what callous spirit drives you out the door and down the corridor into a world without her, abandoned and alone? What allows this unholy separation? Angel put her hand on his shoulder and just said 'I know' and he knew it was time to leave his Jemma be.

Walking to the car, he wondered if that was the last kiss, the last conversation or the last time he'd see those eyes on him. He managed to wait until he was locked up safe in the car before what had just happened played back for him and all hell broke loose.

Back to the Car

Back in this same car on Rancho Viejo on this new day, Salvador gradually emerged limping from this moment once again and wiped his tear-soaked face with his T-shirt. He held his T-shirt over his face, hiding himself from the horrors of where Jemma still was.

He was never more committed to finding his solution, some fucking way to bring her back to him, but now the sounds and smells that joined his face under this T-shirt and promised relief from the pain were not of the green fields and tree lined asphalt of Rancho Viejo. These were the salty scents and sounds of the sea. Salvador unwrapped his shirt and took in his new surroundings. Here we go again.

# The Madness of Hector Valdez

Detective Ray Morres carefully straightened a small photo frame at the corner of his desk even though it hadn't been unstraightened by anything for weeks with the dust collected around it.

Once he was happy with it's new position, he was annoyed by the dust trail he'd just created. He lifted the frame up, took out his handkerchief and dusted off the offending piece of desk ensuring a perfect square of it was free of dust. He then dusted the face and top edge of the picture and ran his finger over its smiling images of a woman and two young children.

Once more the room was heating up as the sun pounded through the windows. Air con wasn't high on San Juan PD's list of expenses and in an hour or so he'd be fidgeting, removing layers of clothing and fans would turn over in their keen but futile effort to help.

But for now, his breathing eased to signal a departure from the troubles of the day of a detective. He tilted his head slightly to absorb the picture, suffering an involuntary swallow as he ran another finger around the faces of the two tiny people held by the woman.

Morres was a big guy and fighting fit. He was a man with a hard, *don't even try it* face, a face that looked like it had been immersed deep in the shit for way too long. His cheekbones could injure you. He was classic Hispanic fighting stock and his glare into the picture changed from one of peace and the tranquility of love to one of the thousand curses of his ancestors. It was a glare to terrify even his own colleagues and served his purpose when it came to confession time. He was accustomed at regular intervals to two very different types of confessional.

He endured the deep breathing, snap-at-any-moment interviews with suspects of all shapes and colours and usually extracted something from them with the not so subtle positioning of his eyes deep into them, like those eyes could shoot lasers and split them down the middle at any moment. That was what he wanted to do to them and they sensed it. Even the hardest scar faced assholes took a few breaths more when Morres's eyes were on them.

Then there were the weekly visits to Father Sanchez at San Juan's Serra Chapel, a beautifully understated little church with all the warmth and peace of the Holy Mother herself.

His first order of business, once inside the womb of the confessional was to hear the low calming voice of Father Sanchez and close his eyes to the place he was about to put himself. He would seek forgiveness for the thoughts he had about those other confessionals he attended at the precinct and would then surrender to the tears of his troubles.

Nothing had changed, he would say, he still harboured the thoughts he always had about it. He didn't know if the pain and the anger would ever leave him. He would take his penance like a solid citizen and use that handkerchief to dry his eyes before his exit, leaving a saddened Father Sanchez to pray for a man most in need of it.

Morres took a seat at his desk and quickly shifted to pull an electric razor out of his trouser pocket, placing it on the desk in front of the picture at exactly ninety degrees to its face, almost like a runway to it. He folded away his handkerchief and placed it back into his top jacket pocket but not before giving it a little kiss. Here was a man absorbed in the most tender of rituals.

He was a man who maintained a well groomed moustache, not too bushy but not too skimpy to suggest it was a frivolous effort. It was a Magnum PI tash of similar steel to the man who owned it, strong, obvious and the only part of his face he didn't need to bother with three times a day. For men who qualify as scarily hairy and need to look the part, in control, subject to no natural obstruction, keeping a well kept visage is a must, hence the ever present razor, which served also to draw his attention to the picture at regular intervals.

For men who have developed chronic OCD, as has this decorated and troubled detective, the removal of surplus fluff is even more important. Morres scanned over the little razor wondering if he should give it another blast but couldn't help once more caressing the three people in the picture frame with a softness of an acoustic guitar on a summer evening concert in the last of the sun.

A few years ago Ray Morres emerged from the most horrible of life's little tests. He was with the DEA in El Paso, staking out a cartel house over the border. Things had gone balls up and he'd been captured by the cartel, eventually ending up in front of its main man, Hector Valdez, a seriously mean asshole, liked playing with bits of humans, kept someone's heart valve in a glass vial round his neck and ever since anyone could remember, the major face in the local cartel.

Manacled in the basement by legs and arms to whatever was around, Hector had got Morres's ID straight off and returned half an hour later with details of his address, wife and kids names and even their school, which had encouraged Morres to sit up and take note in every conceivable way. Hector said he'd sent a couple of guys off in a truck to see his family so he had about twenty minutes to hand over a little info and turn them round.

For Morres, it took not even one second of those twenty minutes to conclude what really mattered in life and he went on to break every code in the book and cough up some serious intel, enabling Hector to avoid agents on a shipment that night. He never found out what the shipment was, it was all over the south west or deep underground inside hours but Hector really wanted to do this.

Hector was initially true to his word. Once Morres was released, he was still feeling guilty and planning a confession to his lieutenant but his family were safe so he thought it mattered not about suspensions or even if he went to jail, all that mattered was they were safe.

But then he came home one night to find his babies, Dani and Eva, propped up together, still and breathless against his bed headboard. His wife, Abril was equally still outside.

Hector liked this, giving someone just enough time to feel safe then doubling their pain. He threatened to apply it to anyone, a challenge to his kind to rise to the top then risk his frivolous love of a meaningless killing, what a buzz. He offered it to those who fancied it, and many did, the thrill of escaping a madman.

Morres never revealed the real truth of his time with Hector although festering deep in him was his mission to dismantle the asshole. Tequila quickly took over and became his only ally after months of failed attempts by fellow officers and the world at large. There was no floor to his world, he'd been handed something worse than death so what do you do? You seek the end whilst pretending it's not suicide. If you're lucky you have a pretty good time doing it. Morres wasn't having a pretty good time doing it. He wasn't nearly finished with the stuff he had to do. Not yet, but soon.

So here he now was in sleepy San Juan, transferred for obvious reasons and given the chance to establish a life without cartels or other such horrible assholes. The last time he smiled was that day he came home looking forward to his babies bouncing and squeaking into daddy's arms.

Sinking sad, lonely and angry into sedate local police work was a less than clearly announced imposition on San Juan PD but the ear and heart of his lieutenant, Big Bob Stefano, good friends with his former commander in El Paso, guided him to some level of acceptance, perhaps even the will to keep living. Everyone can see something of themselves in a desperate man.

He had one thing on his desk that would stay on top of the pile until it was done, that missing little girl. If anyone was going to get hold of the sick fuck that took that little girl, it would be him. Every suspect was Hector Valdez, every lead smelt of Hector Valdez and when he got him, he would be Hector fucking Valdez in Morres's mind. What wasn't entirely clear to him was what he might do once he had and here was perhaps the method of his exit from this stage.

5   Ghosts

Salvador found himself on Coronado beach, a forty minute drive from San Juan. It was a bright sunny day and he was here with his buddy, Tony the Shoe, and a few of the guys. They were all camped out with a few beers at the Bolas Quemadas beach bar just across the little track from the beach.

Salvador turned to check the big bamboo calendar clock thing on the wall at the back behind the bar. His throbbing head, his fucking still throbbing head, really didn't like moving in this way. Apart from the blues band due here tomorrow and a generous happy hour planned between 7-9pm tonight, this was the day the guys had all come here a few months ago. Salvador hadn't been able to come because he had a deadline but he was here now. He remembered the guys talking about this day as possibly one of the funniest Tony had ever produced for them. It was that day.

The clock said 6pm and Salvador had an internal chuckle as his watch and the day in general shouted 2pm loud and proud, being the fact that it was 2pm. In all the years he'd been coming here from childhood to now to after now this daft clock had always said 6pm. It was a standing joke with the punters and the staff said it didn't matter what they did, new batteries, new clock even. It just got to 6pm and stuck there. So as far as Bolas Quemadas was concerned, it was always 6pm in Bolas Quemadas.

Clearly, whichever force of supernature was jumping him around like this seemed to object to him getting any sleep, unless of course he had slept somehow, and it sure didn't feel like it, or was he actually sleeping now?

A black dog was racing about on the sand offering the occasional happy 'woof.' The place was pretty much as Salvador remembered it from the other times he used to come here, not too busy, a few folks crashed out on the sand, some in the bar, some in the cafe, browsing the shops and a few more in the water. There was no real noise apart from the breeze teasing the palm trees, the sea tickling the beach and him and the guys.

Tony was the life and soul of anything any of them ever did. He was priceless, with an energy and disdain none of them could match. He was delighted to see Salvador catching up though. Others had tried and found themselves on the thick end of a separation or down the fat end of a toilet.

Tony would manage in one sentence to piss off women, Mexicans, Asians and anyone who had an opinion he could have fun with. After mucho bourbon, Tony was ruthless. He loved locating breaking points, he knew he had them, playthings for his abuse. He was first to admit it. A person who does that can sometimes trip over their massive clown feet and rub the odd spud head up the wrong way.

Salvador would get coded texts from the big man, lured to the bar by fine spirits and fine ganja and an occasional messy dabble in wrongness. When Tony had finished building his work of reefer art under the bar top, he'd slip past Salvador with a subtle nudge and a wink and Salvador would be drawn outside with him to his van to return smiling, freshly instructed.

The bar became a different place, the music driving deeper into him, sunlight through the window found only him on his chair, the people there were more interesting and everything had the potential to be created. His brain hummed to him like next door's washing machine and all was right and smiley with the world.

Today on Coronado beach though, Salvador needed to

have a chat with him. Tony had known Camille at school as well. He did what buddies do to each others girlfriends, rip the shit out of her all the time and Camille loved giving it him back. He was hilarious. Guys liked him and girls liked him and every so often another wayward soul would share herself with him. Tony wanted love like everyone did and he wouldn't admit that until the day it arrives.

Tony was center of attention at the bar, in the middle of a classic Tony rant under the heading 'fucking shops, man' about the ever shifting sands of retail and the chaos that can befall a man entering a supermarket.

'Every so often,' he started. 'Your plotted route around the place, your sanity in a vast world of stuff you don't need, is thrown into disarray with a wholesale reorganisation of all the shelves. It leads you to paella rice where once there were cornflakes, to chocolate chip cookies where once there were olives. You eventually get the things you need but only after you spend more time trawling round things you didn't, or do you?' He already had the crowd.

'Do people normally buying cornflakes have a secret unfulfilled yearning for paella rice? When they take the corn-flakes out of the bag at home do they stand in quiet longing for their true grainy love?'

Tony's look of honest but cross-eyed helplessness in this horrific world he painted sent a few of the guys over the edge and several more from around the bar had diverted from their own private conversations to grin broadly at the comedian at the bar. But Tony wasn't done yet.

'At the airport,' he continued, expressionless. 'Once you've got through security and there's no escape back to the world of the Earthbound, you're funnelled like a grad school experiment like rats down a shining, perfumed path of fifty buck t-shirts before emerging into open space smelling like a hooker's handbag.'

As all and sundry lost control of beer and humility and passers by were drawn to the commotion, Salvador emerged from his own laughter to take that chat with old Tony.

'Hey Sally how you doing?' said Tony, giving Salvador a weighty flat hand to the chest. Tony always called him Sally. He was the only one allowed to because it didn't matter how many times Salvador asked him not to, it just kept coming.

'Jesus, Tony, look man, got a question for you.'

'Shoot, Buddola.'

'Do you remember Camille from school?'

Tony looked up and then right, sent a hand to rub his chin stubble and finally did.

'Shit yeh Camille, smoking hot right? You tapped that, you cheeky fuck?'

'I didn't tap anything dude, we were friends,' said Salvador realising what was to come, a succession of 'you did too, you slut' and 'no I didn't' and 'yes you did' and finally 'no seriously dude I didn't, we were thirteen,' which itself, Tony thought, didn't prove a point.

'Do you remember she just didn't come back to school?'

'Yeh, she died or something right?'

Salvador wasn't expecting this. He was all geared up to see if Tony knew where she'd gone. He must be thinking about someone else.

'No she didn't die, bud,' continued Salvador. 'I saw her recently. She's back in San Juan.'

'Nah I'm pretty sure she did, man. Didn't they tell you back then?'

'No dude no-one told me she died. No-one told me anything. I just thought they'd moved away. I went to her house and everything but they'd all gone.'

'Yeah, her parents moved back east apparently. Her mom just up and went, couldn't stand being in the same house and her dad had to follow quick smart.'

'Are you sure you're thinking about Camille? Little blond girl, cute as a chocolate button.'

'Well I think so. Are you sure it's her you saw?'

'Pretty sure. No, totally sure.'

'Well maybe I'm thinking of someone else, it was a long time ago. I was sure it was her though.'

Salvador reeled from this chat. Not what he'd wanted. Tony was full of shit, definitely thinking about someone else. If it was Camille, his folks and the school would definitely have told him.

Tony gave him another flat hand on the chest, put his arm round him with a 'you ok bud, come talk to us over here, you big nosed fucker?' passed him one of the big frothy beers and returned to his adoring fans.

The frothy beer was paradise. Don't get wasted, he told himself, focus. He turned to the calmer image of the beach to process things, and not least had to wonder if they'd kept it from him because him and Camille were so close. No fuck that, he thought, he saw her this morning, Tony's full of shit.

At that moment there emerged from the waves the athletic, fine and wiggling shape of one Megan Fernandez. Megan hadn't been at their school, she was much younger than them but she and Tony had shared history.

Megan made it into the bar and bless him, Tony had her a glass of wine all ready. 'Hey,' she said, caressing Salvador's leg on the way past and settled in with the guys to listen to Tony's second set.

Tony had his crocs on. He always wore these weird rubber shoes called crocs. The kids loved them, they attach little badges to them through the holes, small metallic flowers, love hearts, aliens, Cartmans or Bart Simpsons. The occasional cheeky kid, destined for greatness or some other life of crime would sport a tiny metallic naked lady with big boobs.

Tony broke from them briefly. He'd spotted possible

shenanigans. He went up to the very attractive wife of some guy sitting at bar and started by announcing in the clearest language available to him that he wasn't a misogynist, accompanied by some fine beer spray.

'I love women, I've got all their albums.'

There was a blank look from this unfortunate couple, nothing, just wishing they'd taken the table over there like she fucking said they should, but there was more.

'Vaginas. Jesus,' he said, actually pointing a finger at the nearest vagina on this stool. 'Little furry cave system designed by God in his Giger phase, fucking mystery.'

At that moment, probably just prior to being thrown out of the bar, Tony had a moment of the strangest clarity and he knew what he had to do. He downed his beer, slammed his glass down, avoided the confused incoming gazes and hammered down the beach and headlong into the shallow sea, his wake catching him quickly and driving twenty five bucks worth of his thirty buck shorts right up his ass.

When he emerged from his splashdown, eyes wide and wet, extracting cotton from his butt and shaking like a shitting dog, he was shoeless and confused and turned to the ocean with heat and curse, troubling some of the ladies at the cafe. Then a sign, a single shoe washed up right in front of him, it was retrieved and held close with a smile as Tony searched for its twin, spotting every ripple and break as the very same. But minutes passed and no twin could be seen.

More minutes passed and Tony resigned himself to the fact that the twin was lost to the waves, never to return. Tony felt a small welling up at his failure to keep safe this poor shoe but soon came round, taking his remaining shoe, a pointless item on its own, apologising and launching it with a big 'fuck off then' of substance back into the ocean over the rocks and far away and he stood to contemplate his loss.

Seconds later, his arm barely back in its place, as he

considered turning to return to the bar, he was drawn to something in the waves a few yards out. A cold feeling rose up in him like an old girlfriend coming up behind you and whispering in your ear. There bobbling casually over towards him was the other shoe.

Tony resigned the day to being a day of one shoe. It's harsh but the other shoe had peaked too soon and was cast away to appear again one day in Acapulco or thereabouts. This successful shoe had played the long game and had prevailed, if one prefers California to Mexico that is. Who knew the plan was to unseat his brother and at that very time become redundant.

Tony returned to the bar but Salvador and the guys were already unable to breathe with laughter. This was the moment. It was like being there on the grassy knoll. It was never clear what exactly drove the great man to this watery mission but he was, on this very day, at this very moment awarded his title of Tony the Shoe, the man, the story, the legend. Salvador couldn't remember the last time he laughed but odds on Tony would have been there.

Salvador didn't know why he was part of this day where once he hadn't been, maybe it was just a bit of laughter therapy, but he did feel drawn to the beach and not just because of the memories of when he'd been here before, something else.

The Camille thing made no fucking sense at all. Tony's full of shit, Tony must be full of shit. Salvador thought maybe a walk on the beach would settle his thoughts. He slipped over the low front wall of the bar and onto the track. As he walked along the track, he looked in at the little shops and stalls dotted alongside but his gaze came to rest on one shop in particular.

His favorite shop on the beach was next to the cafe. It didn't have a shop sign but did have a vintage metal Pepsi sign propped up against the wall on the counter. No-one ever knew what it was called so it got called the Pepsi shop. It had the coolest things, just one of each thing, miniature rope and balsa wood boats, an oil painting of the sun freshly risen over a primordial rock and abstract sculptures that looked like they'd been chipped right off that primordial rock.

There were clearly master artisans of all flavours tucked away around the vicinity of Coronado supplying this little shop. What a fine way to spend retirement, camped out near the beach selling a boat or sunflower fan every so often and not needing much at all apart from that.

Today the shop was dark inside. All he could see were two off-white eyes looking right back at him, unmoving, unblinking.

Salvador felt strange. He wanted to avert his own gaze and carry on to the sand but couldn't. He was still walking but more slowly, unaware of what was in front of him, unaware of anything else apart from these eyes, which gradually followed him as he moved. A sudden feeling of fear came over him, like waking in the night to a door slowly opening in the blackness or a huge spider under your pillow. He had a growing feeling that death lurked nearby and also started to feel his head throbbing again.

The only thing that allowed him some peace from this evil glare from inside the shop was the fact that he had to close his eyes to deal with the pain. He stopped and put his head in his hands. It was getting worse. He tried to open his eyes again but when his eyelids made their intentions known his head would pound and pound even more.

He was seconds from letting out an almighty roar of pain when suddenly the pain subsided and he found himself in familiar surroundings yet again.

Coupe de Ville

This time he was back in San Juan at the Net Nano building, casually strolling in through the front doors heading for the elevator just like he did every day until recently.

It was a tricky induction jumping to a place where he was already in motion, whether it was in the car or walking or running into that battle hell. It was a bit like taking off on two skis and suddenly find you're landing on one, getting acclimatised to this body. At least the dark glass panels that lined the walls of this lobby showed him it was his own body, always good to check just in case he's come as a monkey or something and everyone starts chasing him around.

He checked around to check some roar of pain hadn't arrived here with him. Back at the beach he'd already pulled in all the air needed to make a solid noise, a mix of pain and fear, but the other people here seemed nicely unconcerned.

He did carry the feeling from the beach though, the pure evil staring at him from inside that dark shop. Who the hell was that? He shuddered under the electricity those eyes now shot up his spine. He hoped he'd never see them again. It was unholy. He didn't know if they stared at everyone walking past the shop like that or Salvador had been singled out for a special dose of evil. But he preferred being here than there.

He'd never felt that before. He then remembered his chat with Tony and Tony's insistence Camille died when they were all thirteen at school. He held firm to Tony being full of shit, just a very stoned buddy with poor recall. Otherwise the Camille Salvador had seen actually wasn't Camille.

The Net Nano building was solid and strong, ghoulishly modern, disturbingly naughty and unashamedly space age. There were two sides of it joined by three ascending glass walkways, invisible from the ground. They allowed people to walk in air passing from one side to the other. The left section was a giant graphite tower PC with an array of all breeds of comms on the roof and it bled leading edge tech, the people inside surely being demigods from the future, gliding round, moulding our world with their enormous brains and mastery of the Segway.

The right side looked like an enormous deep recessed window, the light blue panes all seemed as one and this side was slightly lighter and more shiny than the tower. Occasionally you could see flashes and trails through a window. It was a quiet green space with firs and oaks randomly dotted around.

There was bound to be someone inside who'd secretly briefed the landscaper to arrange the trees in a certain pattern, maybe a galactic alignment that tied in with some Fibonacci numbers. Overall the building shouted 'big square brain' and it was a very cool place to be.

As usual, Salvador didn't know why he was here but again it was useful he was. He knew there were things he needed to do here but was this some time in the past or some time in the future? Was he here to see his researchers, Chen and Annalise? Maybe today there'd be some progress, some answers.

Maybe there were reasons for the jumps after all. Were the jumps here to help him or hinder him or were they totally random, a glitch in the universe, no reason for them at all? Maybe God was a kid with a spider in a jar, just sending it round in circles.

Salvador's boss, Yuki had been tampering with the elevator music again. He always liked this Japanese zen music on the way up to center him. Salvador couldn't get on with it at all. It was 'twang' then nothing for about five seconds and then a lower 'twong' and finally it sounded like some guy's fallen down the stairs with a tray of beers. In the fifteen seconds or so it took to get Salvador up top, there had only been two fairly uneventful 'twangs,' one 'twong' and a surprise 'twing.'

Salvador was out of the elevator and head down focused on his office door. He crossed the floor thanks only to the prospect of peace on the other side and maybe sooner or later a glass or two of the golden liquid, single cube cracking away in it. He needed to calm his nerves, get centered, but not too much, promise. He made it to his sanctum unmolested, closing the door behind him. He was safe, heart rate lowered, breath returning, all good.

Much sooner than later, in fact immediately, that cube was in that glass and joined by that liquid. Salvador crashed back into his chair and closed his eyes to feel it go down his throat. A deep breath signalled he would hopefully soon approach his center.

He swivelled in his chair to face the window and it's composed view south over the countryside. He was getting more than the flashes of Coronado. He was getting flashes of home.

He'd been staring out of his open kitchen window taking in the warm breeze tickling the blinds and making some papers on the table shuffle in hope of flight. He was standing there in that kitchen lingering in some memory.

He was sitting at the edge of a mountain at peace with the world, looking out at a massive moonlit landscape, fabulous and beautiful. He felt different, his head was cloudy and confused, a constant dull hum preventing thoughts from hitting that next level, not processing like they should.

He wasn't alone, something big joined him for just a

short while, made some noises then left. That's all he could remember apart from he felt in sync with this big thing, like it was meant to be there when he was, he just wanted to follow it and keep it safe for some reason.

He didn't remember having that memory standing in the kitchen at all but now he had it. Sitting here now, Salvador was sure the last time he was here was when Yuki sent him home after the Jemma thing happened. Who knew when another flash was going to come to him of something he didn't remember? For all he knew he could have been here earlier yesterday or next week, he could have been a bird on the window ledge or a blade of grass swaying in a tiny breeze, who knew? Maybe he'd walked naked through the office but for a pink headband and matching socks, something you have to try at least once.

Suddenly an effervescent grinning Yuki, hands outstretched, exploded into the room like a game show host coming down the stairs. Yuki was a gentle intellectual giant, energetic, positive, a complete operator and perfect in front of the money people. A doer of deals, an awesome person to be around, always smiling. Yuki's big smile was made even more smiley by virtue of his Thai and Japanese extraction. There was something infectious about the deep broad smile belonging to folk of that ilk.

Yuki could smell someone's ability to annoy and their ability to be useful as soon as he set eyes on them. It was a cracking skill and it was why Salvador had this hall pass to get his shit together. Yuki wouldn't let him try anything meaningful here if he was still no more useful than a Maasai barman and he knew Salvador wasn't in the game he needed to be in.

Yuki had been inspired by one life-affirming instance when he was at college. He said it made him the him of today. It taught him to expect a rip in logic at any turn and helped him learn how to exploit it.

Yuki wrote a polite letter of complaint to the Happy Puss Kitty Treat Company Inc. of Dayton, Ohio, mentioning that his cat didn't like their kittie treats. He wasn't asking for his money back, just wanted to offer some suggestions like a solid citizen. The Happy Puss Kitty Treat Company Inc. of Dayton, Ohio wrote back promptly and said 'we're really sorry your cat doesn't like our happy puss kitty treats, please find enclosed a cat that does.'

Yuki instantly transformed Salvador's office into the epitome of fast smart youth, delivering an electricity and vibrancy to the air in the room. A solid man hug was folded in, then a less than subtle chest bounce, which Yuki had to jump for, and finally a more than sensible number of back slaps. He was a strong little guy, Yuki and when he got hold of Salvador, he knew he was got hold of.

Yuki had got it straight away, he'd given Salvador a load of shit for even daring to turn up to work after the Jemma thing and said everything he had was at his disposal. Yuki was his boss for sure but this was what friends did.

Yuki knew about his mission to bring Jemma back but Salvador's new and very odd temporal situation was a matter for Salvador alone and would stay that way. Yuki was genuinely keen to know where Salvador's mind was taking him on the Jemma thing and Salvador was genuinely keen to sell it to him. This is how Salvador found out if he was on track, try and sell something to Yuki.

Yuki already knew most of it. Doctors couldn't get to the area safely let alone try anything surgical and that, folks, is where they seemed to have folded. But Salvador wasn't having that, no sir, fuck that, there was something out there, there had to be, he just had to find it. He'd been having ideas. One or two maybe had legs and one needed to be the answer.

'Yuk, our new Neuronet VR system.'

'Yep.'

'Doctors should try using it on coma patients, insert feelings into the part of the brain that caused Jemma's shut down, remind it what it's meant to be doing, maybe bring it round?'

Salvador's crowning devotion at this moment in time was to ruthlessly ignore medical opinion, not because he didn't respect the prevailing excellence of medical opinion but when it accepted its own defeat it assumed this was final, by proxy your own surrender. It switched focus to last rites, funeral planning and insurance. When they said 'there's nothing we can do,' your only option was step up and do it yourself.

'Yeah, Chen and Annalise told me about this one,' said Yuki. 'It's gorgeous theory, bud, but even when someone suggests a new treatment that isn't right out of Star Trek, it's got to jump so many hurdles. Maybe I know someone with a bit of sway with our little Mission Hospital.'

'Thanks Yuk, that's a kind thought but I'm pretty sure even the capo di tutti oligarchs of Mission Hospital couldn't jump that much regulation.'

Salvador was right of course but you try, and then you do it yourself. He'd already initiated this plan covertly. Today was hopefully when Chen hands over the system so he can try it with Jemma.

Salvador and Yuki sat on the opposing couches near the door. Salvador was always grateful he had this man's ear.

'So what else?' asked Yuki.

'Thanks for Chen and Annalise, by the way, Yuk, they're awesome.'

'Long as you need them, bud.'

'I've been looking at pretty much everything, Yuk, supernatural, magic, mystic eastern stuff...' but he didn't have time to finish.

'Sceptical,' Yuki said with a most sudden force of gay abandon. Yuki remembers the day he finally accepted being gay, or as Yuki liked to say, a giant homo. So many long years with only dreams but no longer. He'd been cornered by his distant cousin or what not from Manilla and she'd backed him into a coat cupboard. As she took him in her mouth Yuki looked through the coats and saw a man changing his shirt. From that moment the mouth around him belonged to the unsuspecting guy in the fresh new blue shirt. Yuki was loud, proud and endowed and cared not who knew it, or who saw it for that matter.

He shot to fame in local gay circles and far beyond into the land of YouTube one night a few years back. There was this bar called The Banished Beaver in downtown LA. Yuki was already the life and soul of the place but when he hopped up on the bar and decided to stir cocktails with his old fella, the place went mad for it and he was asked to, and did indeed deliver his own light creamy topping to at least three lucky punters. It does still literally make Salvador gag thinking about it.

Although Yuki realised the limits of western medicine, Salvador thought his reaction to mystical ideas was a little symptomatic of those limits. He should have known better.

'And don't look at me like that with your eyebrow thing going on, like my fine Asian features should know that shit, dude, we're from Anaheim,' said Yuki and there it was, the laughter began with a modest chuckle. It refused to be fleeting and persisted, becoming deeper, more painful and allowing far too little breathing. People probably don't do this nearly enough in a lifetime, completely lose it all ends up. It's a superdrug, forcing abandonment of all cares and several bodily functions. Salvador had no idea what really kicked them off, tension, relief, but he did know the tuneful wind mutually released during the ordeal poured fuel on it.

'Anyway, dude, I've got the DOD in here in ten minutes. Keep trying and keep me posted, yeah?' said Yuki.

And that was that. Yuki got up, impeccable, and with an ease and grace that can only be enjoyed by a light man.

'Oh, wait, I wanted to mention,' Yuki reminded himself, edging a few yards back towards Salvador. 'I was playing a round at San Juan Hills a few days ago and I saw your dad's old car. Coupe de Ville right?'

'Right, yeah a '49,' said Salvador.

Yuki pointed to one of the photos Salvador had on his wall, their office party at the golf club a few years back. To the side of the group shot out front Salvador noticed the unmistakable form of a '49 Coupe de Ville in sky blue.

'Unreal,' said Salvador. 'The exact car my old man had when I was little. How come I didn't notice it when I was there?'

'That's the one,' said Yuki. 'I knew I'd seen it before.' It was even the same colour apart from his dad's car had a silver roof and this one was black.

'Who's was it?'

'This guy got out of it and went into the shed. I guess he works there.'

Yuki fastened his middle button and after a quick hug he was at the door. He pulled back for a moment and looked at Salvador.

'Literally, anything you need buddy, I mean it,' he said, and with an appreciative nod of respect and love from Salvador, he was gone, taking a fair bit of the room's energy with him.

Salvador was pretty sure Yuki will have talked to Chen and Annalise already on their various ideas or he would have been more enthusiastic. Maybe it was the DOD meeting he had but Salvador didn't get the impression any of it had really grabbed him.

Salvador finally found time to check his calendar. He was definitely in the timeline he was meant to be in. This wasn't the past or the future. It was the present, back where he should be, like in the street earlier.

Today he was going to the hospital to see Jemma's consultant, Dr. Ramirez for a chat first and then see Jemma. He was pretty sure how it'd play out with Ramirez. The good Doctor will try to convince him to turn off life support. The hospital's view was that her state is irretrievable. The letter said 'terminal' and so it was. He had nothing further to say to this than what he'd said before, namely 'over my dead body, doc.'

He would lie next to Jemma and talk to her, his senses primed to detect anything from her, hearing every noise as a response, a sign of recovery. Then he'll try the VR idea. Sure he felt guilty not telling Yuki but he had no choice. Just thinking about it working, Jemma opening her eyes and saying 'hello Baby, what's up?' threatened to send him into the most wonderful dream, a dream he would happily live in forever. Maybe these jumps could just send him there, plant him in a time where it was all OK, keep him with his Jemma forever. Why not?

One of the many things Yuki had done for him after the Jemma thing happened was give him some time with a couple of smart grad students, here at Net Nano learning the ropes. Chen and Annalise were available to help Salvador research the slightly left field ideas he was looking for. Yuki knew this was all Salvador thought about and all he had to keep his hopes alive after western medicine threw down its gun and legged it back over the hill, and he knew Salvador wouldn't stop trying until he succeeded or ran out of time.

Yuki had seen how deep into the bottle Salvador's persistent dead ends were sending him. He was close to taking Salvador off for an intervention to some cabin somewhere with no booze, perhaps a small medical team and Chen and

Annalise for a devoted think tank, extra brain power and leg work to his mission.

Chen and Annalise were perfect. They were both doing their masters at Berkeley, smart, quick and organised and they had ideas. Yuki will have asked them to drop in on him as soon as he left. A knock at his door confirmed it and soon brought the two of them inside.

'Hey Salvador, how's it going buddy?' said Chen, instantly in for a hug.

'Not bad, crazy kids, how about you?'

Salvador sat them down where he and Yuki had just behaved like people half their age. Chen couldn't wait to get on topic.

'The VR rig's all here buddy,' he said pointing to a small bag he'd brought in with him. 'All ready to hook up. God, I love that idea.'

Chen did love the VR idea. He'd said it should be enhanced by electroshock. Despite some early problems involving sending current shocking through the stairwell and other places around the building, he was unmoved and wouldn't stop trying until he'd proven it.

Genevieve from accounting certainly wasn't unmoved after getting a solid few volts up her and almost falling over the stair rail. People said after that day she became strangely attractive and soon after that her hemline started to rise. Salvador would not be enhancing Jemma's set up with elec- troshock though but here was the method to his madness in this bag.

Chen and Annalise were seeking out every occurrence of fooled medical opinion and things modern medicine thought were silly, tribal miracles and brave new ideas and they were presenting Salvador with their thoughts as they came along.

'It's a long shot,' said Annalise, giving Chen a few extra seconds to get his adrenalin back down. 'But I guess everything is. We've found these people called the Luiseño Indians. They practice these rituals designed to release the hold on a spirit. Australian Aboriginals also do it, quite a few tribes do but the Luiseño are right down the road.'

'You're gonna love this,' chipped in Chen. Salvador was hooked already.

'The incantations happen around a fire,' continued Annalise. 'They have to be next to a river. Your spirit is drawn through the darkness and towards the firelight. You may have to go through trials to reach the light. When you do reach the light, the fire is meant to pick up briefly into the air. This is your spirit waking up and announcing itself, it's returned. The fire passes your awakened soul into your body and you're then cooled in the river.'

'It's so cool,' said Chen. 'Can you imagine emerging from that wondering what the fuck...?'

'They've never done anyone in a coma before,' said Annalise. 'But people who did the ritual said they had visions of monsters and ghosts and all the things that were super scary to them. They were pursued everywhere they went but then they found they could generate super strength or speed or some other ability as their journey progressed towards the light.'

Salvador was absorbed in this idea. It made perfect sense.

'That's exactly it,' he said. 'Jemma needs her spirit woken up and released,' but Annalise wasn't done yet.

'Yep. They wake up in a state of wide eyed delight. They've discovered their essence but it's confusing. They immediately try and process it. They have to be submerged in the river so they don't get a chance to process it, this is what needs cooling. They'd quickly forget what happened in their quest for the light and remember it only as a feeling, a transition.'

'A silent epiphany,' said Chen with a triumphant, theatrical prayer to the ceiling.

Salvador didn't bother asking to get any sort of permission from Mission hospital to take Jemma to this ritual the same as he hadn't bothered asking them if he could hook her up to this VR rig in the bag, That's why he'd told Yuki not to bother.

Annalise had a solid plan germinating for the ritual idea, the extraction from and return to her hospital bed undetected. This was his next move if the VR idea didn't work.

'The Luiseño elders have agreed to do it so it's just getting Jemma there and getting her back again afterwards,' she said.

'But we're onto that,' added Chen.

'It has to be overnight' said Salvador. 'Maybe I'll hide myself in Jemma's room until lights out. I need a method to transport her once I'm inside.' Suitable notes were made.

He'd been there late before many times, when Jemma first came in, and he knew that after midnight it was a pretty quiet back route out. Leaving the door to the parking lot open, he could slip her back in afterwards although, if the Luiseño did what they said on the tin, maybe he'd take her home for a drink afterwards instead. He certainly didn't want to get Yuki involved with this felony, the owner of the equipment and certainly not these researchers at the start of glittering careers. He couldn't help thinking some help would be really useful though.

Salvador got up and gave Chen a big enthusiastic hug again and this time tugged Annalise in for one as well. She was initially reticent but ultimately couldn't help a big genuine grin and she appreciated it, blushing and punching Salvador on the arm. These two awesome smart young people were coming through for him. He felt more vibed about life than he had for ages. But how soon before he's dropped down the plughole again? Did he have time?

As the door closed behind Chen and Annalise, Salvador dropped another cube in his glass and pointed his chair at the window again. He was still for a few seconds. Then he remembered Yuki's words about his dad's old car. He turned his gaze back to the photos on the wall, which told stories of UCLA, Jemma, Net Nano and good times.

Look at him, a freshman at UCLA before he ever got a sniff of Jemma. He was looking at a Salvador that didn't even know Jemma yet. He tried to imagine that but quickly called himself a bonehead. He needed to be imagining exactly the opposite.

That was the party when Yuki got funding in for something. Messy. Yuki worked hard but he played hard and paid even harder. There were trips in fighter jets, chilling on the beach and just about anything the questionnaire suggested. The office was always given the next day to recover but that party shut them down for three. Yuki admitted it was worth every minute.

That's the office party at the San Juan Hills golf club two years ago. He remembered this one all too well, Jemma's sublime thy length chiffon mini dress. This wisp of a thing, a sexy light orange affair with lilac flowers, glided over her like cool water over a glass ball and offered just enough transparency to focus on her incredible body but only imagine seeing through to it.

Salvador was a persistent pest to her all evening and finally got hold of her outside the bathroom, surprising her a little at the door then pushing her back inside and locking it. He blew that little dress up with breath to spare and pinned her face flat against the wall. Nestling in behind, lapping at her back like a thirsty St Bernard, he took her right there. By the time this moment arrived, he'd been blue-balled for about two hours, wandering around the party just needing to do this to his Jemma. Downstairs, at any given moment, she might find his hand stroking through her dress, making her jump like she kept finding insects in her pants but enough was enough. He could take it no longer.

He had a lot to give but gave it quickly. There wasn't even a queue to use the bathroom when they left. He looked at her smiling, pulled his jeans on and they emerged as invisibly as possible. His short term performance embarrassment was nothing compared to the grief she would assign him later. She could barely contain herself as they seeped back into the room and back among the unsoiled other guests. If a man can't make his girl come like the ocean on a Tuesday, then let him give her mirth.

And then there was the car, his dad's old '49 Coupe de Ville in sky blue. It was a real beauty and Salvador wallowed for a moment in the many trips they'd all taken in this wonderful car. How strange he'd never spotted it on the day or when he put the picture up on the wall.

Salvador didn't remember all of the drive but it wasn't a jump, just wandering focus and he did at least remember the component parts of it. He knew where he'd parked the car at the office but only because that was his spot, he remembered getting into it, kicking it over and heading out onto Ortega for the hospital. From Ortega to here was the only blank and that was only because he couldn't get Jemma out of his mind. Maybe this was finally a change of scene under his own control.

The smell hit him first, that overly clean scent of death or no death. He was quickly up onto the third floor of Mission Hospital and was upon Dr Ramirez sooner than expected, checking charts in the hallway outside his office. Ramirez invited him in with a warm smile. Salvador suddenly became a little conscious of his bag of tricks but he'd brought little gifts for Jemma before so another cuddly fluffy toy or something was not unknown to the folks here.

Dr Ramirez was a solid Guatemalan with a strong ethnic South American look about him, regal, you can imagine his forebears standing on the top of a Mayan temple waiting for their command to not so surgically remove the heart of some poor local and getting the buzz from the masses below as he held up the heart to them, rock and roll. Salvador thought it was perfect preparation for modern medicine.

Ramirez's office was where Jemma and Salvador had initially heard the bad news, that day a cold clinical space with the walls closing in on them. Today it was sunnier, not as grey but still a place he'd prefer not to be.

Pleasantries were exchanged with a degree of sincerity but Ramirez had something to say. He had an authority about him. It was a shift in posture, a lowering of the head and a slight raised eyebrow and it made Salvador feel like a schoolboy.

'So Salvador,' said Ramirez. 'By the way do you know your name means saviour in Spanish?'

'I do, doc you've told me,' said Salvador sensing an attempted softening of the air prior to a firestorm.

'Sorry, of course. I know you're keen to see Jemma but what are your thoughts about her situation?'

'Sad' said Salvador. 'I've just got a feeling I'm not going to like what you're going to say.'

'Look Salvador. I know you think the whole idea of switching off life support is...'

'Abject surrender,' interrupted Salvador. 'And not going to happen.'

Salvador felt a little guilty going on the attack quite so quickly but it was every damn time, is Salvador sure he shouldn't be thinking about switching her off. Ramirez was a really nice guy. Getting annoyed with him was like getting annoyed when you catch an old lady picking your pocket. Salvador was frustrated being here having to run over all this yet again when all he wanted to do was see his Jemma.

'Yes I understand but the hospital has to think of so many things,' returned Ramirez, his agenda unwrapping in rhetorical bursts. 'First, can Jemma ever make a recovery to normal brain function? I'm afraid not, that'll be due to the permanent vegetative state, emphasis on permanent please. The longer she stays in it, the less likely she'd ever come out of it anyway.' Ramirez leaned forward. 'And there's never been a twitch and it's been a long time, Salvador.'

'I know all this doc,' said Salvador, also leaning forward. 'But nothing is permanent and a long time, as you put it, is only three months. I swear only the end of days is a long enough time.' Salvador relaxed back in his chair. 'Doc, I get what you're saying but you're trying to sell ice to the Eskimos here. As long as Jemma is alive, my answer will remain, and please excuse my language, fuck no.'

Ramirez took a few seconds to allow the room back to room temperature. He did understand this was a horrible discussion to have but today he had to have it. What Salvador didn't yet know was that this wasn't the regular stuff, there was more. Ramirez wasn't finished.

'Second,' he continued. 'Are there other people who need Jemma's facilities? Yes, and third, Salvador, there is the insurance question and the fact that your cover only goes up to a certain point.'

'Indeed it does, doc,' said Salvador 'It goes up to the point we stop paying for it. We pay through the arse for it and have done for years.' Salvador managed to take a little time to enjoy the word *we*, something he hasn't been able to say for while.

But Ramirez was reaching his point, the crux of this conversation. He looked down and ran his hand through his hair. He wasn't at ease.

'Doctors report to insurance companies on patient status,' he continued. 'When that status is capable of improving, the cover continues as per policy, when it's not capable of improving, there's a cut off point.'

He looked Salvador clean in the eye and both men prepared. Salvador raised an eyebrow of his own to prompt him.

'Then they have to withdraw cover. I'm sorry Salvador. They'll cover Jemma for one more week.'

'Bullshit,' was the only response a quickly numbing Salvador could offer. 'Says who?'

Ramirez handed over the letter, another fucking letter,

this one with just as much nastiness attached. He read it closely. The room was silent, quiet enough for Salvador to hear a dripping tap in the room next door. Ramirez sat quietly back in his chair to allow digestion and placed his two index fingers together against his chin priming himself for Salvador's response. He'd got to know Salvador reasonably well over the past few months and knew he was a rational man but news like this can take people in irrational directions.

Salvador read this second filthy letter coming across phrases such as 'there's no point' and 'would be better for all if...' He felt something grizzly about his midsection, something angry starting in him, poking him with a sharpness and wanting him to get to his feet and have a go, clauses and contracts and waivers and bullshit. Fine, if you didn't know you had a to fix the landlord's roof if it blew off that's all well and good but not his Jemma's life.

He knew about controlled breathing from an old girlfriend and he slowed his to avoid the anger this letter was conjuring. Fuku Insurance certainly didn't stand on ceremony and told it like it was, medical opinion was that Jemma's status was unrecoverable and so in seven days they would cease cover and so would the hospital.

Salvador did actually appreciate being told the contents before reading it. It eased the blow slightly and his freezing stare on Ramirez dropped away to something less Hannibal Lecter but something you still needed a jumper for.

'What if I funded treatment myself?' he asked.

'I'm sorry Salvador, it would make no difference. When a patient isn't terminal and a recovery is possible yes of course funding can come from anywhere but you have to understand where we are coming from. There are people we can save and they need her space. The hospital has to give it.'

So that was that, another seven days, this time to step up and think of something. Yes he was about to try two more ideas but the pressure had just risen. Seven days. Jesus. Ramirez offered some tenuous wisdom albeit hampered by the appreciation he was talking to a person looking at the organised and precisely timed death of his wife and a person now lost in a fog. Although Ramirez's voice had started to tail off and reverberate round the room, Salvador still heard him suggest he try and spend the time remembering not fighting, getting his head on ready, making his peace. Salvador got up from his chair and offered his hand. Ramirez obliged. There was no further debate to be had.

'If you'll excuse me, doctor, I'm going to see my wife.'

Salvador reentered a corridor that looked very different now. Everything had an urgency about it. People were moving faster, looking more concerned, even the machines were beeping faster. His head was thumping like a school band, the brass section tearing at his sanity, time was speeding up all around him and his hyper fog stayed with him all the way until he made it, dizzy and ashamed into Jemma's room, two three two, and shut the world out behind him.

So far, he'd failed to find a solution. He was ashamed. He had a decent brain on him, he had the help of others with much finer brains but still he'd failed. He had seven days to pull it round and find his answer, to bring her back to him, start his life again with the only aspect of it that made it worth living. But he needed to put the horror of seven days behind him for now, enter a space where peace reigned. He knew his Jemma would sense the angst. He couldn't bring that in here.

Two three two was a nice long room with a window either side of the far end of it, a pair of comfy chairs in front of them and an aztec design rug. Salvador always brought a flower, usually from Emilie at Flores Apestoso on El Camino but today it seemed confusion had left that out of the plan. The sun's louvred entry through the blinds created a real peace in the room and was joined only by the sounds of the machines.

One or two of the simpler ideas they'd come up with were still playing their art in this room, taped incantations and rare fragrances said to be the only thing to stimulate certain parts of the brain. Risking the danger of creating a small internal Woodstock in room two three two, Mission Hospital, Annalise had it all recorded and installed a while ago but Mission Hospital couldn't possibly have imagined what was plotted against it over the next few days.

He always took a little time before looking at Jemma. He had to adjust to her as she was now, the invaded, wasting away, only capable of outsourced movement thanks to her technology.

He moved over to her and asked her 'what's up then, Wiggle?' Wiggle was a name he conjured one evening soon after they first met. He and Jemma had gone to bed early and he was already under the covers with some Hunter Thompson book. She was taking an age in the bathroom but when she emerged, she did so in a burlesque costume that would melt glass and certainly closed that book quick smart.

She performed a slow striptease for him and danced and wiggled over to the bed never dropping eye contact, seeming like she was going to eat him alive. By the time she'd got within sniffing distance, Salvador was drooling and hard as a lamp post. That very evening she became his Jemma, his baby and now his Wiggle.

She got her own back soon after that when they went to a 70s disco night at a friend's house in Venice Beach. Salvador was never usually the keenest dancer but he'd been coaxed up to dance by his Jemma when 'blame it on the boogie' came on and he seemed to find his rhythm at last, even started enjoying it. Unfortunately it was a rhythm belonging to some other song altogether and Jemma failed to continue her own sublime moves from laughing so hard. That very night, Jemma, and several of their friends re-christened Salvador 'Boogie' given that he had very little of it.

There was only one way these conversations could go and that was Salvador delivering his monologue and imagine her responding. In his head she looked up at him, took his hand and smiled.

'Oh you know, Boogie, just hanging around,' said Jemma. 'How's you?

He hopped up beside her on the bed and squeezed her hand, rested his head back on the board and exhaled for what seemed like a full minute. This seemed to be the only place that allowed him the deepest peace, just as it was before this all happened, next to his girl. They sat quietly together for a few minutes just enjoying each other's company but he couldn't resist telling her his surprise.

'Guess what?' he said.

'You crashed the car,' said Jemma, squeezing his hand right back.

'No, Baby, Net Nano has loaned me something.'

Jemma waited for a short while and clearly she needed to say 'What's that, Baby?'

'Well, I've got a full VR system. Chen gave it to me today.'

'Who's Chen,' said Jemma. 'Is he the one you always say is so chilled he fogs up the windows, you know, huggy bear without the purple velvet crimped pants, hat like a tart's umbrella?'

'No Wiggle that's Leroy at the bar.'

'Ah OK, so what are you doing with a full wotsit system then?'

'Well we had an idea,' said Salvador. 'We'd been wondering if we should try convince the hospital to give this a go but there's no way they would so I will.'

'Give what a go Boog, come on spit it out, seriously I've got stuff to do.'

Salvador grinned at his cheeky little wife and gave her a big smacker right on her warm head.

'Might work,' he said.

She gave him a last chance nudge to make himself heard or she'd take a nap. Salvador lay back and examined the ceiling for some endorsement, the faintest upward eyebrow from some VC with a few mill to drop on you. Maybe this VR idea would jog something inside her.

'I'm going to hook you up to our latest VR test rig. The idea is it sends signals into your brain and stimulates a response.'

'Sounds like fun, Baby, go for it,' said Jemma with a chuckle. Sometimes Salvador could really hear her in this room and so it was with this chuckle. It was most likely a combination of machines, reaching some kind of occasional synergy with each other, or the breeze through the open window or just a scuffed shoe somewhere outside, but this chuckle closed his eyes and he remembered the times he heard it, so many times, such a light little chuckle, the sort of chuckle just before a tickle happens.

'Right then, Wiggle, I will take that as your official consent. Hang tight while I get it set up.'

He was normally allowed to visit undisturbed but on occasion a nurse would arrive to check something. Over the months He'd talked to all of them and he had a good idea of Jemma's exact daily ritual, who comes and sees her and when. This was fine provided one of the machines didn't do something really stupid. He'd be setting up a covert little VR session and a freaked out machine did not need to happen. The only early warning system of a resulting human invasion would be the footsteps and that gave him four or five seconds to dismantle and hide, doable but pretty tight.

The sender unit was the size of half a shoe box and he plugged it in and initialised it. There was a little rack space behind another group of machines and, worst case scenario and he only managed to bag up the headset, its single green light should go unnoticed among the many others.

The display was about iPad size and the rest fitted snugly to various parts of her head and didn't assume too much real estate. He centralised Jemma and ensured she was comfortable, brushing her hair aside and placing the goggles and neuronet. Annalise had asked. 'Er, why goggles, she's in a coma?' but if it did work and she came round she needed to see what she'd been seeing in her head before the programme gently wound down and he could introduce her to the here and now.

Salvador wasn't a stupid man but he has been known to do stupid things, sometimes gold star level stupid. To him, this wasn't one of those things but to literally anyone else it certainly was. There was real jail time waiting for people who did stuff like this, not to mention the abduction he planned if this didn't work, and the hospital would have every right to give him a good kicking for it. But for him, what price is too high for success?

He sat on the armchair next to her bed and the display booted. He checked the neuronet could deliver signals and then checked on user feedback. He'd loosely prepared for his emotions at this stage of it but still wasn't quite ready to see the first message on the display and quickly overrode the 'not receiving signal.' The system would record the session anyway.

His plan had always been as highly targeted and logical as this scene allows. The emotional response part of the brain, the amygdala, the place that's been invaded, it will be targeted and he'll see if it makes something happen, try and draw something from Jemma's brain.

It was all set up so he switched it on. He looked at Jemma's eyes and prayed for the one hundred percent all winning start of an instant awakening, Jesus, the birth of a science and his Jemma at home for cocktails by 6pm.

He hopped back up on the bed with the display and continued.

'In other news, you know I've still got no idea where I'm going to be from one moment to the next? Latest development, I keep seeing people from the past. Who knew? I'll keep you posted. The thing is Baby,' Salvador said rolling over on his side and engulfing her in an almighty cuddle. 'You will be subjected to me again, woman.'

'What do you mean no idea where you're going to be, Boog?' said Jemma. 'Getting wasted with Tony too much?'

'No Baby, not that much, well actually yes, a lot, I think, but that's not it. These jumps. Can't figure them out, they might be to trip me up, might be to help, might be completely random.'

Then Jemma said something that threw one right back at him. When she saw something clearly, anyone who didn't was an idiot, plain and simple. Her confidence made people think she was being dismissive but it was usually filled with such delicious revelation.

'There must be a pattern, Boogie' she said. 'Just find the pattern.'

Instantly Salvador saw patterns in his head, lots of them, patterns of code, mathematical patterns, assembling an Ikea chair, a line of ants just doing what they do. Then got to the patterns Jemma was talking about.

'Patterns,' he said, dismounting the bed like a bug had just crawled up his butt. 'That's it, Babe, patterns.'

What if there was some sort of reason for all this jumping around, a pattern, he thought? Was he being jumped around to find the answer to this, the only thing that mattered to him? If these jumps were here to help him, some kind of guide, find a pattern in them, reveal its component parts. It had to be to provide the answer for Jemma. Whether he ended up jumped into a short soldier in the Napoleonic wars or president Eisenhower's shoe guy, there had to be a pattern, there had to be clues.

Was his brain giving him an extra dimension, trying to point him to the answer? In an infinite number of universes and infinite number of time frames all existing at once, it would be an unfortunate dimension that had access to no solution at all.

Salvador leaned over and gave his clever girl the fattest hug and a kiss right on the tip of her nose. Every so often one of the beeping machines got a little out of step with the others and had to catch up. One of the machines in the far end of the rack missed a beat or coughed, generally had a whinge. It concluded his revelation. Maybe it would all become more obvious now.

If he hadn't witnessed this digital arrhythmia before, he would, as he did the first time, haul arse wide eyed and furious down the hall and find someone to get involved. But he'd certainly witnessed it over the months and realised it was just what machines did but was this a techno cough that would bring a nurse in? Salvador continued his news.

'There's something else, Baby,' said Salvador.

'More? Surely not,' said Jemma.

'There is you know. My little helpers, Chen and Annalise have a cunning plan.'

Again Jemma waited but she knew he was in 'What's that plan, Baby?' mood.

'If this VR idea doesn't work right away, we're going on a road trip.'

'Yay, where we going?'

'We're going to see a local tribe. There's this ritual they can do, maybe bring you back.'

A signal from the VR display stole his attention. The programme had come to an end as would his visit. At no point during the experience had Jemma beeped, signalled or moved, same as it ever was, but she'd just come up with some solid words of wisdom. Had this VR started working?

Salvador felt like a kid getting his prize, proud mom and dad and smiling faces, applause and *bright future that one*. His corner was about to be turned.

'Patterns,' he said again as he looked at this unbelievable wife of his. How like Jemma to be showing him how to save her.

The VR gear was bagged up in seconds and he smiled, pulled her closer and gave her a goodbye squeeze, lingering slightly to allow for any possible reciprocation.

'Don't be sad, Boogie' she said.

'I love you, Wiggle, see you in a few days.'

He kissed her on the forehead, hovered at the door and left the room. He wouldn't shake the feeling of abandonment until he was in the car.

It didn't take more than a few steps to re-acquire the horror he'd left outside Jemma's door. The buzz of patterns was quickly overtaken by the reality of seven days.

He found an empty elevator and the doors closed all too slowly on him. He slid down the back wall and closed his eyes as his tears exploded. Seven fucking days. He pleaded with himself not to melt down again. If Jemma still possessed the sentience he knew she did, she'd be feeling him. He knew how she'd be wrapping him up safe and tight right now.

It'll pass, he thought, it'll pass, let go of it, let it go. And then the floor of the elevator pushed back, his descent slowed and seven days became a desire to smash the shit out of a bottle of Pappy Van Winkle's Family Reserve twenty year old bourbon.

 Coronado

An unexpected breeze calmly whispered across his face and he could have sworn a soft voice accompanied it. He pulled his hands away. This was no longer the elevator. The sun was drifting red and resigned into the sea, his car was parked sensibly in his driveway and there he was sitting on the front step of his house. He remembered his last thought of having a drink and it felt like he must have done that in spades but that bit wasn't an active memory.

'Patterns,' he said, wondering if one might suddenly become obvious but it didn't. The creatures of the evening, wondering if he was talking to them, quietened briefly but then turned their little noses up and got back to their stuff. Salvador tried to piece something together from the jumps so far but nothing came to mind. There didn't seem to be anything that kept cropping up. If he sees two bears, that's a start but if he sees two blue bears, there's a sign.

'Two sevens,' said Salvador. Its the only thing that's repeated. Two seven day letters, one says *terminal,* the other says *time's up.* They weren't jumps but it was all he had right now. And then *seven days* was back. No, not this again.

'Fuck you, demon,' he said, and as soon as he did, he felt a breeze drop by and off across the fields and he felt the presence of that demon, crackling like dry wood in his ear, telling him how deliciously close he was to failing, but today, folks, he would say 'no, fuck you, fuck off' and so he did and lo and behold his demon went right ahead and fucked off.

'And stay fucked off,' he added, slurring a little.

The sun had now sizzled into the sea, it was legally night

on this front step. His face was still wet from his tears and he wiped it down with the sleeves of his shirt. His brain was tired. All the creatures round here knew it and they all agreed he needed to get his head down and leave them in peace, stop making them wonder what he's on about.

He did feel a bit cheated though. Here he was in the aftermath of a few drinks without remembering having the drinks. Not fair, it was time to put that right. That might jog some clues loose.

He should have asked Ramirez about these headaches. Now he was home, he can have a look at it at least.

He'd clutched at that letter in the elevator at Mission hospital and here it was still in his hand. He felt like breaking something with the baseball bat inside the front door, that massive green pot, those smaller red pots, and then he thought about Jemma watching him break things. He would not break things.

'Right stand up,' he said, ready to re-enter negotiation with some half drained bottle of Pappy's. As anyone bordering on alcoholism may tell you, another drink can always be justified. This one would start to help him find the answer although he was sure he'd heard that before.

He hopped up the two steps from the door to the main hall and dismissed the door back into its hole with a well-practiced touch, listening for the most subtle of clicks as it rejoined the house. The creatures of the night breathed a collective sigh of relief.

He was instantly greeted by the big hall mirror, which had him weighed and measured and trapped in its truth. He approached himself towards it as he grew inside its frame. After a battle and probably numerous bars, he didn't look too shocking and he couldn't see anything up with his head. Allowing for a shave, he was in good shape.

Jemma's dad had died a few years before Salvador met

her. She'd been left a boat load of cash otherwise this fine house would have been twenty years distant.

The inner hall was a vast vaulted ceiling of solid oak beams, giant abstract pictures of pretty weird things, a few pieces of antique wooden furniture and a few rugs and couches, and the massive open fire. It was more a lounge than just a front hall.

Salvador strolled through the small stone arch to the kitchen, pulled an ice bucket from a cabinet, a chunky broad based glass from a shelf, threw ice in both of them and smiled at himself reflected in the glass. He looked up at the bourbon, which was hopping happy to be in this scene and dropped it in the bucket

Autopilot moved him fluently through the kitchen and its functions but he was now done with it, thanked it and headed down a few more stone steps to the real lounge, the den.

Lamps settled with a dark yellow glow on several knee high tables. Three dark burgundy couches formed into a half square stronghold lay on soft white pile carpet and all bowed in submission before the tech wall. Flanking the open fire in the middle of the wall, the corners of the room showed off several lumps of big chunky speakers, advancing icebergs and above the fire was an eighty inch curved plasma screen. On this sleek slice he could see any function of the house from heating the attic room, watering the office plants to checking his email.

Ironically, Salvador did like to whinge about technology not being as advanced or reliable as it should be but when it works, it's a beautiful thing. Every day is Christmas, every day is a joy to get it moving and see it fly until something even cooler comes along and then Christmas day starts all over again. The system was voice controlled and moved its sound, vision and obedience between rooms as he went. First pair yourself with its infrared sensors, establishing your infrared image as you and from that moment you're the pied piper. Jemma had it all installed as a surprise and then gave him lessons on using it, lessons usually conducted with her wearing a classic schoolgirl outfit, ponytails and the whole nine, lessons rarely completed.

Salvador collapsed onto the couch facing the fireplace and slammed the ice bucket on the oak coffee table. Two cubes were teased into the glass, made a couple of slippery circles and awaited the three fingers of pappy's.

He lay back, put his feet on the table and slowly rotated the heavy glass in his hand. Ice in an empty glass is of no use, a wasted forlorn scene, but when joined by pappy's it becomes flawless diamond, rich, burnt deep orange and clean, a sepia lens with emotion. With fine bourbon, he thought, you deserve fine music. Voice control was instructed. *Ordinary Man* by Chinese Man.

The next few minutes set him on his path for the evening. He laid out on the couch, remembering girls night out, licence to do exactly this, knowing a drunk horny wife would be back later to inflict carnal niceties on him. Salvador turned on the TV, no volume. Images of Laurel and Hardy added to the space. He pretty much knew what they were saying by heart, he'd watched them so many times. Volume wasn't required and this completed the backdrop of his boys night in.

The music machine carried out its shuffle orders and the room awaited the cut of it's DJ jib. Along came a rare version of 'Going to California' as perpetrated by Messrs Clapton, Page and Beck at some point in time. It was time to chill with the three acoustics. If there was something going to make itself clear let it be listening to this.

He tore his eyes away from the fireplace and looked through the main window into the dark open countryside.

The low blue light outside highlighted the tops of the trees, gently swinging to the music. Salvador's California. It felt like he'd always been here. He was born in Boca Raton but his folks moved to San Juan when he was about three so it's all he's known. Going on trips with his folks, places embedded in his childhood, then taking Jemma there. None of the magic was missing, just transported to a perfect new stage.

Salvador upended the bottle and discovered the end of it but 'worry not,' he reassured the rug, and hopped up and headed through a door in the back for a brand new gold bar of bourbon. The new bottle made its heavy impression onto the table. That's where it sat, and that's where you could find it and nothing else.

Text from Tony.

'You are required to assist me getting fucked up.'

'Sorry dude, gotta sleep.'

Home Movies

His trips down memory lane called for a few home movies, bring him closer to his girl. He issued new instructions for a random order home movies medley. He stretched out as long as he could stretch on the couch, his toes almost touching the far arm, and, as the first movie faded in, the three maestros faded out in sync, but only when they were ready.

'Sunny Jim's Cave!' shouted Salvador like he'd just seen Mr Punch's stick behind his back. He was starting to feel bourbon joy, that warmth that loosened the odd button, found the mundane tragically amusing and made everything else just about alright.

Nothing spectacular happened, it was just a day where the humours were balanced. Sunny Jim's cave is a sea cave that had been tunneled through to. It used to hide Chinese immigrants and contraband during prohibition but now offered a show that only glorious nature could provide, sheer echo space, other-worldly decoration by the multi-colored crystals and the sea just outside lapping up at the door.

Mucho chuckles flowed from all around when the guide, a young lad and clearly new to all of this, needing simply to rant on about this very cave, started reeling off a curious tale of being somewhere in the Caribbean being chased by the French navy. He got about a minute into it before he felt that stab of realisation and knew there was no going back, stopped abruptly in mid word and a short silence was followed by 'French you say?' from some comedian in the ranks. That did for the rest of them right there, not least Salvador and Jemma, who endured a painful laughter and wondered if it would ever stop. The cave echoed with much mirth, a sound that would have reddened the hardiest tour guide's face, but to his credit, the lad dealt with it and calmly accessed the correct page.

Sunny Jim's Cave faded out in favour of 'One Sunday,' one of Jemma's. Just seeing her there. 'My Wiggle.'

She'd set up a camera in the bedroom and put on a show for him and the unanticipated later watching world. She'd hoped in vain it'd be just for her and him, dear girl. She teased him and danced and frolicked and pursued him in the very finest tradition of seriously porn fucking him. The middle two minutes of that movie were what it was all about. If he hadn't been fully controlled by her little wiggling form, he might have smelt a rat but Jemma wanted this porn and she wanted it recorded and she wanted it now.

And with such a recording, it just has to fall into the hands of others. In this case, those hands belonged to Jemma's mom, who was visiting and got to the house before either of them got home. She knew the place well, made herself cosy in the den and eyed the controls coldly. She wanted TV but feared the uphill tech task associated with getting it.

The remote control was easy for them what knows but pointless otherwise. So she pressed all of them in various combinations and suddenly things lit up above the fireplace, bingo. It offered her the movie options and, whilst initially keen on some live talk show idea of TV, she was instantly swayed for some godforsaken reason by 'One Sunday' by Jemma Legada.

When Jemma and Salvador got back Jemma's mom seemed a little more upbeat than usual and over dinner picked the perfect moment to reveal her afternoon viewing highlights. Salvador was on the floor and when she was through hitting him, Jemma cleverly had her face in her hands and her jaw in her soup for a very long time. Her mom then said something that didn't relieve Salvador's laughter or Jemma's embarrassment.

'Close your mouth dear, you never know what might crawl in.'

Salvador thought Jemma and her mom got a little closer that night.

Salvador felt the call, it was time to bleed the lizard, leaving 'One Sunday' to do its finest in this room. When he came back down the steps he immediately looked over at the TV. He recognised this one. 'Coronado Beach,' where he'd been jumped with Tony and the guys and Megan the other day, or today, whatever.

He used to go to Coronado with his mom and dad when he was little and then when he was at college. The most recent trip there was probably only about three months ago with Jemma just before it happened. They'd filmed the beach and the sea, and them playing silly idiots and he'd done a walkabout, shooting just about everything else, a snapshot of a perfect day.

There she was his fine little Jemma. She knew he'd just started recording and she wanted in shot now. She ran away from camera across the finest sand towards a sea some twenty yards away. Then she stopped in her tracks and turned with a dramatic star shape 'ta dah!' She bent herself double laughing and ran back to him, failing to account for the camera and slam-hugged him with black screen unfriendly vigour. He'd never seen her so completely happy and this made him never so completely happy. The week that followed would change all that and Salvador let out a deep exhale on this couch and felt a tear or two start to threaten.

They'd laid out on the sand, tickled each-other and generally messed about until they realised where they were, absorbed its mandatory slowing and relaxed. When the sun demanded it, Salvador got up and legged it to the sea, briefly receiving the attention of someone's black Labrador running free. Calculating an entry into the waves that was least likely to embarrass and committing to it, he felt it went well and there was applause and a little whoop no less from his Jemma, up there and tiny in a vast expanse of sand.

The place was nicely unbusy, people ran up and down the beach, a few frisbees sailed past and all was well with the world. Then he saw the '49 Coupe de Ville about twenty feet away along the access track to the shops, like his dad's old car, and that angry parent, chastising his young daughter into the back of the car. Salvador remembered thinking how come solid shitbags like that get kids and him and Jemma don't.

It was such a cool car. When he was a kid, his dad took him and his mom out in it to Disneyland for his sixth birthday. It was his earliest memory of the car and how huge it was in the back, like a big moving play den. He had all sorts of toys and games and general kid stuff in the back with him and every so often everything would slide from one side to the other as his dad misread a bend. He was pretty sure he learnt the word 'fuck' that day.

Disneyland was a blast and the pirate next to him was one seriously messed up dude, but eventually he just wanted to get back in his own private ride and chill out at home with his folks, a few candles strewn about, some Billie Holliday and the warmth of the TV womb.

Tonight though, here in his cosy man den, his focus was on the day rather than the video of the day. He closed his eyes and let the sounds of the day take him there again, smelling the sea and listening to the various birds and goings on around the place. He came to after a small but unscheduled nap and the video had cut to packing away to go home. Typical, dozing through the best bits, but it did tell him he was too sleepy to rewind it. He didn't like watching this last bit, this thirty seconds signalled the day was almost over.

His car was on a sand strewn gravel parking lot closest to the beach and, as he and Jemma loaded the car up, a young girl walked past chanting 'can you hear me' into her cell phone, the all too frequent cry of your average cell phone user. The screen then went black briefly and there was a shot of driving the wiggly windy little roads up the mountain from the beach, and the day was over.

Here on this couch, Salvador was pleased with himself. He'd dismissed the idea of going to the bar to get fucked up with Tony and dismissed it again between glass number three and four. Was this a step in the right direction? A coffee was in order, not because it would assist sleep. Sleep was inevitable.

The coffee was quickly generated and a little bourbon added for good measure. Salvador put the milk carton on the table and lay back and looked around the room.

He sipped his coffee, feeling his eyes planning to close but then noticed something familiar. There was something on the milk carton. Most of it was scuffed off and he couldn't see what it said but there was still something familiar about it.

The blue image on the milk carton blurred into another realm and so did Salvador as he lost his fight with consciousness and brought to an end another boy's night in.

 Six Bells, Six Days

As Salvador slowly drifted into the realm of the freshly awake, his brain tried to tie something together, swirling it around only to lose it again down the plug hole. The essence of a new day emerged from the night's anaesthetic and started to reveal itself in birdsong and the sunlight on his face.

Still not quite ready to be released from a long overdue sleep, he thought he'd roll over and grab another few minutes but an unexpected and impertinent gravity opened his eyes wide as he toppled off his seat onto the hard stone floor outside La Mona bistro in San Juan's old town. The place went quiet.

And then, as he lay there staring up through the elm trees to the blue sky, a feeling came to him, he was missing something, something obvious, it was right there, come on, he thought but no. Whatever was missing stayed missing. And then Salvador sat up. The beach. Coronado beach has cropped up more than once, that day with Tony and last night in his home movie. He had no idea how it could relate to his mission unless there was a yet to be discovered rare plant to bring people out of comas tucked away among the secret bushes of Coronado.

Some of the other customers at La Mona were turning away politely, some kids were cracking up laughing, looking right at him and there were various mumbles. He thought any folks here that knew him over the last few months wouldn't be surprised to see him fall off a chair at any point of the day but if only they knew what was really going on.

Then he heard his mind remind him *seven days* and he felt the same nasty growl wake up and start to rip his stomach open from the inside. This demon was back and it was inside him.

He got to his feet to retake his seat and had the oddest sensation someone had just whispered in his ear. He turned to look over his shoulder but there was just a wall and a waitress standing in front of him, pen poised to capture something she could use against him in a court of *please get on with it.*

It was morning and the sun was shining down this little street onto him and the waitress was waiting. He avoided asking her if she'd just whispered in his ear and sat back to expect double espresso and a couple of melon slices. He might think about dropping some brandy in a second espresso a bit later, hair of the dog, if yet another hangover didn't subside, but at least he knew were he got this one.

The original old town of San Juan was a maze of tiny sandstone streets with bars, bistros and shops provided around every corner. The color and vibrancy supplied by flapping fabrics and spices reminded him more of a market in Marrakesh than anything in the U. S. of A.

The bells of San Bartomeu started ringing out. This church and its sunlit square were the centerpiece of the old town. The square was a meeting place for worshippers and all-comers before and after church services and the cafes would bring them shots of filthy stuff and nibbles to reward their piety, often sending a few of the veterans home covering more ground than they needed to.

Soon after San Bartomeu's lead, its bells were soon echoed by The Serra Chapel, a way down the hill and finally from the New Harvest church in new town San Juan, a beautifully blended example of catholic and protestant just getting on with each other, until the bell ringing competition crops up and then the gloves are seriously off. In a world of agnostics, atheists and true blue believers, it was easy to feel the womb warmth of the bells, a chain of events that inspired peace and relaxation, not to mention confidence in the time-keeping of San Juan's worthier souls.

The waitress returned with Salvador's order. He couldn't help notice her theatrical skipping off as she held eye contact and a smile, throwing her bottom in the air as she went. This flirtation arrived at a vinyl scratching finale as she tripped over a chair leg, just about keeping her balance but feeling pretty silly, and was forced to retreat inside La Mona to update colleagues on what a dick she was.

Salvador couldn't help a secret grin. Women were almost as silly as men, a hairy and deeply worrying thing. Men yield sovereignty, or it's deftly wrestled from them, either way, on face value, a champion idea, and so they're rightly surpassed by the fairer sex and then the fairer sex go right ahead and make dicks of themselves, prove they're just as daft as anyone else.

The melon had been cut into cubes and placed into a bowl. The general idea of melon is grab the thing and sink your face into it. Salvador didn't want it butchered, he wanted it freshly killed.

He dispatched the espresso and signalled a waiter nearby. The waiter was no stranger to cipher, another much under-appreciated quality of that tribe, and acknowledged.

Salvador tucked into the cool melon, instantly addictive, and almost as instantly gone. He awaited espresso part deux and the rest of the day, which he assumed had some kind of purpose given he'd been jumped into it. There you go, now you're getting it, he thought.

Even with his body objecting to him from every organ and *seven days* pestering him relentlessly, he reminded himself to stay on top of the day, look for the signs, find a pattern.

There was a florist opposite La Mona and, next to that, something haute couture. The wispy little summer dresses in the window wrapped softly around mannequins of a certain slice and a fan coaxed the material snugly to form. That's where he got the dress for the golf club party, Jemma's awesome dress.

Down from the dress shop was one of the oldest shops in San Juan, the bootmaker, Wm Mullins, emporium of all things leather, floor to ceiling Butch Cassidy, fight club, bike club and saddle up, and it ran the florist close for scent. They would re-heel, re-soul and supply you with just about every-thing from whips to classic southern cross biker jackets, a peek at the old west, immerse yourself in the essence of America.

The new espresso arrived from the waitress with a smile and a card with additional handwritten numbers. A black dog of uncertain stripe sprinted past, weaving around assembled humanity and round the corner into Lasille Street. From the unconcerned reaction of everyone, it seemed dogs would happily run and weave around de rigueur in this part of town but Salvador had spotted another familiar item.

It's not my dog on the noticeboard, the dog on the beach and now this one here in the old town. The beach, now some dog or other? Two things. Were these really the signs he was looking for or can most people see this sort of thing most days, nothing unusual? Is there a pattern from them? he thought. Only Coronado, which only brought him back to the same question. Why?

He turned over the card the waitress gave him...'Jenny from La Mona' and a number. Salvador was agreeable to most women but not Brad Pitt, fall-at-his-feet kind of agreeable. Beautiful girls didn't fall at his feet. Camille then that tickle from Megan at the beach, now this Jenny. It was like some kind of parade suddenly. The briefest of flashes showed him

Camille looking into him as she came in his dream and the street saw a grown man slap himself in the face.

The sun once more erupted from behind the clouds and lit up the street. In an instant, the hidden colours and smells of the street materialised. Salvador ambled off along the stone arched walkway towards this bootmaker. If he stood still and quiet enough, he could just about meditate in Wm Mullins and maybe that wasn't a bad idea. There was a pair of ankle length boots on the rack outside. He wasn't looking for any ankle length boots but there was no harm putting his nose into a new leather boot and taking a deep snort.

Something then arrived into this space that didn't belong. Salvador took his face out of this left boot and was quickly brought down from his leather high. He noticed first a slow methodical clicking sound. It seemed to react to the other sounds in the street. It played with them, ever so slowly overcame them. The other sounds started to surrender, gently fading out, leaving behind just the clicking noise. It was like the sounds were flowers that started dying the instant this new sound arrived, poisoned.

Salvador looked around. He saw the people at La Mona still chatting and laughing but now muted, he saw the flower shop throw spent flower water from a vase silently out into the drain in the street and one or two people walking along, their footsteps drawing no sound from the cobblestones. The vision of a town going about it's normal noisy day persisted and yet the sounds had followed the water down that drain and everything was now quiet apart from the clicking. It was like someone had stood up, tapped a spoon against a wine glass and everything was silent for the best man's speech.

Then a slow whistled version of Dock of the Bay faded in to join the clicking, adhering to it's rhythm perfectly, controlled by the pace of it but its sound was unstable, its tones sinking and rising like it was having trouble breathing, a record player losing then regaining its desire. The music echoed off the old stone walls and shop windows, off humans and tables and chairs and Salvador could see its rippled pathways consume every inch of available energy and make their way towards him to resound and terminate in his head.

The wonderful combination of coffee, leather and floral smells had also deserted and been sent down the drain, gradually being replaced with a smell Salvador recognised, that horrible cleaning chemical at the hospital but even more overwhelming, enough to pinch his eyes to stop them watering.

Out of the corner of his eye he noticed the form accompanying this musical dominance and had to turn and look. A man who could have been anything from thirty to eighty, a sick looking grey face in a black retro suit, black trilby and a thin black tie was already searing a look straight into his eyes as he walked his demonic music down the street.

He had a bad limp and a beautifully carved steel tipped cane to ease it. He swung this cane like a circus announcer in time with his music and everything about him was coordinated, fluid, filling the street with his metronomic clicking and Van Morrison.

His twisted ensemble of senses grew on Salvador like a giant spider was holding him, making him watch this. Salvador noticed the man was the only object in this street casting a shadow and a shadow much longer than it should be. All other shadows had been flushed down the drain to join the sounds and smells and all of the other imprisoned life of the street.

The man's intense stare and broad, large toothed disturbing smile tightened on him. Salvador wanted to turn away but he couldn't. He'd seen those terrifying eyes before.

The man didn't blink once on his way past, he just seemed to vanish and reappear younger or older every other pace in time with the wobble of the music. His aged yellow eyes hypnotised him like the eyes in the shop did at the beach. He'd never wanted to see them again yet here they were, fixing him.

Salvador had no option but to track every step of his route past him. The man's head twisted to maintain his God-abandoned stare as he moved past until it had twisted almost 180 degrees looking back at him but still he whistled and still his cane clicked on the stone and still he walked on until he rounded the corner and was out of sight into Lasille street, finally relieving the tyranny in Salvador's head and allowing him to regain his breathing.

Salvador bent over and put his hands on his knees. He was sucking in air like an outclassed sprinter, leaking and spitting out the taste in his mouth onto the street. He felt like throwing up. The sounds and smells of the street returned slowly, popping their head over the top of the drain to check the all-clear then gradually resuming their place in the world, shadows slithering over the stones to re-attach to their owners, the flowers were the first smell and then the idle chatter of La Mona.

The man was now invisible but still clicked slowly up the street. He moved out of earshot as he'd be approaching the busier Del Obispo Street. Salvador felt like he'd just avoided the devil entering his soul. Here again was a sign, an evil sign. He didn't know why, and every cell in his body pleaded with him not to do it, but it was out of his control. The demon in his stomach pinched and cut at him until he followed the man round the corner.

By the time Salvador rounded the corner, the man was turning left down an alley. He hurried to make ground and peeked round the corner but the man was gone. Did he live in one of these little terraced houses or had he gained limp-free super speed?

He headed down the alley and through the old town gates out onto Del Obispo. He had no idea what he'd do if he did catch up with him. He hit Del Obispo and hung conspicuously out onto it like an emerging butterfly and before he could complete his analysis, there he was, standing right opposite him on the other side of the street.

He was flanked loyally by the black dog, and his enslaving stare on Salvador resumed like it had never gone away. He was pulling Salvador to him and Salvador's left foot stepped off the curb but, as it did, a car passed right between them and stopped for the light.

Salvador's foot reclaimed the sidewalk. The spell was broken and he felt his body return to his control. His attention was drawn to the car stopped at the lights. The driver turned his head in staggered slow motion and the unmistakable broad toothy grin of the man, no longer standing opposite him on the sidewalk, welded him to the spot. The light went green and his gaze persisted as the car pulled away down the slight hill. The dog's little black face studied him from the back window and seemed sorry not to meet him.

Salvador tried to wrestle logic from a place it had abandoned. Logic had been overturned and had its pants pulled down to its ankles. His mind was clogged by tar in place of reality, cerebral dark matter. He got that feeling in his stomach before an unravelling, a steady poke by his demon, reminding him things were not alright.

His mind then returned slowly to Del Obispo street and another realisation came to him. Another sky blue '49 Coupe de Ville, just like his dad's old car. It was the car the man just appeared in at the lights.

Salvador was released from the man for the first time since he first saw him. Again he felt out of breath and sick. Why had he been jumped into this sudden evil? He was certainly no closer to the truth he needed to find. What did any of this have to do with a solution for Jemma?

He was also troubled by the fact that, at the exact moment the man had vanished from the roadside and magically appeared in the car, someone else had taken his place right where he'd been standing. Salvador had noticed it when it happened but was too focused on the man to process it properly.

Now he did. It was something familiar. His heart stopped racing and his temperature cooled. It was the very real and definitely not dead form of Camille, a welcome diversion from the bizarre, maybe a witness to it.

Camille had already noticed him and, now closer than outside Brannigans, he knew it was her, the unmistakable smile and that partly raised eyebrow. Tony was an butthole and clearly had his brandy confused with his rum.

She waved, assessed her green cross code and navigated red light static traffic over to him. The red light held firm for her. She skipped hello and handshake and headed in for the big hug. She sunk into him and held on, not unusual after a fifteen year gap. Salvador held on right back, not sure which of them needed it more. He was happy to see his friend. Just as the morning had threatened his sanity, maybe here was his relief.

Camille slowly took her head off his left shoulder and a long strand of her soft blond hair remained on his shirt. She looked up at him and asked if he was OK.

Salvador wasn't OK by a stretch but he said he was OK. He noticed there may have been a hint of a tear in her left eye. They linked arms and started walking back down the alley and back into the old town.

Not until Jemma came along was Salvador truly over this childhood love, that feeling he had of wanting to be near her all the time, the sadness when she had chemistry and he had maths. Girlfriends had come and gone over the years but none had diverted him from wishing she was still around, until Jemma and then all bets were off. After he saw Jemma on the steps of the California Nanosystems building, his head was purged of all others, no-one else qualified.

He didn't think too closely about how Camille had materialised where she did just now. He preferred to focus on her and on learning what happened to her. But slowly slowly catchee monkey. Let's not attack the poor girl before reintroductions are made, thought Salvador. He hid a quiet hope that maybe she could even be a more sensible reason to have been deposited here today. Maybe Camille was a top ranked medical consultant specialising in coma patients, with an unmatched ability to bring them round, or possibly a voodoo witch doctor or even a superhero who can breathe life back into a sleeping brain. Camille always had the ability to do something exceptional. Salvador made a mental note to look into witch doctors as well, something voodoo. He'd seen some of it when his dad took him to Cuba once.

He was aware that their venture back into the old town arm in arm could look like they were a solid couple and tongues do wag in San Juan. He'd told Jemma all about Camille ages ago. If they'd known each other, and maybe one day they will, they'd be best buddies so wagging tongues were no concern.

Salvador had to adjust. Few thoughts were hitting him without interruption from that fifties government looking horror movie dude, those eyes that cliff dived him into the supernatural, so he started their first conversation since he was thirteen.

'So,' he started.

'So.'

'I just wanted to ask you something,' he continued.

'Go on then,' she said under cover of a slight chuckle.

Maybe that chuckle hid a wariness it might be the obvious 'where the fuck have you been?'

'When I saw you you just now on the sidewalk,' he said. 'There was a man.'

'A man.'

'Right before I saw you there and then a blue car stopped at the lights.' Please let her say she saw him, thought Salvador. 'You saw him, right?'

'Nope, don't think so,' she said.

'Are you sure? It was like you literally morphed into where he was standing,' said Salvador, but still she hadn't.

'Nope, why?' she said.

Salvador then thought he'd withdraw from further comment about it. The best way never to have a second conversation with someone is to terrify them during the first and say exactly what he decided not to say.

'Nothing,' he said. 'Just thought I recognised him.'

Salvador knew well the razor sharpness of this Camille and was in no doubt since the age of thirteen it would have sharpened, a terrifying prospect. She was always able to spot a diversion from the truth in anyone, even then and if he wasn't careful his attempted swerve from what he really wanted to say would be easily uncovered. Perhaps the merciless tickling from her that used to accompany this uncovering might not follow now they were thirty odd but he couldn't be sure.

As they walked, he gave her a fairly solid shoulder charge. Camille struck back without hesitation, there were more than one or two escalating retaliatory charges and, as they rounded the corner and passed Wm Mullins, Camille parted from his arm and launched into a definitive head down shoulder charge into him, the Defcon 1 of shoulder charges, effectively ending the battle with a glorious victory, celebrated by a flamboyant huff, nose turned up, right out of vaudeville.

Salvador and Camille had returned to the thirteen year old versions of themselves. Neither of them seemed to have grown up. Salvador took more than a passing interest in their reflections in the shop windows to make sure they weren't smaller than they should be. Maybe this is how such a reunion is meant to play out after so many years, reminding each other how they used to be before moving it onto an adult level.

Past Mullins on the right was another small alleyway decorated with plants and lights and the alley terminated about thirty yards down where the tables of Cafe Bruja occupied the space. Salvador prepped a chair for Camille.

'Having lunch are we?' said Camille and punched him on the arm.

'Kidding,' she said. 'Let's drink wine.'

At that moment the bells of San Bartomeu cast off their shackles and filled the old town with themselves. Six strikes and that was that. Usually people realise church bells are happening around them but rarely count exactly how many chimes there are. Here in Bruja everyone else fell into that category but Salvador didn't. He checked his watch and it was midday. He wondered what could have happened to the bellringers. Had there been a downing of tools at the six bell mark in protest at something or other or was this the second string bellringing crew, just not bothered if they were never going to be given the prime slot for Sunday mass?

'What time have you got?' asked Salvador.

'Midday,' she said.

'The bells only rang six times.'

'Did they? I didn't notice but it's always six o'clock Salvador,' she said, flipping open the wine menu.

Salvador got a chilly spike up his back. Jemma used to say

that. 'It's always six o'clock.' Six o'clock was the time they had their first drink when they got home after work so anytime she fancied a drink, she'd call it six o'clock.

Salvador sat back in his chair and looked at Camille. She was unconcerned by bells or six o'clock or much else apart from the idea of a nice Chablis.

Under the guise of checking out some of the gorgeous plants lining this tiny street, he heard Tony's insistence Camille had died back when they were at school but here she was. Then there was this six-o-clock thing, 6pm when he checked his watch in the heat of battle, a fraudulent 6pm at the Bolas Quemadas bar at Coronado with Tony and a fraudulent 6pm here in the old town. As his dear old Cuban grandma, Charo used to say, particularly at her birthday parties. 'What the fuck is going on?'

There were too many signs and none of them meant anything to him apart from simply recurring. He could feel that demon's bite again. He needed to turn the gas down on himself. He was threatening to boil over. Is this what it feels like to lose it, flirt with reality but live supernature. He had visions of men and vans and institutions.

If he was unfit to make his own decisions, it would mean only one thing for Jemma, passing the only decision that mattered to the mercy of Fuku Insurance and Mission hospital. He needed to bottle it, he thought. Stop. Stop. It'll come. Baby steps. His impending meltdown was averted by Camille, who touched his hand. It would be the Chablis after all.

'You OK?' said Camille. 'Can you hear me?' and he slowly brought his wandering mind back to the table here at Bruja.

'Salvador, really are you OK, you're all over the place, wassup?' she said.

Salvador shook his head and smiled. A tall Hispanic waiter had introduced himself during Salvador's rabbit hole experience, he'd deposited menus, bread and olives and reeled off the specials, something about bouillabaisse.

Almost immediately after that, a different waiter of curiously indeterminable sex or age with a T-shirt saying *I'll turn gay for you* asked them for their drinks order. Salvador was trying to make eye contact with Camille but she'd spotted this waiter and wasn't handling it well. She was buried in a menu, trying not to generate the explosion of laughter just round the corner. He quickly requested 'Chablis Grand Cru,' extracting a low hum of approval from Camille as she simmered and scanned over the seafood.

Salvador had to admit to himself he was looking at this Camille very differently now. There she was right where the man was earlier and Tony was convinced she was dead but, he thought, push on through, was it really her problem? Was it her fault? So she was just standing behind the dude and Tony's full of shit. She was just his best friend from school, reunited, having lunch.

'Grilled sea bream, little bit of ground black pepper, lemon juice please,' said Camille, and she was done, menu snapped shut and discarded in favour of the fast incoming wine.

'Lamb,' for Salvador.

Glasses touched with a C sharp and Salvador re-established his decorum.

'Happy whatever day it is,' he said. There was bound to be one. The wine hit his nose and he fell in love again, that first smell of the booze, every day. He took a sip of something that might take him the wrong way but, seriously, fuck it. He was here with Camille and he would get his answers somehow.

'So what are you doing here in the old town then, Scrunchie?' said Salvador. She'd finished her first glass already and he topped her up. 'And when did you become an alcoholic?' He still wasn't quite ready for 'where the fuck did you go?'

Camille delivered a raised eyebrow that been improved by the years apart. 'My drink problem only extends to places that serve it and I was looking for a dress actually.'

Salvador's mind immediately strayed to the shop where he got Jemma's dress and pinched the back of his own leg, picturing Camille in it. But fuck it, he thought.

'Have you seen Dressed to Chill back there opposite La Mona?' he said.

'My God, yes I have' she said. 'I know it. I love it and I'm going there next.'

Salvador remembered the day he took Jemma there to buy that dress. That dress. They'd been in there for just a few minutes before this tiny wispy masterpiece, no more than eight grams worth, made itself known to Jemma with a cheeky wink and quiet whistle and that was that. She was hypnotised, completely unable to form coherent words, seeking only the dressing room, already knowing the outcome.

He couldn't remember to this day what it cost but that single moment was priceless. She could have fitted the dress in her purse. Jemma had to avoid trying it on too much at home unless she was ready to be savaged by Salvador. The fact that the dress even made it to the golf club party that weekend was more a testament to its construction than Jemma's abstinence.

For some reason Salvador felt a joke was the next logical step and risked entering the realm of the raised eyebrow.

'Hey Camille. What did the pirate say on his eightieth birthday?'

Camille tilted her head back and examined the roof gutter, contemplating this sudden transition to unproven stand up. She smiled and looked across at him out of the top of her left eye, demanding satisfaction, challenging punchline delivery but he coped.

'Aye Matey,' and he added a little outstretched hand 'tada.'

Camille shook her head and placed it in her hands and just in time, their glasses were topped up and the food duly arrived. It's ritual to scan the appeared plate in fine detail, which would have been worthwhile if he actually remembered what the menu said should be there.

'Yummy,' said Camille.

Salvador examined a baby carrot and imagined a tiny farmer extracting it from the ground, then he remembered what was lacking from this morning's recollections. The milk carton. He knew he recognised something from the milk carton, just the blue edging and a shoe, about all he could make out from it. He'd seen that same blue edging and little shoe on the town noticeboard, that missing little girl.

'Who's that little girl?' he said, assuming Camille was more in his mind than she was.

'Little girl?

'The one who went missing a while ago?'

'Ashlen?' said Camille.

'Maybe. There's a poster on the noticeboard over from Brannigans.

'Yeh, Ashlen, only nine the poor little thing.'

It was worse now. She had a name and she was nine.

'When did they last see her?' said Salvador.

'About three months ago.'

'Three months ago, holy shit,' he said. Forget the first forty eight, Jesus, how could she still be alive? What are parents going through?

'It's horrible,' she said. 'Little Ashlen was at San Juan Elementary.' Camille took a moment to compose herself. 'Surely someone would have seen her going home, such a short distance.'

When a nine year old is a little late home, maybe five minutes, parents get on with things but develop a small nagging in the top of their belly and they're minutes away from calling round. If an hour passes, this becomes a burning panic, all available stones are overturned and the world is now involved. Suddenly Salvador realised something.

'Jesus. Jemma must have known Ashlen,' he said.

'Who's Jemma?' said Camille. Of course, why would she know?

'Jemma's my wife,' he said. He saw no particular reaction from Camille. However much you love the one you're with, it's always nice to see at least some disappointment on the face of others that you're taken. He covered the basics about Jemma and he could see Camille was right there feeling him but Salvador wasn't going down that hole right now.

Ashlen must have been taken before Jemma went into hospital. Why didn't Jemma mention anything? Why had she kept it to herself and not involved him, her true soul mate, the single human that should be polled about it?

'Little Ashlen only lived a couple of hundred yards round the corner from the school,' continued Camille. 'What the hell happens in a couple of hundred yards?'

She was right but something had, and Salvador needed to know if Jemma was at the school the day Ashlen disappeared. This might be part of a clue to a sign to a pattern, whatever, but something he could get his teeth into, finally.

Even if Jemma wasn't there that day, come on, surely she had to mention it to him. He didn't even remember a change in mood, maybe she did tell him, maybe that's where she zoned off to at Coronado and other times after that. Or was Salvador drifting towards his messed up state for longer than he thought without realising it?

'The cops had no idea,' said Camille. 'Still don't. They

said it seemed to fit the stripe of a random circling asshole, someone whose brain has just gone over to the dark side.'

'Jesus,' said Salvador. 'The poor parents.' All this was no comfort to the parents. They wouldn't give one shit what breed of sicko had taken her, just get her back. Any random circling asshole is terrifying enough. They just casually drive around and take people's little girls as easy as dumping off the trash.

The table was quiet and lost some of that energy that Salvador and Camille had brought with them to it. Lunch was re-engaged and minutes passed and Salvador thought now might be the time to bring up 'where the fuck did you go?'

'So where the fuck did you go?' he said, slightly less subtle than a CEO paying his wife a billion dollar dividend just before the company goes bust owing the pension fund, oh let me see, a billion dollars.

Camille stopped eating, put her cutlery down and took a sip of wine. She shot Salvador a little glance out of the corner of her left eye and there was that sadness he saw in her outside Brannigans. She seemed to be planning how to respond. It wasn't like her to need to plan anything. Whatever she needed had always been right there on tap like some supercomputer. She must have known he'd ask this at some point.

She was still and quiet for a few moments and then took his hand and looked him in the eye.

'I really can't say,' she said and looked down at the table again.

'Yes you can Scrunchie, it's me, tell me why you left. I missed you so much,' said Salvador, giving her a flick on the hand. She looked back at him with the saddest smile he could ever remember seeing on her face. He started to get that feeling when someone you love is sad, that sadness transferred right into you, telepathic sadness.

'Are you OK Scrunchie?' he said, taking her hand now in both his hands. Her hand was cold and trembling and it looked like tears were on their way. Her face went pink and there was definitely movement in her bottom lip. She did the only logical thing.

'I need the little girl's room,' she said and off she went inside Bruja.

Salvador was an idiot, way too much, way too soon, but what happened back then? Was she sad because her parents moved her away from him and everything she knew? She could have fucking called. Was it Ashlen? Was it her sadness for him over Jemma?

He finished off his glass and refilled it just shy of over-flowing. He'd lost his desire for the rest of his lamb and would offer her a big fat sorry when she got back and promise not to ask her again. He really was an bonehead. Maybe over time, as they rekindled that friendship, she might feel like saying but not within an hour of seeing her again, idiot.

As he sat and waited for her to come back, he tried as best he could to put earlier events out of his mind, deal with that later but right now he needed to make his friend feel better.

The minutes passed and she still hadn't come back. She'll enjoy him guessing she had a poo, he thought. This Jemma and Ashlen link was the closest he'd been to seeing any sort of light at the end of this fucking tunnel.

Many more minutes passed as did a waiter asking if he needed another bottle, which, curiously was 'no thanks.' He was starting to worry about Camille. He asked a waiter to check on the ladies room, he was worried about the girl he was here with, she'd seemed distressed.

'Girl, sir?' asked the waiter.

Salvador was getting a little annoyed. 'Yes, Blond girl.

Could you please check the ladies room, I'm a little worried about her.'

'Certainly, sir,' and off he went.

In quick time, the waiter returned and confirmed his previous diagnosis of an empty ladies room but didn't bother confirming his diagnosis that Salvador had been alone for lunch.

'Thanks. Is there another way out of this place?'

'No, sir, this is the only way in or out.'

Salvador thanked him and asked for the check. Camille had vanished, part two, he thought. Had he been away with the fairies contemplating his horrors and she'd come out, possibly announced she had to go with no response and gone? Or did she just vanish into thin air plain and simple? Was she the superhero he'd imagined earlier but her super skill was invisibility? Why do it to him again?

Salvador threw down more than enough to cover the cheque and packed himself up for a slow thoughtful stroll around the old town. His mind was racing with this link to Jemma.

As he passed shop after shop, bar after cafe, heading closer to the church, he was showing little cause for interest in what had become the mundane chatter of a world he didn't recognise any more. His head was full of a bizarre day. He walked back past La Mona, scene of his confusing arrival in the day, earlier a place of relative tranquility given what was to follow for him. And then he was drawn to the colours and vibrancy, the sheer design beauty of the little dress shop opposite, Dressed to Chill, where Jemma got that dress.

He saw himself in the window, a dull, design free entity, faded blue jeans and white T-shirt in a sea of radiant wonder. The mannequins in the window, all seeming alive and smiling, were looking right into him, swishing their fabulous coverings around themselves with a catwalk cheekiness no other shop could match, and they were beckoning him in for a taste of paradise.

Camille had said she was coming here to look at dresses so maybe. He went inside. The shop had a few customers and a couple of staff members milling around.

That day, once Jemma had been lured by that naughty dress, the dress with a soul and a story, into the dressing room, Salvador, rather than seeking something else to do somewhere else, had an overwhelming urge to sit on the little couch they give you outside the dressing room and watch for however long it took for his Jemma to emerge wearing that dress. He realised it had to be special for her to give way to it so easily, the little hussy.

Today he found himself, as single men do when they stand in a dress shop, nervous, decidedly out of place, alien. It was like wandering into a lady's private boudoir, catching her doing things that ladies like to do alone. There's not normally enough places to avert your eyes without someone capturing you with that look and finally the ceiling is the only place for your eyes to hide, unless it too has a mirror and then it really is time to leave. It is a function of men in dress shops to know more about the ceiling lights that the merchandise.

'Hello, good afternoon,' said a smiling young shop assistant, hands clasped together in a de facto prayer for purchase. 'Are you waiting for the young lady?'

Fine, thought Salvador, Camille had slipped past him at Bruja after all and was indeed here. Embarrassing.

'Yes thanks, I am,' he said.

'Super,' said the assistant. 'She's trying on one of our Henri Faitderien in the dressing room. She won't be long, out in a minute or two. Do take a seat on the chaise longue.'

She pointed to the very couch, or indeed more accurately, chaise longue, that Salvador had pitched his tent last time he was here. And the dress Camille was trying on was the very same designer as Jemma's dress. Salvador wasn't a betting man but if he had been, what are the odds she was about to stroll out in that exact same dress.

Salvador took up position. Tricky things to sit on, chaises longues, unless you want to stretch out and have a doze like a slob. Them with class cross their legs and recline with a degree of panache, others wiggle and squirm not knowing where to put arm or leg and eventually wander around looking back with hatred at the ridiculous thing. Most opt for a stool type approach, waiting, wringing hands impatiently.

Suddenly Salvador had a thought. He hoped Camille hadn't deliberately given him the slip and would be less than happy to see him stalking her here to the inner sanctum of a lady's finest day.

Then there were one or two twitches in the curtain to her dressing room and it seemed finally Camille was ready to emerge to the adulation of the assistant, who stood eagerly preparing words of wonder and encouragement, commission sparkling her eyes.

When the curtain finally drew back, Salvador's face changed from someone awaiting the appearance of what was bound to be a Camille in a wonderful dress to someone seeing the love of his life, his very reason for that life, awakened and here with him in this shop. Jemma's smile gripped him, picked him up and threw him round the room, bouncing him off walls and ceiling, floating over all the customers, bouncing off the mannequins and finally set him to rest where he started.

His head was suddenly fizzing like the seconds before they put you under, 100, 99, 98, 97... Here was his beautiful Jemma, standing before him, modelling that dress, that very same dress they'd bought all those months ago.

Salvador rose gently from the chaise longue, strolled

slowly over to her, never releasing her eyes from his own and took her in his arms, the air scented with her, pouring over him, holding firm an inch away for just long enough, and kissed her like he was going off to war. The staff and customers in the shop stopped what they were doing, joined the two of them in a thousand of their own moments and the young assistant could safely consider this a sale.

Salvador pulled away from her sweet face, her very sweetest little face looking up at him, blushed pink from the attention but lost in this moment. To make matters better, one of her little ears was poking through her hair to create elf ear. Salvador could only caress its little edge and kiss it, smelling something he'd only been allowed to dream of. He nestled his face in her neck, released his tears quietly and breathed as deeply as a man could ever breathe into the neck of his one love, summoning up every last instant of her, unable to release her. 'Where the fuck did you go the other day?' didn't get a chance. She was here now.

'Wow, Boogie, what's all this about, its only a dress,' said Jemma, stroking his hair back and wrapping herself up in his warmth again. She noticed the rest of the shop's focus, the tears gently rising in one or two of them as they witnessed what man and woman are born to absorb.

So could these jumps deposit him wherever Jemma was forever? He knew where Jemma really was but was that a dimension that didn't need to exist?

Camille, she'd been a vehicle to lead him to Jemma. It's why he was brought here through horrible hell to get to this point.

Salvador didn't know how long this would last before he was jumped off somewhere but maybe, just maybe, he thought, sparing a thought upwards, that was the end of all that. He had to entertain the possibility it was an illusion but prayed it was permanent.

Here he was the day they bought the dress, many months ago. She would wear the dress this coming weekend at the office party at the golf club but today it would remain tucked away in her light blue bag with the orange rope handle straps and they would wander round the old town, a rare day off work for both of them.

He wouldn't burden her with the questions he had of the world. Maybe that was the old world. Those questions were now gone. All of his questions had asked just a single question. 'How do I save my Jemma?' but here she was, saved, so go with it.

They left Dressed to Chill and headed towards the church.

'Seems like six o'clock to me, Boogie?'

'I guarantee it is.'

There was a little bar, soaked in the early afternoon sun, Bar Triskell to the south side of the square dominated by the beautiful church of San Bartomeu. Wine would be had.

Triskell was buzzing. It seemed like the sun had been winched up over the mountains this morning simply to hover over the people here. Jemma loved the sun. She could sit in it all day with no factor whatever on. She wouldn't burn, just ever so slightly change tones.

The only little table available outside was half cast in the shade of a big canopy gently ruffled by the old town breeze. They raced for the sunny side of it and Jemma had it but paid the price with a tickle.

For a busy place, a waiter came along pretty quickly and Salvador's second bottle of Grand Cru was just as quickly delivered. Jemma put her little nose in it and drew it in, loving its nose and its thinking.

Another C sharp jumped off the old stone walls of San Bartomeu. Jemma purred an affirmative from the depths of her glass, adding a cautionary bubble for good measure.

'So who's coming Saturday, Boog,' she said.

'Yuki and everyone from work really, Wiggle,'

'Awesome, I haven't seen Yuki for ages. How was his trip to Japan?'

Yuki had gone to Japan to meet a major games company, hopefully ready to turn Net Nano VR into a serious product. He was in the boardroom. Pleasantries had been observed.

'He'd just put the goggles on all of them,' began Salvador. 'And Yuki was watching what they were seeing on the big screen. He was in the middle of his presentation and it was going pretty well, their heads were moving around with the action, there were plenty of smiles, all the reactions he wanted.'

Salvador had to break off and overcome the anticipation of a tale she didn't yet know. Jemma leaned in.

'He was just getting into the bit about piloting the space-craft in this game, and one of their senior guys sneezed. Along with the usual oomska of a decent sneeze, his false teeth came out, they flew across the table and landed right in the lap of his CEO.'

Salvador and Jemma lost it right there but Salvador wasn't done.

'The executive obviously knew his teeth had abandoned his face. Yuki started to really lose it. It was the reactions of the players to the things happening in the game. They knew nothing about this guy's emergency. When the teeth had finished their skim across the pond of boardroom table and landed in the CEO's lap, their mouths opened in horror right on cue as the exec's frantic hands fumbled all over the table to try and recover them, but he couldn't find them.'

'What happened?'

'The CEO had no idea he had this guy's teeth in his lap. He was flying around in his spaceship having a great time. The toothless exec had no option but to take his goggles off and look for his real world teeth. He wandered round a room of de facto blind people, all leaning forwards nervously. He finally located his teeth in the lap of his CEO, he tried to retrieve them but his touch was tragically heavy. The players sat back in horror as the CEO was brought back from his trip around Cygnus Five with a jolt and this guy's hand resting on his Johnson.'

'Holy shit,' said Jemma. 'Then what?'

'The CEO looked at this executive and the executive looked at the CEO and suddenly all hell broke loose, shouting and bowing and all sorts of horrors. It was the gravest affront to honour and swords needed to be considered. The CEO, all eighty years old of him, stormed out followed by everyone else at the meeting, all bowing and pleading for his forgiveness'

'What was Yuki doing?' said Jemma.

'It was a downward spiral for Yuki from the moment the guy sneezed and he completely lost it when he saw the look on the CEO's face with this guy's hand on his Johnson. Later Yuki felt a bit guilty. He said it might have been his sudden halt to the presentation that allowed the CEO to re-enter the real world only to realise he was being fondled, and not in a good way. As they all filed out, Yuki was free to hit the floor in hysterics.'

Small moments passed and husband and wife lost it all ends up. They had to quieten it in this public space, which made it worse. Finally Jemma retrieved herself.

'So no sale?' she said.

'No, Wiggle, that's the thing. It was a total sale, no haggling, no messing about, bish bash bosh and done. The Japanese were so embarrassed by this freak of denture, they sent two hookers and all sorts of sake and stuff to Yuki's room, brought the recovered CEO over to sign up personally right there in his hotel room.'

'Hookers? But Yuki's gay.'

'Correct, Wiggle, but he certainly didn't have the heart to burst their bubble on that one. Definitely another interesting chat though, convincing two smoking hot Japanese hookers that his Johnson wasn't designed for the likes of them. He was worried they would also feel a deep shame but, if he'd understood Japanese, he might have understood they weren't locked in a trauma of dishonour, they were just calling him a dick before they got dressed and left.'

'Best business meeting ever,' concluded Jemma.

'Totally.'

They chinked glasses and concentrated on drinking, give or take a few spillages of laughter.

'Are you sure he wasn't tempted?' said Jemma. 'You know, just maybe get a blowjob from these girls or something? I mean a mouth around a dick is a mouth around a dick, right?'

'Well you might think that, Wiggle, but it's like me getting a blowjob from a guy. Probably feels good but, dude, it's a dude!'

Again the laughter dropped all over this table. Jemma narrowly avoided a toppled glass.

'OK so turn it round' he continued. You're not gay right?'

A straight left to Salvador's upper arm was her answer.

'OK, so if another girl went down on you, however good she was, it'd still be a girl, as in the same sex and clearly qualifying as gay, right?' Salvador sat back with the smug look of a man who might add 'job done' and slap imaginary dust from his palms.

Jemma looked up left then up right then down at the table and finally straight into Salvador's eyes with a massive grin. Her hand rested on her chin like someone with a chinny wart on a first date. Salvador heard no challenge and, interestingly, no dismissal of all girl action.

'You've got nothing,' he said, attracting another straight left.

'Nothing,' persisted Salvador.

Salvador knew his Wiggle could destroy any sentient being in less than six words if it really put sand in her bikini. He just needed to wait for her comeback, ready to be set back down to the earth of the real world and away from his fancy pants la di da quick smart.

Yet today, there was no such mastery of her art of human dismantlement. Her comeback was delightfully simple. She was able to drop instantly into the sixth grade without warning and, if there'd been food here on this table, there probably would have been the real danger of a food fight.

Jemma extracted an imaginary finger phone out of an imaginary pocket and she slid it up to her ear. 'Can you hear me?' she said. There was no obvious response from this finger phone so she wound out her middle finger and it became the finger phone's aerial. 'Is that better?' Salvador, the husband, the lover, the protector of all things, had just been served the bird, the creative art of flipping someone off. This classic bird had been 'Bad Reception.'

'I see,' said Salvador and found himself right there with her in sixth grade, hitting back proudly with 'The Spiderman.'

The waiter appeared with menus, oblivious to this ridiculous scene, as Jemma and he were performing 'The Wine Cork' and 'The Elephant' respectively. Jemma's response to the arrival of this waiter was simply to continue, unaffected by any external influence, with 'The Wolverine,' which she delivered with delicate but fearful poise.

No words came to the waiter's mind and he began what looked like becoming a fair time trying to process it, which he shouldn't have to do in fairness. So Salvador jumped right in and said 'five minutes please?' but on the word 'please' he glanced at Jemma still holding the final scene of 'The Wolver-ine' perfectly, middle finger held erect as a tube of steel, glaring into him, still like the night, cunning like the fox, and he lost it. The word 'please' was ruined. There was some-thing messed up about this girl. None of this could've made sense to the waiter and he was off for the requested five minutes or maybe far longer.

Salvador had uncovered a long time ago that his Wiggle favoured attrition, knowing he'd fold like a cheap suit under her glare, disarming and gorgeous, just a little bit nosferatu. Salvador's mind returned to the prospect of that dress, the prospect of very slowly removing it, teasing the shoulder straps ever so gently off each shoulder in turn, finally allowing gravity to take control of the dress and reveal her smooth body in front of him. He would pull a little lock of hair over her ear to create a classic 'elf ear,' run the tips of his fingers up her spine to the nape of her neck and there would follow a kiss of head-massaging, deep breathing, as their bodies slowly approached each other and touched. They would part faces to capture who was doing this to them, already out of breath.

He would kneel in front of her sweet smooth brown body, pull down her little panties, gently kiss her on the belly, waiting for her tiny blond hairs to come alive, and embed his face in her, grab her hips and slip his tongue between her legs, moving her to the bed, turning her on her front, licking her thighs slowly all the way up to her little butt, clambering up her drooling, taking her right there and yes he would nibble that little elf ear until they both came.

Jemma had her eyes on him for every second of his fantasy, knowing exactly where he was. There was something flickering and it could well catch the drapes alight. Salvador had often wondered if she was actually an alien, created in error thinking humans could be perfect.

'Back in a minute. Shall we get the cheque?' she said, running her fingers through his hair. She smiled and kissed him on the end of his silly nose and was off inside to the little girl's room but not before saying something that shot a cold spike up Salvador's spine.

'Oh and when I get back I'll show you 'The Demon'?' she said. 'But I guess I've already showed you that.'

Salvador knew she was talking about another bird but dived right back into the demon this morning. His own demon ripping at his stomach appeared again, competing with his hangover for 'pain most likely to succeed.' Something needed to rid him of those thoughts and that something was a healthy erection. He hadn't even felt it start really but his pants were becoming cosier.

It must have been a slow burner from the fantasy he'd just had and he needed calm. There were kids here. Maybe now was a decent time to consider a room at a nearby hotel.

They'd done this several times. Check into a hotel for the night but stay only the hour or so required, was it a frantic affair, a paid engagement or something more sinister? It was secret, covert and messy. Afterwards, they slip down the stairs, disguises re-applied, maybe swapped, and leave in separate directions afterwards, keep the fantasy alive for just that little bit longer. Salvador and Jemma had affairs with each other inside their own marriage.

Salvador's weighty pants subsided, freeing him from the sort of looks that land a person in trouble. He remembered that little boutique hotel just round the corner in whatever-it-was street, that's it, the Emmerton Hotel. This place was unique, you'd step inside and you were transported to early twentieth century Paris, portraits of the great renaissance artists, French poets and writers all over the walls and a menagerie of cats and dogs littered around the dusty place wondering what in God's name all these pesky humans were doing walking on their rugs.

Salvador and Jemma had enjoyed its hospitality once before, more about getting out of a javelin style rain than a demand for coupling but once inside, coupling came easy. Afterwards, the folks there were so cool they'd been invited for a bottle or two in front of the fire in the salon and ended up staying all night. When Jemma's back, they'll pop in for a couple of glasses and see where the afternoon takes them, knowing Jemma would tell him exactly where that would be.

The happy punters here at Bar Triskell were at ease with life and the world it occupied. The kids over in the shady bit were preparing to be taken elsewhere by parents who can't have slept for weeks and he thought a solid boner might not be such a felony once they'd gone, but said boner had already subsided.

He checked his watch and it was now 2pm. She'd been gone for at least fifteen minutes. He closed his eyes as a horrible talon of deja vu grabbed him. Surely not again, he thought. He grabbed the attention of a waiter and had a feeling he knew how this would play out

'The lady I was here with,' he said.

'Lady, sir?'

Again he closed his eyes but had to follow through with it.

'Yes, lady, here, with me, just now, sorry,' he said, realising nothing was this lad's fault unless he and literally the rest of the world was in on some paranoid conspiracy. 'This has happened before. Anyway, she went to the bathroom too long ago for a bathroom break so please can you do three things for me?'

'Sir?'

'Is there any way in or out of here apart from this doorway here?'

'No sir.'

'Did you see any female person sitting with me here?' he broke off suddenly noticing his was the only glass on the table.

'No sir.'

'Please can you check the ladies restroom for signs of life?'

'Yes sir.'

The waiter went back inside but Salvador knew the message he'd return with.

'There's no-one in the ladies or gents restrooms sir,' he said.

'Thank you,' said Salvador and closed his eyes. He put his head in his hands. For fuck's sake. Were there really restrooms in bars in other dimensions with random beautiful women emerging from them? He'd been dropped into the best day he'd spent with her and then lost her all over again. 'Fuckers.' Was it so fucking unfair of him to want to stay in whatever fucking dimension she was? Maybe all this taking the piss out of him was just to remind him what he was fighting for.

At that moment, the bells of San Bartomeu once again began to suggest it was 6pm. Salvador looked up at the old church and its honest intent to do good for the people of San Juan and wondered if perhaps there might be an answer inside. He'd asked its founder once before to help, but hadn't got a reply. Perhaps the holy spam folder had claimed another. Or perhaps the reply was being slowly played out for him over the last few days. Six o'clock. Still. Well, what do they say? Even a busted clock tells the right time twice a day.

He'd been taken in, an adolescent conjuring of innocence, believing that something was as good as it seemed. But 2pm was its cut-off switch, or 6pm according to San Bartomeu. One of his demons would be appearing before long but in all this he had to spare time for a little smile. It's not every day you get stood up by two beautiful women.

The place he needed to be told him to get his shit together and focus. Among all the clues he couldn't figure out, today was all about the link between Ashlen and Jemma. He couldn't ask the Jemma here today about it because it hadn't happened yet. None of the shit that was about to happen to them had happened yet.

His demon poked at him.

'Six days.'

An hourglass had turned, the grains slowly drifting downwards from one chamber to the other.

He had to talk to the school, find out what was going on with Jemma when all this Ashlen stuff happened. Was she there the day Ashlen vanished?

'Six days.'

Elementary

Suddenly there was another jump-me-exactly-where-I-needed-to-go-anyway jump although it always freaked him out when he was jumped into a moving vehicle. Salvador was halfway down a small fir-lined Siset street and managed to bring his car back from its panic wobble. He was still lingering in an alternative place where Jemma would have just come out of the restrooms in Triskell and they'd now be ruining some room at the Emmerton Hotel but this was exactly where he needed to be, San Juan Elementary, Jemma's school, Ashlen's school.

The school was Siset street's principal occupant, nestling into the end of it. The oak trees embraced the little school and there were lemon trees and a small chilling out field, a perfect setting for keeping tiny people comfortable while they get infused with human stuff.

He pulled up out front and noticed a bleeping chain of tiny people attached to a teacher, winding through the little avenue of trees to the open space of the chilling field and fun. The teacher had lost any sort of control of them at the door. A few tiny people had already broken ranks and were into that open space, running around and falling over. It was recess and a fair squeaking racket it was too. Salvador made his way up the steps and was quickly inside, glad the tiny people were out there and he was in here.

School corridors brought back good memories, times of trial and ritual. Tony and the stalking nut job, Candy, Salvador and countless examples of Mandy Murdoch's most wicked mornings, and of course before all that, Camille. Most of the time, boys in eighth grade upwards had their best and worst times in these corridors. Salvador had to reign in the memories and focus.

He route-marched down the shiny hallway, like a thin layer of water sat on its surface, with its pictures of dragons and big orange suns over the sea and little wobbly houses and the smell of feet and grass and a pre-adolescent innocence. His shoes made a forlorn squeak on this shiny floor, like a normal full blooded squeak had been injured, not firing on all cylinders, feeble.

He turned the corner and coming towards him, already warned and looking at him and his feeble squeak, was the very cool Iris, one of the senior teachers and one of Jemma's closest friends.

Iris was a large lady, on no account interested in being otherwise. Her husband was a chef over at some swanky joint called La Siesta in Venice Beach and their love of fine cuisine and a sedentary lifestyle was just fine thank you very much. Iris was about forty with an approach to life that drew kids to her like little baby lion cubs to their mommy.

She understood the little people and she loved the little people. The little people felt safe and comfortable when she was around and they loved her right back. If there was a God placing people into the things they were meant to do, he got Gandhi and Mandela right, bankers pretty close and Iris would be right here. To see Iris with her little people, she calls them smallies, it all just seems to fit, be more possible and our sweet world grins. What power to be capable of this.

Iris saw Salvador from several yards away. She looked nervous. She slowed and then stopped dead in her tracks, like someone opened the lion's cage. She went as red as a cherry and she was confused, head tilted to one side, not quite accepting what made its way into her eyes. It was the closest he'd seen the very mellow Iris to fear. She took a pace and half backwards, swapped her papers from left to right hands and got a bearing on where she thought she was in the corridor.

Salvador wondered if she'd recognised him. Had her eyesight got that bad? She usually wore glasses but surely she knew it was him from what was little more than ten yards. But she seemed to see more some random invader than a Salvador?

After a brief standoff, her expression changed. Her mouth upturned slightly and for the first time Salvador was confident she wasn't going to call the cops. The new improved and focused Iris made her way over, beaming a warm but still strained smile. Perhaps she knew why he was here today and just wasn't ready for it.

But then came the hug. A hug from Iris was a proper hug, a primordial security that only a hug can give you. She gave herself to the hug, didn't faff around it like some coward, she dived into it and this one took him. He was instantly absorbed and at ease. When it had to end, as all hugs do, if they're not to become messy, parting from it was an umbilical tug.

Salvador noticed a very gradual release of Iris from whatever she'd been concerned about and they chewed around a bit.

'Hello Salvador, you're looking…'

'Homeless, I know, been a long few days.'

'Any news on Jemma?'

'Not much, about the same.'

Iris was so lovely, he used to spend ages just listening to her when Jem was around but right now, five days.

'Iris, I've popped in to ask about that day.'

'Which day, darling,' she replied in a voice tuned to her little people with maybe a slight tremble.

'The day that little girl went missing, Ashlen. She comes to school here, right?'

'Oh, little Ashlen,' said Iris. 'Yes she comes here. Jemma knew her very well.'

That day. The mention of Ashlen's name and that day allowed no further words from Iris. Her lower lip tucked under her top lip and she looked down, gripping her paperwork just a little harder. She took a sniff to keep tears away and she looked up at him suggesting 'Give me a sec, darling.' Salvador was so sorry to bring this foulness back to her. She pulled back but Salvador got a little closer to her. He was here for her, every bit as much as she was always here for Jemma. And then she did that smile that tries to mask a sadness but never fools anyone.

'Such a bubbly little thing, Ashlen, always smiling, always happy, skipping and singing, hiding inside mucky things, always upside down for some reason,' she continued.

'Jemma never talked about it. I only found out about it this week on a milk carton,' said Salvador.

Iris put her hand on his shoulder and looked down at his shoes like he had a grazed knee, he knew she knew.

'Salvador, Jemma was going to tell you, darling, she really was. We kinda closed in on each other here, we all spent a few days figuring out how to tell the people we love. It took me about a week to tell Frank.'

'Really?'

'Sure. I know she didn't want you to stress about anything else with the other things going on, trying for kids and all, and then…well… it was only a few days later she got that horrible news. She said you guys needed that week to sort your heads out, and then…'

'I know.'

'It happened. The other thing was she just felt so guilty, we all did.'

'Guilty about what?' said Salvador.

'Well, Jemma was one of the teachers on duty that day at going home time.'

'Jesus, she would have seen Ashlen leave, maybe even give her a little wave.'

Salvador's head went fuzzy and Iris saw it and moved him over to a bench. Salvador had his head in his hands and he was just pleading in his mind. 'Don't you dare fucking jump me, fuckers, not now.'

'Oh my God,' he said. 'And just a few hours later…'

'I know, darling. But She didn't do anything wrong. We always watch out for the cars the kids get into, which way they're going, who picks them up. Anything that's not quite right, not in the usual pattern, gets flagged and tested.'

'So, Jem didn't miss anything? You know she'd think she had, she'd blame herself. Is that why she felt guilty?'

'No, darling, Jemma didn't miss anything. It wasn't her fault. We all felt guilty.'

'Oh, fuck, Iris, what she must have gone through? My poor baby. Why didn't you tell me?'

'Because we respected each others wishes not to tell.'

'And she said don't tell me?'

'Yes. Only for now though.'

Salvador was developing a nasty pain in his stomach, a demon waking up. She'd lost one, inconsolable until it all turned out fine and the little sprog woke up and demanded chocolate ice cream, but this one didn't.

Jemma was a teacher, the best kind of teacher, like Iris. The best kind of teachers are parents in every way bar the birth and the ability to sign things that mattered. The parents handed over their little people to the school and trusted two clear things, love and security and perhaps an occasional learning, basically, 'Keep em safe till we get back from work.'

But this time the school failed them. Jemma must have

thought she'd failed them but at home, it hadn't happened. Maybe that was it. She needed a space where it hadn't happened, an escape from the horror. But it would have been a haunting, a gnawing at her throat every minute of the day, a barrel of tar dropped on her, making her go red and itch and she would just want it gone.

Salvador would have needed his Jemma to make it better, make it go away but Jemma carried this alone. How the fuck didn't he hear about it from someone else? It's not exactly an every day thing here in San Juan. Someone would have written an article and someone would have fucking read it. Someone would have fucking told someone else. The town would be buzzing with it or was it another case of shame and conspiracy? How come he only found out in the last couple of days from a fucking milk carton?

He remembered there were one or two days he just had this itchy feeling he was losing her, words not sinking in or being returned, attention strayed, an overall feeling that he might not be required. The rest of the time she was his Jemma, fantastic, same as ever. It had to be the baby thing so he put his paranoia back in its box. But it had to be this.

Salvador had been instructed many years back by a girl he was quite keen on, that men, and particularly him, the dopey dick, have this ridiculous notion of 'losing her.' She pointed out if you lose something, you genuinely don't know where you put it. For men, they know exactly where they put it, they're just too dopey to find it.

For men, losing her is a gradual process of failing to see the signs, being told the signs then failing to see them again. They find her teetering on the brink of truly thinking he's a complete idiot who cares not a bit for what she thinks, leaving the one they love feeling pointless. If men could remember why this happens, their recovery would be swift, polished and ready to dazzle, but they never know why and therein lies the rub.

Iris recalled the countless wrapped up scarfy hugs as Jemma and the rest of them gradually slid down the slope. The demon in Salvador's stomach reminded him he'd been excluded, and excluded by his soulmate nonetheless. A shitty but fair observation, demon, he thought. If she'd shared it with him, would she be where she is now? Did her lonely sadness feed the demonic growth invading her brain, giving it air and water, encouraging it to take over?

'Jesus, was she ever going to tell me? I mean, was it a take-it-to-the-grave thing or was it a need-a-bit-of-time thing?'

Iris could only offer a half smile that referred him to her previous comments. Was he someone who'd gone over the edge to where he is now long before this? Did Jemma finally feel completely alone? And now the demon had him. The pain in his stomach tightened enough to think about bending over. Without Iris's hand resting on his shoulder, he would've been in prime spot to let out the wince of pain he felt and dive into a much unwanted contemplation. He was getting dizzy again but Iris's hand squeezed on his shoulder and he was back in this corridor. Fucking keep it together. He pulled himself back from his demon and pulled Iris back to something she'd said.

'One of the teachers.'

'Darling?'

'You said Jem was one of the teachers on duty. What other teachers?'

'Well, there was a young sub, a student teacher, Jesse, she was the other teacher on duty out front with Jemma that day,' said Iris.

'Iris, I'm really sorry but I need to figure this out. Is there any chance of having a chat with Jesse?'

'Sure. I'll text her and ask her to come inside.'

Iris pointed him to a classroom door that would in a very few minutes be invaded by small dirty fidgeting urchins. Jesse would slip down the corridor and be there any moment now.

'Thanks Iris.'

'Anytime, my darling,' she said, tightening her grip on his shoulders. 'Just come get me if you need anything.'

They hugged again, this time Salvador recalling the sort of hugs he had with his mom before she passed, a total safety and a hug he didn't want to let go, but Iris separated from it and carried on back along the corridor, turning back just the once to smile.

Salvador looked back towards the classroom door, spotting a shape heading down the hallway towards it. He marched over a little too keenly. She slowed and skirted the wall, her shoulder flicking a picture of a whale with a trumpet on top of a house. For the briefest of seconds Salvador wondered what these kids were smoking.

A possible thumbs up from Iris behind him eased Jesse a little. She smiled and asked him into the classroom. She said they had only a few minutes before bedlam and slowly shut the door, lingering by it long enough to see where he was going to be before it came to rest in its hole.

She didn't seem the type to be nervous looking someone in the eye but today, she preferred the window and the outside. She was only about twenty, seemed underfed, broad southern accent and looked like one of those studious hard working young girls with bags under their red eyes, looking generally unwell. The truth of it was though, those bags under her eyes were more Ashlen than textbooks.

'The parents had just started arriving,' she began. 'Some kids had started walking towards them and there were patterns we always recognised in the ritual. Zanda Mitchell always got into his mom's blue Mercedes and instantly thrashed his brother, Tristan, apparently held in that car purely for his amusement. Others kicked a ball and others just waited and the rest held hands and skipped away across the field to Brannigans to meet their parents. Ashlen and her little friends always wandered up Siset taking turns to chase each-other.'

'So what happened that day?' asked Salvador.

'From out front you lose track of the tiny shapes halfway round Siset at the bend. Ashlen lived just off Siset near the junction with El Camino. Me and Jemma saw all our kids leave like they always did. No flags.'

But it was the biggest flag of all they missed, thought Salvador, something he wasn't about to say.

'Did you or Jemma sense anything unusual, smell, anything?'

'Nothing,' she said. 'It was all like it always was.'

Salvador hadn't noticed Jesse's fledgling tears from his profile view and then she looked down briefly.

'Apart from one thing,' she said.

'What?'

'I'm sorry, I've just remembered. I can't believe I didn't notice it then,' she said, leaning forward on a desk. 'All the kids and parents had gone. Jemma had gone back inside. I stayed out front for a bit longer in the sun. It was such a beautiful day. I just stood in the sun for a while looking into the trees, took a moment to...you know... have a little think about things.'

Salvador did and threw her a warm smile.

'It was the trees,' she continued.

'The trees?'

'The trees were so quiet,' she turned back to look out the window, like she was bringing in the essence of that afternoon, and closed her eyes. 'There were no other noises at all, just the swish of the leaves against each-other.'

'What noise do they normally make?'

'The birds.' said Jesse. 'The birds should have been humming all over the trees. That was the time they usually did, flapping and squawking and generally carrying on, but there was nothing. No birds.'

Jesse was stuck in her fix on the outside. She brought a finger up to her eye and pre-empted another fledgling tear.

'I'm so sorry,' she said. 'It's not nice to think about it.'

Salvador could feel how much she was hurting. He moved closer to her, ready to handle any possible crumbling and she just repeated 'There were no flags, all was as it should have been?' Jesse was helpless, only the teenage years between her and being one of the smallies about to invade this room. She would have prayed only for Ashlen and might have been defeated by the randomness of their failure if it wasn't for her commitment to the others.

So why don't they accompany them to the car or walk them home, thought Salvador. Who cares who pays for it? Just saying it's only little old San Juan, nothing ever happens here, doesn't cut it. It doesn't happen normally of course, until it does.

Jesse sent a momentary glance at Salvador and returned it instantly to the window via the floor and her right outstretched hand. After a moment of quiet in this classroom, she summoned the bit that caused her the pain.

'We should have felt something,' she said. 'That's where we failed, a parent would have felt something.'

'You can't blame yourself, Jesse. You can't blame any of you. You'd need to be telepathic and most parents aren't telepathic either.'

Jesse managed the same half smile Iris did earlier. She was just a kid herself, thrown headlong into this horror way too soon. One day she'd be a great teacher, she had the love and the belief. She had to deal with it or she'd end up depriving the various little people of San Juan her perfect synergy with them.

'So who were Ashlen's friends, the ones she always walked home with?' said Salvador. 'They'd know about the walk round the corner. They would've headed on to El Camino as Ashlen turned left down her drive, right?'

'Tammy and Eliza,' said Jesse, a more natural smile returning to her face. 'Ashlen, Tammy and Eliza were the three musketeers, inseparable. They were just noisy, mucky and so cheeky. The cops upset Tammy and Eliza pretty quickly and their parents said 'OK forget it, that's enough.' The girls said Ashlen turned left for home just like every day and they went down El Camino to the cafe just like every day and that was it.'

'So she was taken from her own driveway?' said Salvador. 'Man, that's cold.'

'The thing is,' Jesse said. 'I know it a horrible thing to say but... isn't it possible the parents did something?'

You couldn't rule it out, he thought. Apparently this little nine year old found her way onto home turf so what was more likely, a random pervert hiding in a driveway or something happened at home?

'The cops said they can only focus on the suspects they can see,' continued Jesse. 'In the absence of a known nut job you had to focus on someone.'

Salvador thought a chat with Tammy and Eliza would be useful but forget ever being allowed to do that. Slipping a VR system on Jemma was one thing but pestering nine year olds, not a chance, a nailed on reason for cops to have words with him. But hang the fuck on, the cops would have spoken to Jemma as well. Maybe they could add something. He needed to have words with them.

'So did Jemma ever say anything to you about that day?'

said Salvador. 'Maybe if she noticed anything at going home time?'

'Not really. I mean, we talked about how horrible it was and beat ourselves up all the time but neither of saw anything weird except me today and the trees.'

Salvador thanked Jesse with a smile as a herd of very small bundles of noise brought the smell of cut grass rioting into the classroom. Salvador escaped and hit the corridor, hearing various versions of 'Alight already, sit down and be quiet' from each classroom door along it, all falling on small deaf ears.

Salvador swerved a few straggling little people and stepped back outside into the hot sun, breaking step to apply shades. He wasn't sure all this had got him anywhere. Jemma was there on the day. She would have seen Ashlen leave the school to wander up Siset street with her friends. He wished he could to find something that told him Jemma wasn't tearing herself apart blaming herself.

Jesse handled her sudden drop down the rabbit hole like a veteran, which pulled Salvador's attention back to what next. Now he needed to talk to the cops. Anything about what Jem went through that day, anything.

He wasn't far from the car, getting his questions straight for the cops then he heard something, a sound. He kept on walking and the sound became clearer, more precise. At the moment he realised he'd heard it before he was flashed back to that man in the old town. All his demons grabbed on tight and this time he did bend over to squeeze out the pain. It felt like boiling water had just been poured down the back of his shirt.

Someone was whistling 'Dock of the Bay' over by the lemon trees, occasionally branching out into a wolf whistle to summon back a quick black dog, enjoying the green space and offering one joyous *woof* every few paces.

Someone was definitely there, doing something amongst the trees. Salvador could see moving body parts. He moved a few cautious steps closer, straining his eyes to see clearer glimpses of who it was. The feeling of dread had returned him here but hadn't vanished altogether.

The closer he got, the more his throat tightened, like the demon was back in him. He wasn't sure he wanted to see whoever was there and he definitely didn't want to be seen by him. For a moment he thought about checking his step, backing away, but the music pulled him closer. Not again, he thought.

Finally he saw something of the source of this song and started to breath. It was just a silhouette but it wasn't the demon in the old town street. It was just a normal looking silhouette, maybe a floppy hat, stacking up tables and chairs after recess. Pretty quickly the man felt he was caught in a pair of eyes. He turned to see who it was and the whistling stopped as he realised Salvador's attention was on him. Confident there was nothing to fear from Salvador, the man waved and turned to continue his work. 'Dock of the Bay' and several more woofs resumed. Salvador claimed the song as a clue but could make no more sense of it than that.

Salvador felt he should really reward whichever power was confusing him so effortlessly as it was doing a bang up job, but would it be arrogant to assume he mattered to it?

Onward to San Juan PD, just right out of Siset on El Camino.

11   Trees

The desk sergeant was comfortable, taking time to get some filing off his desk and professionally managed to ignore Salvador's entrance. Chat, crackles, phones and squeaky floors were the soundtrack.

Nothing really happened in San Juan, bar fights, barfing and the occasional graffiti incident capped it, until this Ashlen thing. Without looking up, the desk sergeant asked if he could help.

'Thanks,' started Salvador. 'I'm looking to talk to whoever's handling the case of that missing little girl, Ashlen.'

'Why's that?' said the sergeant, now taking the time to make eye contact.

'I might have a little information for them,' said Salvador.

Without anything further required from Salvador, the sergeant made a call.

'Someone here about Ashlen,' he said and waited patiently for the other end of the phone.

'Right,' he said to the phone. He gave Salvador an up and down look then came round the front of the desk, patted him down and buzzed him through, flicking a thumb thataways. 'Down the hall, last on the right, Detective Morres.'

Salvador thought Morres lingered a little on first glance. He stopped what he was doing quickly, staying bent over his desk in putting something away mode and looked instantly very interested in Salvador.

It looked like whatever expression he'd been carrying folded in favour of this one, which reminded Salvador of

Iris's confusion back at the school, head tilted and nervous, like a naked ex had turned up at a wedding.

What's with everyone looking at him like he's got a bomb strapped to him, like he shouldn't be there? He hadn't checked if his flies were undone but it's the sort of look that greets a man with his Johnson out, swinging freely.

Morres stayed perfectly still all the way up until Salvador was at the doorway of his office. The two men stood and stared at each other for too many seconds and finally Morres changed position, more on guard. Salvador understood that cops look at people suspiciously most of the time, probably more so in this Ashlen case. Morres would be eyeing him up to see if there was an intuition bubbling up anywhere. Maybe just a cop thing.

'Can I help you,' said Morres with a fifty a day voice, without any change of expression, figuring him out.

Christ it's hot in here, thought Salvador. He could almost hear the steam escaping through a window. Time for him to make his words count. Trifling with this detective would make for a sour and disagreeable pudding.

'Detective Morres?' he said, already annoyed at his first effort given there was a decent sized 'Detective Ray Morres' sign on his desk. Poor start. 'Salvador Legada.'

If intimidation was high up on the list of qualities for a detective, this guy had to be a pretty scary detective. There wasn't the hint of a smile, just a blank stare. He didn't know if it would yield a smile or a left cross.

'Mr Legada,' said Morres, gesturing Salvador to take a seat.

The air stirred up by both men sitting down took its time to strike but then dislodged the top sheet of a pile of papers on the corner of Morres's desk, which Morres had to put right, ensuring a reformed tidy pile.

'So what can I help you with?' he said.

'My wife teaches at the elementary school down on Siset,' said Salvador. 'Jemma Legada.'

Morres took his time. Salvador felt probed.

'Right, Jemma Legada. I thought the name was familiar,' said Morres, with an unusual tremble in his voice. He detected it himself and shuffled in his seat, clearing his throat, annoyed with himself. He was waiting for some substance from Salvador.

'I went and talked to a friend of ours at the school today,' he said. 'They couldn't really add anything else to what I heard already, but I wondered if I could ask you one or two things.'

'About Ashlen Taylor?' asked Morres, sparing the briefest glance at the photo on the corner of his desk. It looked like that glance softened him just a little.

'Yes, Ashlen' said Salvador. 'I'm trying to figure something out.' He paused. 'I'm not sure why Jemma didn't mention it to me after it happened, but you talked to her, right? What did she say?'

Salvador wondered if "Any news?" or "Do you think she's ok?" would have been a more appropriate start but in waded his massive clown feet like they normally did. Morres wondered why a wife wouldn't mention this to a husband.

'She never said anything to you?' he said.

'No, I only found out in the last couple of days that Ashlen was at school there and Jemma was there the day she went missing.'

'I gotta say, Salvador, not telling you is a little strange, don't you think?' said Morres, leaning slightly forward in his chair. 'It might be useful to ask her why that is?'

'It would,' said Salvador. 'But she's has been in a coma for the last three months.'

'Jesus, sorry to hear that,' said Morres, again shuffling in his seat. 'Well yes I did talk to Jemma about it,' he continued.

'She said there was nothing unusual about the day, same as ever. She was upset she didn't notice anything, neither of the teachers did. Who was the other one there?' he asked himself, looking over to his perfectly positioned paperwork, initially seeming less than keen to disturb it.

'Jesse,' said Salvador.

'Jesse,' said Morres. 'That's her. Jesse was pretty cut up about it, being so young and all. We had to drive her home.'

'I talked to Jesse as well,' said Salvador.

'Right. Today?'

'Yeh, sweet girl, bit worried about her, not sure she's getting her head round it. She's kinda departed. It just might be a turning point, that's all, you know, hope she doesn't ditch teaching, go off somewhere?' Salvador concluded he was ranting and stopped. 'But if my Jemma didn't say anything else, thanks anyway, detective,' and Salvador stood up.

Morres was aware from the desk sergeant that he should be expecting something from this Salvador, some apparent new info. Morres already had something new, wife not telling husband, but he'd been assured more.

'You have some info yourself don't you,' he said. 'That's what the sergeant said.'

'Sorry, yes of course,' said Salvador. He only said he had some info to get through the door but he suddenly realised he does have some info, the trees. It might be pointless but let Morres decide.

'Jesse. She did mention something else,' he said. Morres moved his head to signal 'right then, and that was?'

'She said something about it being unusually quiet.'

'Quiet?'

'Yeh, she said the trees were normally full of birds making all the racket birds make in the trees.'

'Right.'

'Well that afternoon, she said the trees were completely quiet, like there were no birds in them, no idea if it helps.'

'She didn't tell us that,' interrupted Morres. 'Why didn't she tell us that?'

'She didn't remember it till today when I talked to her.'

'Useful, thanks Salvador,' said Morres, disappearing to the back of his chair, eyes on something irrelevant, allowing thought without closing his eyes. He was gearing his mind up to fit this into his underpopulated puzzle.

'And everything's relevant, even if you only prove it's irrelevance.'

Salvador was impressed by this healthy zen approach from Morres.

'So can I ask something else?' asked Salvador.

'Sure.'

'Didn't Tammy and Eliza say anything?'

'Tammy and Eliza. They did yes. Like everyone else, nothing was different, they didn't see anyone else when they walked Ashlen back, not on the road, not on her driveway. The first they heard about it was school the next day.'

'Do you think they knew more than they said?'

'No I don't. They're nine years old. If we can't tell a nine year old is lying then we're doing something seriously wrong. They'd probably have something else in their little heads but it needs help to bring it to the surface but no, they weren't lying.'

'So have you tried to ask them again?'

'The parents won't let us anywhere near them and the powers that be don't want to make them.'

'So who do you think it is?' said Salvador, realising what a massive pain in the ass question that must be for a detective who clearly didn't know yet, bonehead. Continuing seemed the only logic.

'Jesse said you guys maybe thought it could be Ashlen's parents?'

'We have to,' said Morres. 'That's where she was headed last she was seen. Trust me, it's a tricky interview. If the parents did it we'd be talking to probably the coldest most evil kind of people you'd ever meet, people who'd just killed their own baby. If they didn't do it, you're walking over glass and they're already in hell, slowly slipping over the edge.'

'So you try and find if they're slipping over the edge from guilt or sadness.'

Morres appreciated Salvador's basic grasp.

'So are you still interviewing people?' persisted Salvador.

Morres was well past his sell-by date on little Ashlen, after three months most of the intensive activity tends to stop, combing the countryside, consistent follow ups on anyone vaguely linked.

'Me, damn straight, it's still right there,' said Morres, tapping his forehead and the top file. 'But I don't allocate resources. That's why we're always glad to hear from anyone about it.' Morres leaned forward and placed both arms on his desk.

'You see, Salvador, assuming it's not the parents, these sick fucks don't always look like they live in a shed, they don't have to scuff around drooling over children in parks. There are those freaks, sure, but these assholes can be literally anyone, regular everyday people, they go to the game, have a few beers with the guys, work hard, and once every few months they just drive off and take someone.'

Morres was far more animated now, eyes open wider, like he was telling a class full of kids, drumming it into them, assholes to avoid 101. He kept glancing over to the photo frame in the corner of his desk, once or twice slowing the next word.

'Then you've got the loners. They circle randomly, might

never have thought about doing such a thing, maybe it just occurred to them in the car, maybe the radio told them to do it, anyway something snaps and they just do it.'

'But the worst kind let you know they're doing it. They live for this shit. They get off on the tease, leave only the evidence to get you so far. They know you'll only ever get them by catching them live in the act. They'll be in Alabama one night then weeks of nothing, then Seattle and maybe a month of nothing. Sick chess.'

Morres sat back in his chair, clasped his hands, looked up at the ceiling and back to the photo frame, wondering why God could let the things happen he knew God did. He slowly let out a breath and shook his head.

'It's a war we're losing against a breed that shouldn't exist,' he said. 'That's why these fuckers are so terrifying, it's a game, a pissing contest as they kill children,' he continued and looked straight into Salvador's eyes. 'It wouldn't be difficult for a person to consider this the finest work of Satan.'

'If you deal with something that's got no foundation in logic,' suggested Salvador. 'You have to accept it's supernatural, find it's pattern or you're always chasing ghosts.'

Once again, Morres was still and projected no emotion. Salvador could see a transition back to the Morres he first met. Maybe Salvador had helped. Maybe Morres was already seeing his own ghosts. Salvador realised that the world Ray Morres inhabited may not be too removed from his own.

But there were now more questions that the day was born with and the one true question still had no answer. To confound his map of things, he still wasn't convinced about what Iris said, why Jemma didn't tell him. He got the timing thing and it was a only a week or so but it just didn't sit right. The Jemma Ashlen link. He was sure there would be something but there wasn't and he was running out of people to ask.

Morres got up, offered his hand and thanked Salvador for coming in. Salvador walked away with a head full of questions and what next. He looked back over his shoulder before he headed back into the corridor. Morres's glare was still on him. He didn't know if he'd been useful to Morres and couldn't get a handle on why he was getting such an odd reaction from this detective. It felt like Morres had information of his own he was keeping back.

Salvador stood outside the precinct for a moment and listened for the birds in the trees. He was relieved to hear lots of them making lots of noise.

12

A ping muffled out from his pocket. It was a text from Tony.

'La Mesa, have news, what you drinking?'

Usually, even without the cryptic middle sentence, Salvador would be easily turned towards the rest of the day and a good deal of the next morning being spent in the bar with Tony but today, *Have news* swung it.

'Cuba libre,' texted Salvador.

It was about 4pm and he knew Tony would be long passed beer and wine. He'd be on the hard stuff, probably rum, and now he had someone who could take it on through to the morning with him. In fact, thought Salvador, the only times there hasn't been some kind of clue, something to consider at least, he's been sober, well apart from the patterns thing in Jemma's room but that was Jemma's idea after all. He smiled. This little drink with Tony would create things. Maybe a cheeky reefer would help too.

Usually when Salvador walked into La Mesa bar it was like Norm Peterson walking into Cheers, a big 'Sally' would echo out to announce a cornerstone of the place's Profit and Loss. Today, though, there was no such welcome. Salvador wondered if alcoholics shared a common telepathy when one of their number was considering the wagon. They'd be suitably ignored as the traitor they were.

But it was quiet, that's all. La Mesa Bar was at the Great Heights end of Verdugo Street. There were a few old folks in the corner playing Bridge, shooting the occasional stinging glance at a couple of kids on the pool table and a few lonely regular guys were sitting round the semicircular bar, fixed on the screens above, nursing their beers.

And there of course was the smiling and most welcoming form of Tony, arms outstretched summoning him over. On the bar next to him rested his Cuba libre and the mandatory shot for every new drink, snuggled up next to the rum like the rum was taking its kiddie for a stroll. A big loud 'Sally' echoed round the place from Tony, further dismantling the patience of the old geezers in the corner.

When Salvador first came back to San Juan, Tony said this bar was about as warm as an Eskimo's balls, the waitresses were just nostrils looking down on you from a catwalk and the rest of them looked like they were in the middle of a wide bore shit stalling half in half out. Bill and Sally brought that change and the place was now everything you needed from a bar Tony was allowed into.

Massive hugs were completed and breath re-entered Salvador's lungs. He took a seat at the left side of the bar with Tony. The news on the big screen spoke of insider trading, missile testing and the importance of large shopping malls with an urgency unbecoming of its content. The rest of the world trundled on immune to ghosts and magic and, tedious though it was, the format here provided a peaceful retreat from the strange. Then Tony got right into it.

'Dude, remember Mister Atkins from school?'

'Sure, biology right?'

'Biology, yes he was. Anyway what are you doing tomorrow?'

'Hospital,' said Salvador. 'Tomorrow, fuck knows.' Tony always did this when it was just the two of them. He needed to know if Salvador would be recovered from tonight to do anything important tomorrow if he needed to. That way, he'd know this could be the session he wanted. He also knew all about Jemma of course and why Salvador was going to the hospital but this time perhaps he didn't.

'News?'

'Same, but they reckon they're fucking about over insurance and stuff.'

'Assholes.'

'But I did want to ask you a favor.'

'Shoot.'

'I need a van and a driver, your van and you.'

'No probs bud, when?'

'Tomorrow night, midnight.'

'Midnight, sexy, whats the gig?'

'Dude, I'm gonna take Jemma to this place, see if they can help her, that's why I need the van.'

'And am I detecting this place and the taking of your wife to it is not sanctioned by the hospital.'

'That would be correct.'

'Dude, serious felony action.'

'It is.'

'Then I'm all the fuck over it,' and Tony brought himself to the brink of a high five but lingered. 'Only you and me ever know,' and the high five smashed its way to yet more annoyance for the old geezers in the corner.

'Jesus, thanks Tony, dude, it's a shit ton to ask but...'

'Dude, I get it. It's for Jemma, man, seriously I'm right there. Enough said. I'll be at your place, midnight tomorrow.'

Salvador felt the sort of love for the man that only real buddies get to experience, a soulmate, a partner in crime, someone who will always be on your side. It had to be consummated by a hug and so it was, a big strong, squeezing hug. Salvador held on in there until he was sure the tears weren't coming and pulled himself back to Tony's Text.

'So, old Atkins?' he said.

'Atkins, yeh right. Well I ran into his daughter, Celia, the other day. Haven't seen her for ages, you remember Celia?'

'Yeah I do. Celia. Nice girl. Didn't look much like the parents, right?'

'Black girl, ginger parents, not much like the parents, no.'

'Right.'

'Anyway,' continued Tony. 'I ran into her and we had a couple of beers and I remember a few months ago at Coronado you said you'd seen Camille outside Brannigans.'

'Right.'

'I talked about it again with Celia. I wasn't sure if it was Camille or I was always too fucked up. It just didn't make sense you saw her because the school and my folks and everyone just said she'd died and that was it, didn't say how, so I asked Celia.'

'Right,'

'She didn't die, dude, or at least no-one knew if she did.'

'What do you mean, no-one knew, bit hard to miss, daughter not in bedroom, funeral service and all.'

'No, I mean she disappeared.'

'I know that, dude, I was there to never see her again.'

'I mean she disappeared, dude, like ran away or whatever. I got it wrong about the dying thing, I guess everyone assumed she had.'

'What? Fuck off.'

'No dude, Celia knew more about it than we did. Camille didn't come home after school. Then the parents moved away pretty quick smart. That's all.'

'Where did she go? And you dick by the way. I told you she wasn't dead.'

'That's the whole point, no-one knew where she went. No-one knew where any of them went. She never turned up, well not round here anyway. But, dude, it's not right.'

'What's not right?

'If she'd run away or vanished or whatever, if you're her parents, you don't just move away. You stay till you find her, right.'

'Right.'

'OK well maybe not, right. Look. I've got a theory.'

'Go on, then.'

'Camille's dad always looked like a sneaky fuck, do you remember, always looking at you out of the side of his face like some fucking reptile.'

'Yeah, right. I never really got to know him. He wasn't around much'

'Right, so remember that day, we're round there and he comes back with that massive suitcase.'

'Yeah he could hardly carry it. Looked really angry.'

'Looked really worried, started shouting at everyone.'

'Told us all to fuck off on our bikes with Camille.'

'Correct. So, what if he got into a whole house full of shit with some really bad people and he rolled over on them and the whole family got relocated? That's why they left so fast. That's why all the bullshit about her dying and vanishing and stuff. They were relocated, dude, thats why the parents moved so fast. Camille was already safe and then they were too, hopefully. That's why no-one could tell us. Feds, dude.'

'Must be. She did end up somewhere else, man. New York. I saw her yesterday in the old town. We had lunch.'

'Fuck off.'

'We did. I told you I saw her before outside Brannigans. She's alive and well and looking swell.' Salvador suddenly realized his first sighting of Camille was only a couple of days ago but he told Tony about it at the beach a few months ago. He figured, what's the point in rocking the big man's boat with a time paradox.

Then something else down below forced its way to the surface. The tears he held back wouldn't be told and he dropped his head into Tony's massive chest and let it all go, a release valve. This was always round the corner.

'Woah, dude, sorry I didn't know it was still fucking you up,' said Tony.

Salvador pulled himself out of Tony's middle, leaving behind a wet patch. No wonder Camille vanished in the old town, that's why she couldn't say, him and his big clown feet, wading in there.

'Ah, fuck man, it's just everything, Jemma and now this fucking insurance thing. I've got no fucking clue what to do.'

'Dude, you know what to do,' said Tony. 'Let's get traditionally fucked up. You know you think better fucked up.'

'You know, I said just that this morning,' said Salvador. 'I do think better fucked up,' and a fat high five slapped some of the room back into the room.

'OK bud,' said Tony. 'Don't go away, gotta see a man about a dog for literally ten minutes, know what I mean? Yes you do.' They did the fist bump, handshake, high five thing that Salvador never got quite right. Tony slapped a twenty on the bar and pointed at the barman, stopped and turned like 007 to point a sausage digit at Salvador. 'Ten minutes.'

As soon as Tony was gone, Salvador did what Salvador did when his head was crammed full of stuff swirling around without a hole to fit into. He put his head in his hands and had his elbows on the bar. 'You OK buddy?' said the barman, toweling off the bar in front of him.

'Yeah, sure thanks, I'm fine. Same again please.'

Salvador squeezed his brain for every last drop of reason but he was no closer to the Jemma Ashlen thing than he started and everything else was just a repetitive mystery. Sometimes you just have to leave it alone until the juice starts flowing, give you the confidence you'll have an idea, which is normally when you do.

He'd had a morning of ending up where he'd meant to

end up, simple trips, pretty much start the car, drive the car, stop the car, do stuff. What he definitely didn't need was another jump into some bizarre confusion. Or was that exactly what he needed, brave the confusion, meet the fear head on, extract the truth? If that's what it took then bring it, he thought. What's next?

The answer wasn't long coming and, before he heard it, he closed his eyes and knew it was coming. This premonition dulled all other sounds in the room in preparation, cast the news and quiet conversation of the bar into the distance and brought into him the fear of the old town.

The clicking of the walking stick on the wooden floor was all around him but there was nothing there, no demon man, no nothing. No-one else here was remotely aware of it. But still the clicking persisted, getting louder, closer.

He knew it wasn't long before he'd be back in the black grip of the old town, helpless, frozen and terrified, lapsing into a nightmare. Still the clicking approached. Whatever ghost was causing it had to be standing right in front of him now.

Then a little girl invaded his audio space over behind him singing, *Follow the yellow brick road, follow the yellow brick road.* He turned to see her and again the sound of her skipping off away into the recesses of the bar was there but she wasn't.

When her song had shrunk away, there was no more clicking. Hypnosis was broken so he turned his attention on the near and distant parts of the bar, wondering if that stare would be waiting. There was an unholy essence all around him laying on his skin and the bar top and everyone here, he could see it settling, the demon was in the room. Signs tended to follow this demon and he felt the force of the demon pulling him but there was still nothing there. It wanted him to follow but follow where?

A door opened behind him and he turned. The black tail

of a dog slithered out through the closing door just about making it before the door closed on it.

The demon's pull showed him the way. He had no option but follow the dog. When he opened the door, he walked onto an empty and now curiously dark street. He checked his watch, 9pm. Where had four and half fucking hours gone since Tony left? Salvador scanned left and right, up and down and all around but there was no sign of man, demon or dog. There was nothing else moving in the street, no sounds, not even the birds in the trees. Should there be birds in the trees at 9pm? Salvador knew he'd learn something here although he wasn't master of it.

He stood silent, searching for sounds and took in some evening air. Then the peace was usurped by the clicking sound of a metal tipped cane on the hard pavement floor.

His own demon ripping at his stomach returned, happy to meet one of its kind. Salvador's head started pounding. The clicking sound took him with it, it was coming from right in front of him and moving away down Verdugo but he still couldn't see anything, all he could do was follow an invisible man, and probably his invisible dog down the street. And again with the God-awful smell of bleach or something.

As he approached the town square end of Verdugo, where it hits El Camino, the darkness had become almost total. He noticed a dark shape partly caught in the solitary low light of Brannigans over the street, the clicking had again stopped. Salvador stopped dead for a few seconds then turned to stealth and advanced on the figure. His heart started to race. He focused all remaining energy on seeing his target. His eyes tried to adjust to the deep shades and what he couldn't see.

He was sure the figure was wearing a trilby hat. It was hobbling around the space he'd chosen like he was unsure of it, circling the center of it waiting for something to surface.

He got closer and could make out a few more edges. He couldn't see anything clearly apart from the fact that this was a moving human-like figure. There was no obvious cane and no obvious dog. He moved closer still, energized, becoming unafraid of a connection. The figure changed his moving pattern, stopped and turned towards him. Salvador froze.

Salvador felt him projecting his abducting gaze from the darkness. The demon started moving towards him, his face being gradually illuminated by the light from Brannigans, occupying the former shaded lands of his face, but just as Salvador was about to define something from this scene, that small and solitary light from Brannigans went out.

13   Nriza

The daylight was seeping away from this valley, replacing it with a painted mist. The machinery of oncoming twilight was covered by a sky with three large moons but no stars or planets beyond that, like this planet and its angry star were alone in the universe. The ballet of the blue green aurora was so busy and bright, it felt more like early morning was on its way not the coming of night.

As the valley folded out onto open plain, the town of Nriza became visible and sat emitting its place in this world with smoke and color. There in that town lurked the promise and preparation of an occasion awaited for some two thousand years.

In Salvador's dream head, he knew this place and finally Salvador will be convinced he's slept. He'll have no idea why when he wakes up but this day was the day that would change everything for the people of this town and for the people of this planet, tucked away in the furthest reaches of a hostile universe, far beyond the known dimensions of humankind.

The town was humming and awaited the coming of the visitor, the return of the one that came before. The implications of the visitor were far reaching but amounted to a good thing given the fires already underway. There was fevered dancing and ochre drums and pipes and the feeling something was coming to the boil.

The four thirty metre high stepped pyramids occupied much of town life and right now most of town humanity occupied every inch of them as they prepared, blissful but tentative, the ceremony of the visitor. The sharpest of joy and the terror of misfire, it had all come to this, for as many generations as they could count, this had been programmed. Today was the day.

An incantation, a gravitational pull of the supernatural into their being, live or die, they'd be enlightened. Such was the general gist of the chant across this small kingdom. Tonight, after dark would come the two lights to signal the arrival of the visitor. Everything here was preparing for that moment in time.

Such was the trust in those of millennia past, even the air crackled with anticipation. Atop the north pyramid sat, regal and unashamed, balls hanging from one step to another, a colorful old man draped in feathers and colour. He would quietly oversee the drawing near of this time of ending.

The population was perfectly happy to believe it was all about enlightenment and rebirth and nice stuff but the elders, who knew all the texts, whose ancestors had written all the texts, held back from them that this was indeed the time it all ended, a burden that could only be borne by those of noble disposition. The signs were all appearing as prophesied.

The sun slowly impaled itself on the west pyramid then slithered down its far slope. As it hit the horizon, it cast a light around and beyond the west pyramid that created colors only visible at that time. It was an eerie low light that resonated with the pyramids, giving a low hum of farewell to the day.

The people found themselves silent and focused on this moment. When it passed, life would revert to noise and business. The west side of the west pyramid, being the last to see the day, hosted most of the darker festivals. The east side of the east pyramid was all about happiness and new birth, a creche among worship sites.

The night began itself from the day's surrender, the beautiful flower garlands radiated with the oncoming candlelight. The people would be called at any time to ready for the procession.

It was the start of a sequence that would lead to their nirvana. First they'd see him, then he'd move among them, and after that the mystery would make its fun. They wouldn't remember their place when it happened. They wouldn't remember the darkness in the world. They'd be reborn, free to furnish their new world with their great joy.

The giant bass pipe cleared it's throat and issued its signal. Normally this bone juggling booming sound called them to more mundane things, occasionally a sacrifice, but tonight was special.

It was time. The pyramids looked like their pants were coming down as the people calmly vacated them layer by layer to join the town strong procession. This procession would weave them through their streets, out onto the open plain and onward towards the mouth of the valley, where they'd assume position.

Focusing on the distant mountains, the elders echoed the pipe's hail of the appearance of the two lights. The lights had appeared over the mountaintops as foretold. They now began the incantation to invite their visitor. A similarly feathered old man appeared at the fore ready to conduct, normally a tedious chore for the old man but tonight he'd give it his all.

The great bass pipe from the town once more sounded it's ominous tone over the plain and the old man started to dance. This call to action resonated and the people were drawn to their shaman. The fire was high, hyper-driven by the wind running through the valley. The assembled torches lit up the shades of humanity collected here and, over the mountains, the two lights began to glow.

The masses joined the shaman and the base pipe in a low

quaking chant and here Nriza was glued to its destiny. After ten soundings from the bass pipe there was quiet, the wind alone prevailed, having its fun with the flags and torches.

The faithful of Nriza were hypnotised by the two lights hanging over the distant mountains, some were happy, some sad and most were praying. They may have left their homes and their town for the last time in their current form, they tingled with the unknown but were carried in their belief by the emergence of these lights, exactly as and when prophesied.

The smaller light soon vanished into the mountain then the larger one followed slowly behind it, settling in the mountain as well and together they emitted a soft orange corona around the mountain tops, providing a complement of rich colour to the aurora, which seemed to be getting more excited. The people were unmoved, focused now on the glow. They mimicked the shaman, who dropped carefully to his knees and they raised their arms in the air, summoning their visitor.

They were prepared to stay here for as long as it took, provisions were ready to ship from the town and they'd strike camp soon, there to remain until the finale. This generation were the chosen ones. Since the first visitor two thousand years ago, all things had been leading to this moment about to be experienced by this generation. They sacred task was to guide the people to their nirvana.

When the great volcano across the plain was still angry and arguing, a visitor came to the people of Nriza. She appeared in the draped fragrant rooms of the shaman. The shaman had been drawn to focus on the very space she was about to materialise into but was still more than surprised by her appearance before him in that exact spot, quietly scanning him, waiting for him to find his center.

She told him she brought his future, his people must start

to prepare for another coming, the next visitor, the people of the eightieth generation would need to be ready.

The next visitor would arrive in a vibrant colourful sky that would prepare the people for two lights. He will be unaware of his place in their world and would have to be guided by the shaman to his own enlightenment before he can enlighten the people of Nriza.

The shaman took this as a simple command and had no caveats to suggest. He humbly acknowledged her and she was gone in the time it took for him to blink, leaving him with a really dry mouth and his sacred duty.

Preparing the texts and images was the immediate task of this shaman. He summoned the other elders to him and together they drafted this moment and their future was born.

The artist summoned was guided in his recreation of his shaman's vision. His visitor was wrapped in blue light, a beautiful female of their own kind, soft red hair and dressed in a simple light green tunic. This image hung from every available wall, as it had done for the past eighty generations, worshipped and summoned to the moment of enlightenment now upon them.

The first visit had been fleshed out with speculation and theory but the basics of the occurrence were so recorded. So profound was this on the elders of Nriza that the day was immediately given festival status and the time of day was given to shamanic prayers.

Passed down from generation to generation, none of the core meaning had been lost, although a hint of advertising had crept in. The feeling was as potent now as at the time of the first visit. About three generations ago, the people started fine tuning the preparation and execution and, by the time the generation of chosen ones was born, they had plenty of help to lean on, for it was they who had to arrange the logistics and whipping of the time, ensure a civilisation that believed.

Apart from indoctrination from an early age, real plans had only been in full swing for the last few months, ensuring foodstuff for the duration and planning orderly movement and attitude in what could be uncertain times. As with all things, you can make a lot of fuss about something shiny but if it doesn't do anything, it ain't so damn shiny.

Over the recent generations, people had entertained the notion that nothing might happen and no-one would come and they will all slop back to town in a mood unlikely to excite. What would they do? It was all very well for the shaman to say things like 'it will take as long as it takes' and 'it's not an exact science you know,' and that is clever stuff, ensuring no legal time penalty, but eventually people would start to defect and shamans would become edgy.

How would the masses deal with a non event? They'd have to either blame the entire notion of another magical realm or blame the shaman, a straightforward choice. The shaman, before he could rustle up his gowns and props, would be taken outside and given a solid kicking for starters. He would have some seriously nasty things said to him and by the end of his ordeal he would've found himself upside down with slices hanging off him, awaiting the boiling tar.

It was a more daunting proposition being the eightieth shaman than anything else, the upside was elevation to get-away-with-literally-anything status, the downside was a graphic torturous slaughter. The sadness was this poor obliterated shaman would be taking the boot for the seventy nine former shamans who'd got clean away with it.

He'd try and focus through the blood in his eyes, forget the searing pain and mutter sacrilegious hatred towards the fucker that spawned this whole idea in the first place.

The orange glow of the mountains dimmed to match the

night as the sky further intensified its colour. It was more day than night and the people of Nriza prepared to get comfortable. A group were sent back to town to organise food and tents, fires sprung up and drums started to play. After the more sublime moments of the day, now they would contemplate, aware that at any time lights or holy ones could appear willy nilly and do just about anything. Not many from Nriza would be sleeping that deeply, even after a few jars of the festering stuff.

The shaman and the elders in their quarters, believing the true meaning of the lights to be their demise, were even less likely to sleep. The original message from the visitor eighty generations ago was simple but also clearly spoke of an enlightenment of some stripe.

Her words were simple logistical instructions and one would have thought wholly positive, but woven into it over the centuries was an analysis of enlightenment and ultimately one camp that thought it was a good thing and another camp that didn't.

The elders here didn't, they saw the possibility of enlightenment as a lighting up, an ignition and great conflagration, an ending of times. The presence of just one manic depressive shaman in a historical event stream tends to tweak it all sideways a little.

A simple take on a simple word and two alien positions had appeared. If you're gonna go, go thinking it's all fine.

Salvador's last memory of this dream state was heading out into the open with everyone else.

The fires and the drums died down, the people cuddled and prayed and drifted into half sleep.

Morres came back inside his office. Rachel followed and shut the door. The windows were open but made no difference to the sweat box room of books, files and dust and the fan just blew that hot air and dust into the air.

'Any news on the Legada coma?' he said.

'Same,' replied Rachel.

'So. Ashlen,' said Morres, hoping the sweat above his eyebrows wouldn't drip over his nose and plunge free and downward, only serving to diminish the respect of this younger detective. 'Just a feeling but I heard something the other day that made me think.'

'Think about what, Ray?' said Rachel, taking a seat and twitching her nose to prevent what might possibly be an unladylike sneeze.

'The only thing that even got close to different about that day was the trees.'

'Trees?'

'Yeh that junior student teacher, Jesse.'

'Poor kid.'

'Well she said there was no noise from any of the trees, no birds, no flappy wings against leaves, nada.'

Rachel was unmoved and took a time to compute a response.

'Jesse said that?' said Rachel. 'That's new info, how does that fit in?'

'I don't know, that's what I'm saying,' said Morres, giving her that look she knew so well, think, girl, think.

Rachel was a solid thinker, always had been. Just something about connections being straighter in her brain or something. She was usually first to suggest something useful when others with many stripes were stuck in a place that simply didn't do it much.

'The question is, Rach,' he continued. 'What shuts birds up?' He stood and looked out of his window on this filthy armpit sweltering day and over the parking lot to the fourth fairway at San Juan Hills. He imagined he'd be a decent golfer if he could be bothered or afford the green fees.

'I dunno, noise?' said Rachel.

'Noise,' he mumbled as his gaze fixed on something out of focus. 'Noise. Yes definitely noise but let's find all the other things that keep the birds out of the trees.'

Rachel was up and out of his office and planning her first five searches before her ass hit her chair. And onward to the sort of cross-referencing logic that could find abstract things, tie them together and make them fit.

Morres took a moment to hit a few practice short irons in the small space available to him. He dislodged a small cactus pot on his second backswing but quickly replaced it's teetering form in exactly the same stain ring it came from. He'd been asked to play with some police foursome years ago. He hadn't done well but he reckoned he could. It wasn't the game so much, it was just being out there on the course. He'd walk around San Juan Hills for hours at night and leave all this in here.

The murders he heard from the trees and bushes as nature played its game guided him to his current thinking. Those animals have to kill those other animals to survive. We do it for fun or seventeen bucks or because the lake told us to. He put people like whoever took Ashlen and the people who killed Nadja and Valentina into a file called *Mutations*.

Delete. They weren't meant to exist, they didn't function within logic, they had no place. He really didn't know whether the mutations that created them would die away or take over but all this shit every fucking day didn't look good.

Rachel returned ten minutes later, sat in front of Morres and threw a few pieces of paper on his desk.

'Well, fire obviously,' she began. 'Loud noises, things they do to protect the fruit, nets and spray and stuff.' She anticipated Morres's first question. 'And yes, the school sprays it's lemon trees.'

Some people said there wasn't one hair out of place on the town that day, nothing different, nothing out of the ordinary, just sleepy little San Juan. Others said it felt strange. They didn't know why, it just did. Morres had put it down to implied hindsight but either way, from tiny acorns... and this was the first time the case had a new player since it started.

'Who does that for them?' said Morres.

'They're getting back to me.'

'The school didn't say anything about tree spraying when we talked to them did they?'

'They did not.'

'So if someone was spraying that day, Rach, why didn't the school mention it?' Morres turned again to the window and imagined that third short iron he just played, the one that felt really sweet, pin high, two yards. 'Can you just call Jesse, check there weren't any loud noises at that time?'

Morres was pretty sure there weren't and started getting that feeling cops get when a lead turns the right way. When Rachel returned within a minute with a coffee and a smile, he knew.

'No loud noises,' she said. And there's a sprayer guy.'

Morres raised an eyebrow.

'And he sprays there once a week, Tuesdays.'

Morres didn't need to glance at his file but pulled it open. A welcome little tingle shot up him and he and Rachel shared it.

'Don't bother looking, Ray. It was a Tuesday Ashlen went missing,' said Rachel.

Morres showed almost every sign that accompanies a smile but there was still no smile. He didn't deserve it yet but this new player had suddenly climbed the wall.

'OK so who is he?' he said.

'That's the thing,' said Rachel. 'They had no records at all, nothing about a spraying company, no invoices, no record of payments, all cash. I think she even said something about budgets. No-one at the school could really even say what the guy's name is, one said Bill, one said Gerald, or was that his dog? One of the teachers said he did all sorts of odd jobs around the place when he sprayed. She'd talked to him by the trees last week. He said he'd got married three months ago.'

'Jesus, it's a school, Rach, what the fuck? Some old mut roaming around? She's talking to the artist, right?'

'Yeah, she's doing it later. The boss lady at the school, Mrs Hargreaves, she was seriously embarrassed,' continued Rachel. 'She said it was highly irregular, this never happened. She couldn't figure out where the records went.'

'If they were ever fucking there, highly irregular my ass?' Morres was feeling the anger, the needless mistakes that let in the nastiness of the world when it's so easy to keep it out, locking a window, turning an alarm on, checking people who are around kids, not joining El Paso DEA and attacking people like Hector fucking Valdez.

'Anyway she did say the trees get sprayed every week, always have as long as anyone can remember.'

'And he sprays on Tuesday, right?'

'Right.'

'Fuck that's yesterday. He won't be there for another six days.'

Morres shook his head at this idiotic bad break chipping away at his new lead. He also wondered how a school could let this happen. How easy it could have been if the school just knew who he was. It might be the difference between Ashlen alive or Ashlen dead. But today was progress, first time since it started. It's more important to make that work than get angry at why it might not.

'Did anyone at the school agree with anyone else about what this fucker's name is?' he said, ready to talk to anyone called Bill or Gerald or whatever within fifty miles if he had to.

'Not a one.'

'OK hassle any sprayer crew you can find within fifty miles and set it up, Rach. If we don't find him sooner, next Tuesday we'll be at that school.'

'Got it, boss man.'

'Oh and for fuck's sake don't tell the fucking school. They definitely don't need to know, they'd probably forget or tell him anyway, fucking idiots.'

'Like it always is, Ray.'

'Right.'

Morres could almost smell the lemons on this fucker but fucking Tuesday. Maybe Rachel would find him first. And he wasn't finished with the school by a long shot. Heads would roll in good time but more important was to stay out of sight and don't tell anyone anything until Tuesday.

Rachel stopped at the door and looked at Morres.

'Three months,' she said.

'Three months?' shrugged Morres.

'Someone at the school said he said he got married three months ago.'

Morres wasn't going to bother shrugging his shoulders again, he just started at Rachel.

'So he got married the same time Ashlen vanished.'

Still there was no smile from Morres but Rachel saw one deep inside and that damn smile would come out one day.

Until then, Tuesday, six days.

On the banks of a small stream trickling through its very own rocky fir lined channel, a young deer stood alert as it chewed something. To be utterly terrified in all moments of waking was an odd but courageous way to live a life yet here stood this fit little fellow. The only sounds were the stream bouncing off itself and its rocks, the occasional dropped cone and the metronomic chomping of this small animal.

Trained on the deer from forty yards up the slope was a Nosler Patriot rifle, cocked long before the deer had arrived. Behind that was a man barely breathing, waiting for a really tasty morsel to keep the deer's head straight for the smallest of seconds.

The deer routinely checked all around him. He'd heard the noise that this nemesis produced from varying distances before and was usually away instantly to return to his clan, missing one or two comrades. It wasn't the way of a deer to equate this noise to his missing comrades but it was the way of a deer to get on his little toes and cover quick ground.

The Nosler was aware of this and needed to dampen any notion of escape quick smart, taunting its trigger to stop breathing like a senior step class and act now, but patience and stillness were the hunter's way and a less than perfect kill was not acceptable.

In a twist of fortune for the deer, the shooter detected some troubling news deep down inside himself. There was a feeling that started in his nose and quickly spread to the back of his throat. This would be a sneeze and a sneeze of substance. It wouldn't be one of those girly sneezes they perform into themselves followed by a giggle. He would not be able to suppress this. This'll be a game changer, an explosion. He had no option but to go with it and let it frighten.

The shooter twitched his nose a little in the vain hope of derailing it but it was no use, there's a point in a decent sneeze where you simply can't go back, it's going to happen. It needs all of your physical dexterity to even keep your own balance.

He felt his eyes preparing to shut and his neck begin to tighten under the fast approaching loss of faculty. He pleaded with mind and body to resist but it was now beyond even their control. Resigned and aware of this, and amid vile cursing of all matter, there erupted from his mouth the fiercest dragon fire sneeze. At the moment of this unwanted ecstasy, his trigger finger sent one off into a tree several yards left of the deer.

This little deer, micro moments before taking to his toes and amid bent over laughter from all the other creatures observing nearby, had now stopped chewing and spied the source of this tomfoolery, not completely sure how it could have gone so wrong for the shooter. He offered a subtle but well meant chuckle and was gone across the stream and up the opposite bank. The shooter was forced to deal with the aftermath of the sneeze, embarrassment, regaining sight and wiping off slime.

Expletives that couldn't be repeated other than by the amused animals of the forest, and making them laugh even more, were spewed forth against all manner of flora and fauna. The fir trees, often considered prim and easily offended, were first to object and promptly dropped a couple of cones on the shooter's head. The shooter widened his eyes to this devastating victimisation, stood angrily and wrapped his boot into the offending fir. The fir was unmoved and quite enjoying this, while the shooter now had a time of falling over and nursing his potentially broken foot. The cheekier of the surrounding wildlife were selling tickets to some seriously funny shit.

Unwilling to be still and lay down meekly for a foot, his expletives got louder, these were now noises of plunder and attack accompanying a futile and headlong pursuit of the long gone little fellow. Twenty yards down the slope, the speeding shooter suddenly lost equilibrium and gained flight, his injured foot caught a tree root, he landed hard and gathered foliage on his rapid descent to the stream. You could just about hear a muffled and elongated 'fuckers' as he floundered, landing in a crumpled heap next to the stream. The shooter gathered himself from disarray and got to his feet in installments. He wasn't as young as he used to be for all this.

The hat that was chaotically removed from him on his way down had left behind an unhinged comb-over, an image of tragic abandon, a sight of wonder.

Even confident of no-one around, a man with a comb-over will move to re-lay the tarp first priority. This was completed by the shooter in quick smart time and for a few moments all was still as he reviewed his recent performance.

But the forest around the shooter could hold it in no longer. It seemed like every leaf and living breath erupted in uncontrollable laughter creating a sound of wonder unfortunately inaudible to humankind.

The forest was bewildered by how humans could be quite so completely uncoordinated.

According to Professor Umthondo Fusu, fellow of the District Seven University in Smolensk, the slide to this uncompetitive physical state by humans started some seven million years ago. In his now legendary address to the UCLA anthropological society, he postulated with an unusual confidence that 'The dawn of humanity was an ape falling out of a tree and forgetting how to get back up it.'

16   Assessment

Salvador had a dream head full of rapid images parading in front of him. A chaotic instant of bar noise, a smell of whisky and lilac perfume then a girl, smiling as she looked up at him, approaching to wrap in for a cuddle. Back in eighth grade in the changing rooms. Mindy Suarez said she'd tell he cheated at math if he didn't let her touch his dick and this was the moment she did. The moment his naked body first held the naked body of another girl, Adrianna from France at Camp. Then he was on a bed being ridden by some girl, Jenny from La Mona. Jesus, really? Holy shit, was she all flirty the other day because they already did this or is it the future? The clips started to speed up and in each clip he was closer and closer to the point of orgasm, then in each clip he was physically at the point of orgasm. He couldn't move, stuck in come-face, time and time again. And finally a clip stuck in shot and held. It was Camille's face as she arched her back and came and as he came inside her, snapshots of seeing her in the street outside Brannigans, shoulder charging in the old town and finally looking into her eyes as her orgasm refused to go quietly into the night.

Then Camille looked off to the side as there was a loud buzzing noise and Salvador sat up in bed. 'Fuck!' He was panting. It felt like his juices had been surgically extracted, some alien experiment, he was still just about in his last orgasm. 'Fuck.' He was naked in bed with a boner so had he actually gone to bed and slept or was this arousal carousel not quite over? His head had something inside it smashing nails into his brain. And then the front door buzzer sounded.

He checked round to re-acclimatise himself with his own

domain. That took too long for whoever was at the door and another buzz sounded. The door. If this was someone pitching him double glazing, it would not be their finest moment.

He got himself into jeans and T-shirt and was down the stairs into the front room, asking his boner to fuck off before he gets to the door, but his boner said 'Wait just a minute.' All he saw through the window was a little blue car with no-one in it. Camille.

His dream. She was there. She was in it. Jesus. Fuck, was she in it. His boner definitely wasn't going anywhere. He can't open the door to her like this. He moved closer to the door and put his ear against it. He knew she was there but he couldn't hear her. Then another longer buzz on the buzzer lifted his head from the door and, without adequate thought to justify it, he tugged it open. Once more his brain numbed where he stood.

'Unfinished business, Boogie,' said Jemma with the look he knew so well on her face, the look that conceived, created and drove their 'One Sunday' video. Salvador's mind was immediately back in the old town planning hotels and licking, like only minutes had passed between then and now.

He wondered very briefly whether words could play a part at this point but Jemma tilted her head and was on him like a lion on the throat of a lingering impala. She wrapped herself around him and he absorbed himself into this most X rated of kisses and into a place where words had no meaning.

She pushed him back towards the couches and, as she did, he did what humans do best and toppled backwards over one of the steps and brought her to ground with him.

He planted both hands into Jemma's hair, massaged her head and her beautiful red wispy hair was pure silk. Jemma grabbed on his shirt and slithered herself up him, they joined again and she was under his shirt, dog licking his entire region, deep tonguing his belly button and heading north to the nipples.

There are two types of men when it comes to nipples, men that will seriously murder you if you even think about it and men who equally hate it but tolerate if for the greater good.

She broke from him, stared for two massive seconds into his eyes and retreated down him, eyes fixed on him as she moved. She drove both hands under his shirt and re-engaged with the belly button. Further down she went. He awaited her arrival, anticipating an event that can only have been designed specifically by a higher being. Before he could even pre-conceive her ripping his pants open, she'd done a Houdini on his belt buckle and he dropped his head back onto the oak floor.

If coherent thoughts were ever possible under these conditions, he attempted one. 'Where the fuck did you go the other day,' kind of summed it up but he well knew that never has a greater arrogance been shown than by a man bringing something up during a blowjob.

Jemma broke from him and sat up still fixing her lovely eyes on him, she smiled and slipped off her light cotton blouse revealing a sight also manufactured by the aforementioned higher being. Jemma didn't do bras and he lay throbbing and she slowly, oh so very slowly, unbuttoned her jeans, classic faded Levis and slightly ripped by the upper thighs revealing her delicious caramel skin. As the buttons loosened, the top lace of her panties appeared. He could take it no longer and rose up to her, running his hands around her waist, lightly kissing her left breast and then he took it. Jemma wrapped her arms around his head and started to dance on him.

He rolled her over and set her down softly, he rolled his tongue up her body over her tiny blonde belly hairs and to her mouth as she maintained her grip on his head, retracing his steps back down her, he lowered her jeans slowly as she arched her back to assist. The jeans were gone and the panties remained and were immediately breached by his tongue. Jemma arched her back again and reached out to touch the warm oak floor.

It was time to remove the panties and sink himself into her and she knew it, suddenly an aura of the purest pleasure approached them from the corner of the room and surrounded them, drawing on their energy and repaying it with fine moments, the two of them were now operating as one and they shared the smell and color of the aura.

Jemma reasserted control and was back on top like a righted yacht. She rubbed and danced as she reached climax, falling on him to consume his head from the face inwards. He rolled her over again, this time with slightly less care, deepened his final thrust and he was there with her.

They collapsed back onto the floor and wrapped each other up in arms and legs. Here she was living and breathing like she'd never gone. In the absence of polluting the moment with some of a million possible questions, he wondered if this was to be his life from here on, seeing his Jemma here and there in time, picking up wherever they'd left off. Would he take it in the absence of the ultimate solution? Damn straight. Bring it on.

Jemma shuffled free with a being-squeezed noise accompanying a tricky extraction and did what Jemma always did, flicked his nipple and licked his nose and headed up the steps to the bathroom.

'See ya then,' said Salvador, wondering if he would.

'Toodloo,' sang Jemma in reply.

'Told you,' said Salvador's boner.

Salvador put his jeans and shirt back on and ambled up to the kitchen to get some coffee together. He spared a glance out of the window and Camille's little blue car was still there. After that dream, all he wanted was her to be the other side of that door but she, if it ever was her, materialised into who he really needed here, then Jemma was here, no other thoughts were needed. She's here and that's that. Why not wallow in her being here again, start planning trips and holidays just like it was before? Maybe he'd appear with her in some Greek villa one day or on a boat off Catalina.

He knew a reckoning with his demons was just around the corner. When he opened that door the person he hoped would be there and soon making that face in his dream was Camille, he could still feel himself inside her when the door pulled open. That doesn't come free and, as sure as aliens smoke weed, the demon in his stomach stirred. Before it could rip and tear at him, and before he felt the need to check the bathroom for a wife very capable of vanishing, the bathroom door closed, just as he was convinced restrooms were the de facto portals for dimension-travelling visitors. His demon would have to wait.

Hearing her feet head up the steps, he poured her a coffee, strong, black, one sugar. He turned to hand it to her but there was Camille smiling back at him.

Salvador smiled back but was now in a place that no-one could hope to understand. It was an automated reaction to hand her the coffee but what the fuck? Had he been with Camille the whole time? How about in the old town? Had he just imagined Jemma? Who had he actually opened the door to? Who just did that to him on the floor? One thing was sure, he'd damn well handcuff Jemma to something the next time he saw her.

'Did we just...?' he said, pointing his head down the steps to the scene of much mischief but there were none of Jemma's stripped off clothes. Camille didn't have an answer, just turned her head and gave Salvador the eyebrow.

'Just... what?'

'Doesn't matter,' said Salvador. 'Anyway, where the fuck did you go the other day?'

'Where did I go?' said Camille.

'Yeah, as in you were there and then you weren't.'

'I came out of the bathroom and you'd fucked off. Did I upset you or something?'

'Nah, Scrunchie, you were in the bathroom for ages then you weren't. I thought I upset you.'

'Drugs. Drugs are bad, ok, mmm hmm, too much drugs.'

'OK so when I first saw you on Del Obispo, you just appeared exactly where this really odd guy was.'

'Or alternatively, nose boy, I came out of a dress shop.'

'After I saw you and you fucked off, I saw Jemma,' he said.

'At the hospital?'

'She was in the dress shop you said you were going to. That's why I went there.'

'Dressed to Chill, awesome.'

'But Jemma was there instead.'

'Jemma, your wife who's in the hospital in a coma, that Jemma?'

'The very same. Don't ask me how. We had a few drinks and then she fucking vanished as well.'

'I didn't fucking vanish, you did.'

'Whatever Scrunchie, anyway... '

'Anyway what?'

'Anyway, this is why I thought you fucked off yesterday, because I asked you what happened when we were thirteen.'

'That's the thing, I can't remember much, flashes really,' said Camille. There was this big emergency at home. Mom and Dad were running around. They weren't talking to each other. They weren't talking to me. Then they left without me. No idea where they were going. I must have done something really bad but no idea what it was. They didn't talk to me for weeks. I still can't remember what I did. Do you think we block really bad things out? I mean, can we really totally forget we've done something?'

'Definitely. It's your defence mechanism. If it's off the charts evil, best you don't keep bringing it up but look, Scrunchie, why didn't you call or something?'

'No idea. I'm sure I would have but I can't remember ever doing it. Didn't I call once?'

'No you fucking didn't,' said Salvador flicking some flower vase water at her. 'So what's your story, where do you live and stuff?'

'New York. Single. No kids. I lecture history at NYU.'

'I thought you'd be an astronaut or invent time travel or something. So why are you back in sleepy little San Juan?'

'Ah well that's the thing,' said Camille

'Is this thing the same thing as the first thing or another thing?'

'This thing is another thing but probably the same as the first thing.'

'Thanks.'

'It's kinda fucked up though.'

'Fucked up how?' said Salvador.

'Well these flashes I get. I'm suddenly in a place then I'm not. I can end up in some pretty freaky places or a different time, back in my past. I'm pretty sure a few times I was in my future. And they're not exactly flashes, they're whole experiences, more like...'

'Jumps,' said Salvador, feeling the cold of hearing his own shit from someone else.

'There's something about where I go, where I'm taken, like it's some sort of...'

'Pattern'

'Pattern. It feels like I've got to decode something, find a solution but I don't know what to.'

'See the signs, put them together, get an answer.'

'Well look who's got all the answers why-did-we-never-fuck-boy.'

'Gee, I don't know, because-we-were-thirteen-girl. What you say sound like what me see. Copy and paste, Scrunchie, what the fuck is going on?'

'No idea?'

'I mean, I've got this thing...'

'Thing.'

'To do. I need to bring my wife out of a coma. I've been trying for months but I'm nowhere. Why wouldn't the signs be pointing me to the same thing, to save her? I'm running out of time and running out of ideas. The thing is, the only sign about Jemma is this link to a little missing girl.' Salvador's demon stirred again. 'I think there might be an answer in that.'

'Answer to what?'

'Why she was so guilty. I mean, the school said they all were but this was different. She didn't tell me anything about it all the time it was going on right up until...'

'You might find the answer to why she felt guilty but is it the answer to bringing her out of the coma. Do you want to dive into that?'

'Doctors have given up. All I've got is me. Her life support is turned off in... fuck, five days. Yes I do. I need to know.'

'Fine, well, just follow the yellow brick road.'

'The little girl in the bar,' said Salvador.

'What?'

'Yellow brick road, this girl in the bar was singing it.'

'What does it mean?'

'Fucked if I know, that's the point. Fucking clues, why can't they just write it down and post it to me like a civilised supernatural fucking horror show.'

'Sometimes, I just end up where I was going anyway,' she

said. 'I was heading to the grocery store and then I was at the grocery store. I was suddenly in that dress shop.'

'Where are you staying? Stay here.'

'I'm pretty sure I'm still in New York. I don't have any memory of getting to San Juan or this house, getting a hotel, don't even remember where the car came from. Then I was in the old town with you now I'm here. I couldn't tell you any of this in the old town. It's so fucked up. You would have run sure and swift, my lofty friend.'

'As would you, little Scrunchie and same here. If I couldn't believe you, you couldn't believe me anyway.'

'But we don't need any of that. We're living the dream, same shit, different shit pot.'

Camille offered a high five.

'Team Scrunchie,' she said.

'Team Scrunchie.'

The El Gunto pants hoist was completed stylishly, especially by Camille who wasn't wearing pants. She was wearing a thigh-length dress and all she could think of was lift it up till it covers her breasts. A demon turned over restlessly in its sleep.

'I do remember the last night I saw you. I've dreamt about it, even been there a few times since then. We got the bus down to Coronado beach.'

'Skimming stones,' said Salvador as every sense of that night came back to him in glorious technicolor.

'Whoever won each skim had to tell a truth or we'd be licked by... what's her name, if it wasn't true, that gross old lady on your street.'

'Mrs. Otto.'

'Mrs. Otto. I won pretty much all of them. I think you were due eleven licks to my three... And then?' she said.

'And then, what?' said Salvador and, for the first time since he was thirteen, he remembered.

'You said you loved me.'

'I did. I meant it. What else?'

'What else? Well I said I loved you right back but I don't know what else.'

'Think.'

He looked at her and her little raised eyebrow and then it came to him.

'You said "We'll always find the truth on this beach."'

'I did.'

Salvador was getting the feeling the truth could well be on the beach. It was on his radar but so far, didn't make any sense.

'Oh my god, I missed you so much, Scrunchie.'

'Me too,'

'I've been back to that beach as well a few times. I am getting clues from it but I'm no closer to figuring out why.'

'You will,' she said. 'I get a feeling we'll both get an answer, just how long it takes.'

'So you know what I have to do. What do you think your crazy fucked up shit is all about?' said Salvador.

'No fucking idea. Flashbacks to when I was a kid, you on the beach, school, being in my house and then being in another house but I don't remember that house. And I remember being on my own in the woods, scared, really scared, but I never see what's making me scared. I just wake up. Sometimes I'm pretty sure I'm a seagull on a rooftop, just over and above everything else. I can see for miles. I wasn't afraid being up there. I knew I could fly. I really wanted to fly but just as I started to lift off, I was suddenly somewhere else. I'm pretty sure I'm showering and I might be sleeping but not much.'

'Well you seem pretty fresh to me,' said Salvador, mimicking her skirt lift and getting a pinch from Camille and a rip from inside him for his pains. 'Jury's out on the showering.'

'Maybe I'm dreaming when I see you,' she said. 'Maybe Jemma's dreaming when she sees you.'

'The doctors said she can't dream, no activity at all.'

'Fuck the doctors. They can't possibly know that. What do they really know about our brains? That bit means you're angry and that bit means you're turning left. How could they know everything that goes on in there?'

'Well they don't, Scrunchie, that's how.'

'That is how, smart boy. Maybe I'm here to help you. Maybe you're here to help me. I know I've got something I need to do, I just don't fucking know what it is.'

'I know Scrunchie, we'll figure it out, right?'

They hugged close. Salvador ran his hand through her fine hair and Camille pulled him in tight by the shoulders.

'There's something I have to do later,' he said.

'There's something I need to do now,' she hummed in his ear and started kissing his neck.

'Scrunchie, no, please,' said Salvador, cursing every syllable. The mood was in danger of swallowing them but soon spat them out again and was back in its box quick smart.

There was a loud bang at the door, it sounded angry or official, you don't want both, you don't want either. They sniggered into each-others necks like teenagers behind the bike shed and separated.

Salvador let go of Camille's hand and looked her in the eyes. She smiled back at him. They were both pretty sure in a few seconds one of them wouldn't still be here. He hopped up the steps from the den and shuffled across the floor towards the door.

He opened the door to a young police officer. He had the sagging, out of focus look of a man who'd repeated these words many times today and he was sorry to bother them. The police had some new info and were upping their game to find this little girl, had I seen her, her name was Ashlen. The officer showed him a small poster with a picture of the missing little girl. This was the first time he'd seen her face.

'The milk carton,' said Salvador, drawing a null stare from the officer.

'I've seen her on a milk carton.'

'More than likely,' said the lad. 'Is there anything you can recall about the time she disappeared, recognise her from anywhere, anything could be useful.'

Salvador didn't feel the need to go through what he learned yesterday again. He'd told Morres everything.

'Will keep my eye out,' he said and, with that, the officer smiled and headed back down the driveway.

Salvador closed the door.

'So that thing I had to do,' he said.

'Thing.'

He told Camille about the Luiseño Indians and the visit he and Jemma would be making to them tonight.

The extraction plan had been formulated, had some weaknesses, but it may be the last real world chance he had.

'Fucking awesome, I'm in,' she said.

'What?'

'I'm coming. I'm just coming and I'll wedge the shit out of that fucker Tony as well.'

'OK you know it's trespass and kidnapping right? Definite jail time if we're caught?'

'I'm in. I'm coming.'

'Alrighty then,' he said.

So now he knew what Ashlen looked like, little urchin, so small, school uniform, cheeky smile. She'd have been promised something to stand still for this picture. How many times had he imagined him and Jemma having one just like this? And then Camille said something he didn't expect.

'This mission, the link with Ashlen, save Jemma,' said Camille.

'Mmm hmm.'

'Have you ever thought it might mean something else?'

'What?'

'Let go, get on with your life?'

'No way.'

'I mean, haven't you let go just a little today with me? Haven't you thought about you and me just a little bit?'

Yes he had and now the demon inside him had brought friends. His stomach was biting at him, clawing him, enough for him to stand up and take it to the bathroom. He might just throw up.

'You OK?' said Camille.

'I feel sick.'

'Want me to hold your hair back?'

He locked the door of the bathroom, filled the sink with cold water and put his face in it. He was dizzy and his head was pounding. This demon and his buddies weren't letting go and he knew why. He saw Camille in an orgasmic swan-song to a dream, then she was there in his house. Even after being with Jemma again, still his mind strayed to Camille and yes he had thought about the two of them. Fuck. Camille was right. 'You cheating lying fuck,' he bubbled. Camille said his signs might be telling him to let go of Jemma. Suddenly, was this the first step to doing that, an inevitable slide to a state of 'no Jemma'?

Salvador opened his eyes under the water to keep the images out of his mind. The plug helped by continuing to be a plug, pretending to be nothing other than a plug. He blew out a lung full and took in another one, dunking himself back under. The plug popped a couple of tiny bubbles up past his eyes to the surface.

'Betrayal, Salvador,' said the demon under the plug.

'Fuck off,' said Salvador, losing more air than he wanted. The sink of water had changed. It wasn't the safe haven escape he needed any more. He didn't want to hear this shit. He didn't need to stay trapped with a fucking plug demon. He pulled his head out of the water and reached for a towel but there was no time. He felt an ocean of green slime preparing to jump up his throat and out of his mouth and he fell down on the toilet and let it out. He flushed the toilet, leaned back against the wall and towelled his head.

'Look at you, Jemma's saviour my ass, you've dreamed it now you're gonna fuck that blonde tart all over your sick wife's shiny floors.'

'Fuck off! Not going to happen.'

'Got the message yet?'

Was Salvador seeing what everyone else saw, a sad desperate man losing his mind trying to save someone who couldn't be saved? I mean, VR machines and tribal dances? What the fuck was he doing? Was it an inescapable end and he wasn't facing it, running and looking for new ways to keep running. Again the demon gauged him, sending him over double.

'You know she's gone, bitch. You did that.'

'No. Fuck off, leave me alone.'

'You know what it means, slow boy, that's it isn't it, slow boy. That's what the blonde tart calls you isn't it?'

'She's not a fucking tart.'

'Well, touchy. Like I say, soft dick, you know what it means.'

'What?'

'You know she's gone. You do, don't you. Admit it. Say it.'

'No. Fuck off.'

'Fuck off right back at you. You're already thinking of replacing her with this tasty little stripling, boy would I tap that ass. Go on, fuck her... You know she will. She's begging for it. But she's right isn't she? Even the person you want saved, saviour, doesn't want to be fucking saved.

She just wants you to fuck off and leave her alone. And four days to do what? You've failed, you can't help her. Give up.'

'Why wasn't it your face in my dream?' Salvador asked Jemma. 'It's always your face.'

Then the demon steered him to another idea.

'But who are you?' said Salvador. 'Wife of mine, loyal partner, honest partner, fucking really? Who are you? All those months, not a word about Ashlen. Not a fucking word. Like I'm just some fucking contractor in the house. I could have been there for you. Why didn't you tell me? You didn't want me next to you. That's fucking cold Baby. Why do I see you, why do I talk to you? What the fuck are you doing here?'

The towel was used to cover his face and accept the tears. His demons were quiet, victorious, he was beaten, the game was up. And then he had it.

'Fuck, that's it,' he shouted through the towel. 'What are you doing here?'

This is what Jemma was doing here. The signs weren't benign prophets, pointing him to save her. It's Jemma pointing him to save her. He thought the jumps were in control, the signs were in control but they're not. It's Jemma in control.

'As usual,' he said.

If Jemma had wanted him to back off, don't bother, let her go, why appear to him, talk to him, let him feel her again and share his hope? That's grade A horseshit. She's doing something when he sees her, guiding him somewhere. She's telling him how to save her.

'Follow the yellow brick road, said Camille,' he said.

'Have faith in her, go with her and I'll find it.'

Finally there was some structure to all of this, not some random hotchpotch of repeating signs. She was in control and she'd guide him where he needed to go, as it always was. Of course, how could it be anything else?

Salvador felt a weight lift off him. Jemma was with him in this fight, not lying in a coma bed, with him, here in the heat of battle, working with him. He felt in control of this for the first time since it started, a random shape had become a square. Where would she take him next?

'Maybe she is dreaming when we're together.'

Salvador was a naked man sitting on the bathroom floor with a towel in his hands. Camille.

'You OK? Pretty japey lingo coming from in there,' said Camille as Salvador went past her down to the den and crashed down on the couch.

Six hours later, he woke up on the couch and she was still there with him, left arm draped over his middle. It was dark. He remembered the feeling of hope in the dream he just left behind, the people wandering out onto the plain, full of faith, he was one of them, sharing a feeling of impending enlightenment. The smell of the incense and the fires was still in his nose.

Camille's peaceful head was just about to reanimate and reassemble her dream for Salvador.

'Fucking Jesus,' she said. 'Fuck, fuck.' Salvador cuddled her in. 'Fuck. I was in this room. There was someone in the house who wanted to hurt me. Yellow curtains.'

'Yellow curtains?'

'Jesus, what a headfuck.' She was out of breath and she buried herself in Salvador and gripped on tight to get rid of it.

The shadows cast by the outside lights decorated the room with interpretation. Salvador reached for the low lamp next to the couch. It was midnight. Tony.

17   The Light

Salvador rubbed his eyes. This was it. This was his last chance in the world he recognised, but his faith in the world he didn't recognise had just grown.

Then there were lights in the driveway. Tony. Solid but the lights were approaching the front of the house pretty quick, actually is it going to stop? And then it did stop, with a screech and eyeball panic from Tony in the cockpit. Then he stalled it. Fucking dude, thought Salvador, he's totally wasted.

Salvador got over to the car door and Tony was fumbling to find the window lever.

'Wasted, completely fucking wasted.'

'Not wasted, dude, well not deliberately, real sorry, sedatives last night, maybe a few too many. Fine when I left. Just came over all... funny.'

'Fuck, man, I would of come over to yours.'

Tony was managing an occasional smile in his own defense but this was definitely not a man who should get anywhere near the wheel. Salvador opened his door.

'Move over, bud, you're not driving anywhere.'

'Fuck, am I driving?' said Tony. 'Feels too... still.'

Salvador put his shoulder into getting Tony across the bench and out of the way.

'What are you on, man, ludes or something?'

'I think all the ludes in the world,' said Tony.

Salvador moved to go inside but there was noise from the big man.

'Sally,' he said. 'Sally… Celia… Camille… They did find her…'

'Sure they found her, bud, told you, she's right here, she's coming too, just wait there, chill, we'll be right out.'

But Tony had already lost his battle with consciousness. Jesus, all the blood and guts from Tony about helping, part of the team, brothers and stuff. Now, any getaways would be slower, stunted affairs, running round to kick this old heap of shit over rather than moving off at speed as soon as the door was shut. Maybe it would be the difference between actually getting away and not getting away. Just when Salvador needed him most, he bailed for the sake of staying straight just for half a day. Useless

'Oh my God, he's fucking wasted. Sleepy my ass,' she said, giving Salvador a punch on the arm. 'I'm still gonna wedge the hairy lump.'

'But not right now.'

'Not right now, my friend,' she directed at Tony. 'But surely and without mercy. How long till he's back with us?'

'No idea but it takes a lot to fell this moose, half a house of quaaludes probably.'

'At least we're going to the right place if he starts spazzing out.'

'There'll be no spazzing or any movement at all from these bones, Scrunchie, I guarantee you that, but we'll keep checking the fuckwits breathing.'

'We get there, we get in, get these uniforms from the locker room and get out.'

'Uniforms?'

'Yeh we've got to look the part.'

'A fitting, fabulous.'

Ten minutes later, they arrived at Mission Hospital. The van had a hole in its tailpipe. When they got underground into the concrete void of the parking lot, it's deep grunt echoed around the place like a marauding dragon suddenly appearing, angry and hungry from another dimension.

Salvador located the extraction point door and parked in the nearest spot to it. The lot wasn't too busy, promising for the mission but also for the people of San Juan, who were staying nice and healthy.

'Let's do this,' said Camille, all ninja, covert dark alleys, espresso and lipstick. She was loving this. He was nervous.

There was a quick pulse and breathing check for Tony. Salvador did mention 'keep watch, text me if anyone uses that door' but it was pointless. Tony opened one eye for the first word and it was closed again by the third.

They entered the front entrance of Mission Hospital. There were two girls on reception and only four or five people waiting. The odd doctor or two would swing through one door into another, oblivious to all other things. It was a scene of relative calm.

Twenty yards down the shiny corridor they found the orderly's locker room and were quickly inside but not without a Stan and Ollie *both going through the door at the same time* moment.

Proudly hanging in several areas of this locker room were a variety of light blue cotton-ish uniforms, many stories to tell. Sizes and name badges were selected and put on. For the purposes of the next hopefully-not-many minutes, Salvador was Daniel Bunn and Camille was a very realistic Madeleine Eklund.

A little further down the corridor were two possible gurney targets. Salvador took the first one without breaking step and wheeled it off towards the elevator.

It was all about confidence, looking like you fitted in. If you swaggered like an orderly, like you knew the place, on auto-pilot wheeling your gurney about, perhaps even offering a whistle, you'd fit in. If you looked furtive and shuffled, unsure of your direction, or handled the gurney like a wonky shopping trolley, you wouldn't.

The elevator slowed to level two. They heard voices waiting for it. Here was their first test. Maybe whoever was on the other side was just too busy to scan them carefully, it was late and the uniform was familiar, and assumption is easier than speculation.

The elevator doors creaked open on two junior doctors comparing six irons on the twelfth at Park Hills and they passed without a second glance.

It was a short trip round just the corner to Jemma's room and they were soon approaching room two three two. Camille outpaced the gurney to open the door and they were safely inside.

She closed the door and looked at Jemma, approached the bed and took her hand. The two of them communed. 'She's beautiful' said Camille, stroking Jemma's forehead. 'I can see what all the fuss is about.' Jemma asked 'Who's this little honey, Babe?' and Salvador could've sworn she moved her head just ever so slightly towards Camille, smelling her, learning her and knowing everything. Salvador's demon was happy to remind him 'Of course she knows, idiot.' Salvador wondered how this small frail wife of his could possibly be the one guiding him.

The initial brief had to get round two problems. The first was the machines. As soon as the person the machines were monitoring wasn't there to be monitored, the machines would generally whine and bitch and then go 'fuck it.' Then they'd flatline and the world would arrive. Chen knew the inputs and outputs on these things and Chen's buddy, Alex had coded up a little machine that kept Jemma's machines showing exactly what they needed to show. He even added the occasional machine freak out to keep it real. This little box would hide in the rack where

Salvador hid the VR box last time and there's nothing to see here, Nursey.

The second, her attachments, the things she needed to stay alive. She could do without the feeding tube and the drugs for a couple of hours. She wasn't on a drip. A drip would've been a challenge. How do you take a thing that needs to be vertical and make it horizontal, create natural pressure at the same level? The simple answer is he wouldn't, he'd hang his coat on it and whistle along as normal, if they don't see a drip, is it still a drip?

These were the things they'd be switching off in… four days time.

A triumphant salvo of escaped tones from one of the machines snapped him out of *four days*. He eyed the machine and it folded and righted itself. Maybe Jemma passed a message into this machine but, anyway, it reminded him to get the code box hooked up and crack on.

Changeover was nice and smooth. The machines were doing what they needed to do. They lifted Jemma onto the gurney. Salvador tweaked open the door a pinch, no sound in the corridor, promising. Visuals were clear and so began this extraction stage.

From Jemma's room, it was a few corridors to navigate to a different elevator at the back of the building. The one that took them right near the exit door to the parking lot. This elevator would deposit them small yards from that exit and everything would still seem in line with usual practice here at Mission Hospital.

Winding round the corners was quiet apart from one acquired errant gurney wheel, wobbling like a top at the end of its performance, introducing a potential fail. Camille kicked it and it was improved a little but continued to disobey. Maybe it's the way of supermarket trolleys and hospital gurneys to behave like this if they're not happy, throwing your front right into the biscuit shelves to cause much crunchy damage.

Each corner presented a new squeak. Now more voices could be heard approaching them, a female doctor, who turned to walk away from them, and another male, heading their way.

'Just talk about hospital stuff,' said Salvador.

'Hospital stuff?' said Camille.

'Fuck off. Just avoid eye contact,' said Salvador.

This was now important. The uniform of the man approaching was the dark blue uniform of a security guard and he'd seen them. Salvador's nerves were tingling but Camille knew exactly how to deal with it.

She sharpened her eyes on this security guard, offered him a smile and a wiggle. It would divert any thought of her identity to what she liked for dessert. He smiled back, they all passed each other and Camille enjoyed an internal smile. She had the power to drive most men round the corner to smash one off, testament to the sheer power beautiful women have over the world.

This final stretch of corridor was another shiny place that smelt of disinfectant. With many doors all ready to present a problem, all they could do was get their heads down and focus on the elevator.

The longest time in the open was now over. The elevator was empty again and dropped slowly to their final stage. It was no surprise to Salvador that the elevator muzak was Dock of the Bay. They emerged to the corridor on minus one and all was quiet once the tune was faded out by the closing doors.

Ten yards down the corridor, Camille listened at the door of the storage room. There was no noise inside. Salvador pushed open the door to the parking lot. Tony was still out for the count, drooling onto the window. Salvador opened up the back doors and lifted his Jemma from the gurney. It was the first time he'd picked her up for so long. She'd always been light but this wasn't right.

He slipped her in the back seat, fastening her belt and making sure she was upright. Camille pushed the gurney back into the storage room and got in the van.

Now the critical bit, applying the double strip of draft excluder tape along the bottom of the door. It needed to keep the door just open enough to let them in later.

The van started and they were back on Ortega, heading for Luiseño country, a small tributary of the San Rey River south west about twenty miles.

It was a still, warm night. The quietness of it allowed in the sounds of frogs and crickets. Camille closed her eyes and tuned to the soothing song of this California nightlife. Occasionally a rhythm appeared in the mix, a light orchestra of flora and fauna combining to hypnotize her. It was like any other warm peaceful evening apart from a comatose Tony right here and a comatose wife buckled up in the back.

The Luiseño people were not given to idle chat, plans were set in motion with a good deal of information missing, who does he meet, what does he have to do, are there chickens involved? All Annalise could report from the Luiseño was he'd know when he got there, they'd find him and take this thing all the way so chill out, relax, white man.

There was a dirt track off to the left, bordered by a rusty barbed wire fence. It bumped and slid them about a hundred yards and they were into the woods. Tony's van navigated a slow and steady decline, carefully avoiding some pretty decent rocks shifting the big man around his seat but not close to disturbing him, and eventually they approached the riverside edge of the treeline and a small track to the river.

A small plateau next to the river hosted a large fire and about twenty people. Salvador pulled the car up just beyond the treeline. They were on their way down to who knows what.

Salvador was still churning over ideas even as he walked into the middle of this one. 'We'll always find the truth on this beach.'

'What's that, quiet boy?'

'Nothing.'

As they got closer to the fire, the low alluring hums and chants grew around them as the people there set about the preparation of the ritual. A tent was facing the river, lined with cushions, fir skins and candlelight and formed a midpoint between the fire and the river.

He thought, if this worked, he'd bestow a donation on the people of the Luiseño of pretty much every single thing he had if they got her back to him. But the Luiseño would be happy with a general sense of owing them one. One day they might need to call it in.

One man emerged from the tent, eyes already fixed on Salvador. He clapped his hands once and issued the word for look lively, she's here. Four of them fetched a wooden stretcher from the tent and joined the man on his way over.

The regal looking man was about seventy years old, light white cotton shirt and pants. His long grey hair mixed with the ear-rings, neck chains and the tails of this headbands. He weighed nothing. He was the Luiseño Shaman and would be conducting this ritual.

The shaman welcomed them with a short head bow and they responded in kind. Salvador got the feeling he'd seen this Shaman before but couldn't put his finger on it.

Salvador lay Jemma on the stretcher and they carried her over past the fire to the tent. She was laid down by two women and propped up with a large fir cushion. The candles flickered and flapped as the humans stirred up the air and then settled with her.

According to Annalise's research, this ritual unfolded in four clear stages. First, the lost soul was laid down and prepared for the ritual with a cleansing, a cool damp cloth wiped away the day and a natural oil rub, fragrant incense burners and then the chanting. This stage accepted that the lost soul wouldn't respond now but it was to warn the entity surrounding the soul that it would be forced to yield its captive. It was on notice.

The fire was being loaded higher and the chants increased from the people now circling it. A raised wooden platform had been set up about five yards from the fire and carried one large fir blanket, the lost soul was brought from the tent and placed here facing the fire and the second stage could begin, the incantation.

After the finale of the incantation and, once the lost soul had travelled its path and found the light, it had to be immersed in the river for cooling.

Finally the soul, no longer lost, would be carried once more to the tent where it would be dried, warmed and dressed. This stage once more addressed the soul, this time taunting the vanquished captor and then reminding the soul it was free and could awaken.

The Luiseño were expert taunters and really ripped into the captor on a deeply personal level, raising eyebrows and causing a release on the lost soul. Salvador couldn't understand the exact phrases they used but Annalise had given him some examples including something about grandmothers, barbed wire and fire ants, and honey and testicles.

It wasn't unknown to the enslavers of souls to accept this defeat but then try a last ditch grab on the soul as it prepared to exit, so these taunts also served to remind it that simply wasn't on.

The Luiseño didn't expect the person to simply wake up, yawn and ask for a cheeseburger. This wasn't an exact science. The awakening could take hours or days and could take many forms. They fully appreciated the urgency and the scene was set.

Jemma and the stretcher were laid onto the platform. Jemma was still, so small in her finest green hospital gown. She was then covered in a light muslin cloth. The shaman headed over and whispered to Salvador. He had a voice betraying many peace pipes. He said his friend was over there the other side of the fire, as in 'Go over there,' then he entered the theatre. The drums started to play more complex rhythms. He waved a long staff adorned with thin streams of colorful fabric over Jemma to introduce himself.

The drums and chanting stopped and the spotlight was on the shaman. He started a different song, standing over Jemma like a sacrifice.

The song was telling all those gathered about what was to come, he'd ask Jemma's soul to listen, tell it where it was and what it had to do to awaken, it had to find the light. There would be trials and challenges along the way but it had to accept this task, gain courage and it had to start right now. Once these challenges had been overcome, Jemma's soul would see a light in the distance, a solitary light in the inky black of that world, she'd head towards it and be reborn into her world.

The shaman then looked over at Salvador and gestured him over. He asked Salvador did he have the love for this woman and of course yes he did.

The shaman directed him to place his hands on Jemma's head with his little fingers resting on her temples. He told him to talk to her, tell her he loved her and he wanted her back, not to be afraid on her path and, most importantly, to head towards the light, he had to send his love into his Jemma to remind her soul of it.

Salvador bent down over her face and kissed her on the end of her little nose.

'Hey Wiggle, how's it going in there?' he said.

He listened for a response but there wasn't one from his Jemma.

'Well, here we are by a big fire next to a river and you're the party, Baby. I need to tell you something. It's about to get hairy in there. I love you so much, Baby and I need you back. You need to be brave now. There's gonna be shit flying at you from everywhere but just remember the light and see me standing there in the light. I'll be with you whenever you need me, just turn around and you'll see me. And guide me where you want me to go, Baby. I know it's you. Come back to me. I love you so much.'

Salvador's hands were shaking. He avoided tears but only just. He turned to the shaman, who nodded and gestured him to step back. The shaman then started a new song, a slow melodic hum of a chant and he circled the platform maintaining his intense gaze on Jemma.

He stopped where Salvador had just been and also placed his hands on her head, he told her that was the love she needed to overcome her darkness, inside her, she'd be galvanized into action and would start her journey, wild animals would come at her and spirits would haunt her but she'd have the means to defeat them and she had to keep going.

As the shaman's song increased its tempo, the drums started up again and the others joined his chant, he started dancing around the platform, summoning up the spirit to assist her, telling her to look out for this spirit because, with it, she would gain the advantage to defeat her enemies. Faster the drums beat out and faster the shaman danced and sang, finally stopping dead as did all other human made noises. The only sound was the crackle of the fire and perhaps the sound of a soul coming to the surface.

The shaman knelt beside the platform and bowed as four female bearers entered to take Jemma to the river. The shaman got to his feet and signaled Salvador to follow him there.

The bearers waded into the river and stopped at a point where Jemma was wet but not submerged, they were joined by the shaman, who said a few words and Jemma was bodily baptized, she was being cooled after her trials and being asked to relax as she'd present herself soon. There was a moment of silence. The shaman looked into Jemma's face and moved over to Salvador. The bearers left the river and took her up to the tent to being the taunting.

The shaman pulled out a pack of smokes and offered Salvador one. A few drags had gone in and out before the shaman spoke.

He told him Jemma had now completed the ritual and he'd have to wait for her to emerge, there could be many outcomes to this, she may want to just wake up and return to her world or maybe not yet. If she didn't, Salvador wouldn't see any difference but somewhere inside her, something would be awake, he needed to be aware of this.

'We all have to go through this ritual, Salvador, if we're to find the truth we seek,' he said. 'We all have to be ready for our own.'

There was another brief silence to focus on the smokes and the shaman spoke again.

'At the beginning of time,' he said. 'A great god was laid low and didn't move, nobody could wake him and the people were suffering with his loss. A simple man came to the house of the god and delivered him with an incantation and the god awoke. In his sleep, the god had been pursued by a winged demon and been forced to hide in a small cave to escape it. In this cave he found a leopard looking at him from the shadows in the corner. The god asked what the leopard was doing there. The leopard told him he was the god's spirit guide, he was the god's true soul. He could guide him on his journey and convey the powers on him to prevail against all things. Evil spirits taunted the god as he and the leopard progressed but he stayed his path, all manner of guides and signs were sent to disturb him and lead him astray, the wolves that approached one night were driven off by the leopard and the god knew the leopard's presence showed him the truth in these signs. Familiar sequences of sounds, smells and images drew his attention and reminded the god where to follow, eventually the sun started rising over the horizon and the god approached the light, he looked at the leopard and thanked him. The leopard told him he could now rejoin his world, the leopard's work was done and he vanished to the shadows of the god's soul. As soon as the god was back in the land he came from, he made the simple man a shaman, the first shaman, this is the ritual she has undergone tonight, Salvador. Inside Jemma, she'll be walking in a dull grey haze, her spirit will show itself and lead her way, if she's there, she'll find the light.'

The shaman threw his smoke in the river. He turned to Salvador again and offered a smile.

'The goodness of the human soul will go to great lengths to save itself but it'll go to far greater lengths to save another, you can take your wife now.'

The shaman put his hand on Salvador's shoulder for a moment.

'I will see you very soon, Salvador.'

Something moved in the trees, swinging from one branch to another and stopped, just watching.

Salvador looked out to the river and flicked his smoke in, turned to thank the shaman for his words but the shaman was gone.

Camille was standing outside the tent waiting for him.

She gave him a warm hug. He sank into it and felt safe. He waited for a demon but none came.

'You looked so lonely down at the river. I was going to come and join you but I reckoned you needed some head-space,' she said.

'Not lonely,' he said. 'I was talking to the shaman. We had a smoke, told me a story, and then he just vanished.'

'Sal, the shaman has been in the tent all the time you were down there,' she said. 'There was no-one with you down there.'

A cold chill crept up his back and left a black lump in his stomach. Salvador had been gifted a sense of normality as San Juan and the machinery of its memories offered him just that. But when ghosts appear in that normality, it ain't so normal anymore. He could no longer tell what was real and what wasn't real.

'We should get her back,' he said.

It was time to replace the patient and who knows, maybe he'll get a call tomorrow morning speaking of miracles and please come and get her.

Heading back up the bumpy track, Salvador wondered what the shaman meant by "See you very soon." Maybe he had met him before.

The parking lot door still had to be open but look closed to anyone else. It all hinged on this.

Suddenly, Salvador was forced out of his self-imposed autopilot as a truck came round the bend and reminded him of the right lane with sound and light.

'Fuck!' he said as Camille clung on to anything.

'Want me to drive, soft boy?' she said, clipping him round the back of the head.

'Fuck off.'

The parking lot was now empty apart from a VW camper van sat quietly at the opposite end to the door he needed. It didn't look like anyone was inside it.

He pulled up in the closest spot to the door. The door was still ajar. The door was opened and Salvador looked into the empty corridor. All good, final stage. He got the gurney from the storage room and soon Jemma was inside and en route.

Salvador smiled.

'What?' said Camille.

'Nothing, just some thing.'

'Some thing.'

'Nah, it's just a stupid thought.'

'Naturally. OK, come on, out with it.'

'It's just we've left the hospital totally open to anyone. There's at least one sick fuck in San Juan. What if we came back and there was some *Texas Chainsaw* scene or something?'

'Dude, where do you get this shit from? Inspiring.'

'What if we get to Jemma's room and there's all holes in her bed. The killer thought she was there, but the bed was disguised to contain her absence. We'd saved her life by abducting her.'

'The irony, soft lad, and are you doing anything to keep your head in one place ever by the way?'

'Bourbon'

'Good choice.'

They were quickly into the elevator and out onto the second floor, still no sign of anyone else. They rounded the final corner to two three two. At the distant end of the corridor, the other side of a swing door, he saw a nurse, looking down at a file. He recognized her, she'd been in to check Jemma before, lovely woman, huge feet but 'shit,' she was coming this way.

Before the nurse could look up, the gurney was useless, given a gentle shove southwards and the two of them were in room two three two. Jemma was replaced and covered, tubes back in normal service and Chen's little code box gave control back to the machines. There was no time to do much about the prospect of the nurse seeing a gurney coming to rest with no driver or the aroma of essential oils and smoke in this room. This would have to do.

The footsteps outside two three two slowed and stopped at the door. Salvador dropped under the bed and Camille tucked in behind a curtain.

The nurse came in, still focused on her file. She threw a glance at Jemma and took a note of some of the readings from the machines. Salvador held his breath for the twenty seconds she was there and she left, wishing Jemma good night with a touch on the forehead.

As her squeaky shoes faded into the distance of the corridor and the squeaky doors opened and flapped shut again, Salvador felt safe enough to emerge. He hopped up on Jemma's bed and took a little time for a cuddle.

'Hell of day, Wiggle,' he said.

He waited a long few seconds but nothing came back from his Jemma. Maybe, just maybe.

'Baby, you there?'

He gave her an extra special squeeze and big kiss on the nose and hopped off the bed.

'Find the light, Wiggle, just find the light.'

He pushed his ear to the door then opened it wide enough for his head. It was clear, just the door swinging from the nurse's retreat. Within a couple of unbothered minutes, they'd exited the hospital and were back on the road. He'd either wake up tomorrow to a call from the hospital or not.

'Tony alright?'

'Still fucked but breathing,' and at that very moment releasing a low flute of wind.

'Reckon he should stay with you tonight.'

'How are you, Scrunchie, you OK?'

Camille took longer to answer than normal.

'I keep remembering things.'

'Things?'

'Things. That time when I was a kid, no-one talking to me, still can't remember why. The beach with you, always the beach with you, but every time there's less people on it. The smell of lemons and chemical, like disinfectant. Every time I think of something I already know, there's more to the story, something I've forgotten.'

'Tell me, say it out loud, it helps.'

'When I'm not on the beach with you, it feels like I'm scared most of the time. I get flashes of this man, he's the one smells like lemons and chemicals. Then I'm in a room. I can't leave. I'm trapped there but I can move. The only light is through this little window with yellow curtains. They're always shut. The car, really old car, light blue. I'm cycling home and I remember it stopping next to me. Then there's just a long line of cars.'

'Light blue?'

'Mmmmm.'

'How old? Coupe de ville?'

'I don't know. Do I look like I know? 40s, 50s?'

'It's the same car I'm seeing Scrunchie. My dad had the same car when I was a kid. It keeps cropping up for me. That one time, you came out of the dress shop in the old town, that was the car that the demon guy was driving. What else about the car?'

'Just those flashes, red seats, always the same, just me in the backseat, trees whizzing past.'

'And the guy you see. He's driving?'

'I think so, can't remember what he looks like but I know I'm scared of him. I still cant fly. I'm still just perched on the roof getting ready to fly, I really want to take off, see what it's like, but I never do.'

'You always jump before you can?'

'Yeah. Where do you see the car?'

'Old town, some photo I've got, office party at the golf club, I'm pretty sure I was hiding behind a burned out one in this battle, and...' Salvador hesitated just enough for Camille to sense it. 'In this home movie I've got, me and Jemma on the beach one day.'

'Coronado beach?'

'Coronado.'

'Tomorrow,' said Camille.

'Tomorrow.'

'Maybe it's just because you and me went there so many times but there's something about the beach.'

'The truth, Scrunchie.'

There were a few moments of quiet as the nightlife reasserted audio control.

'If Jemma's trying to tell you how to save her, or whatever it is, is there anything else you can look at?'

'Like what?'

'Like stuff of hers, diaries, stuff lying around, her stuff, you know, any tapes she made.'

Salvador remembered 'One Sunday' and smiled but then remembered the VR session in her room that day.

'I did record a VR session with her.'

'Mmm, stuff like that, lightning boy.'

'There was no signal feeding back from her, nothing was being recorded.'

'But it was recording, right?'

'Yeah.'

'Play it back. What have you got to lose? You can't tell what's in a black jar till you open the jar,' she said, remembering Miss Hoadley's stirring chat with them about never being afraid to try new things.

'You know what's really weird?'

'Go on, surprise me, everything, right?'

'I've spent such a long time in the world I recognize, pretty much two days now. It's starting to make sense, Scrunchie,' said Salvador banging both palms into the steering wheel. 'Normally, by now I would have...'

The problem for Salvador was that double palm smash 'come on!' on Tony's steering wheel hadn't made contact with Tony's steering wheel. It had made contact with the large chest of a pretty big guy in La Mesa bar and this guy had just stacked it backwards over several tables and chairs in front of him.

Tony's laughter was loud and strong. It rose against all other sounds in the room and taunted this felled monster. He stayed down for several seconds, considering all sorts of possible realities and then selected spitting fury, but it wasn't to go well for him. He rushed his getting up process and only deepened Tony's laugh as he tripped over a chair and hit the deck all over again.

The pain of what might be about to happen to him started showing itself early, his head started throbbing, or had this monster already hit him?

The car, the countryside, Camille and the dust were gone, replaced by booze, music and a decent number of people with mouths open, now witnessing this monster once more struggle to his feet.

Salvador got the impression here wasn't a place he should be hanging around. What looked like three even bigger buddies of the monster he'd just toppled, he imagined all employed to pull metal out of concrete, were starting to arrive in support.

Salvador had no energy to summon the jumping juice and deal with any of this and why should he? He had no beef with this monster and he certainly didn't want one. These tractor pullers were about to remind him how to flee a scene, with or without grace.

He turned to navigate his exit and had to applaud the strength of the comic timing with this one, same as jumping into the table at O'Hara's. Someone out there has a sense of humor.

The doors to La Mesa bar burst open with Salvador's escape hatch into the street. There was the comical falling out of the same door by his pursuers, tripping over the step, themselves and each-other. They were now a floundering pile on the floor. Salvador heard another massive roar from Tony inside. He turned and got himself on his toes and the risen monsters lumbered after him at burger king pace. All he could hear behind him were timeless classics such as 'I'm gonna kick some real ugly into you, boy,' 'you fuckin' dead, princess' and, he was almost sure, 'No Mr. Bond, I expect you to die.'

There wasn't a sound from any of the trees as he jogged towards the golf course but he wasn't sure whether there should have been at two in the morning.

Soon he was out onto the twelfth hole at San Juan Hills Golf Club. He could hear the puffing of four drunk angry men. He hid in the bushes by the large bunker on the far side of the fairway, a nasty steep one, forty yards from the pin, set fair to turn a four into a five.

The monsters headed off in the wrong direction down the fairway towards the hole, a handy downhill for them. They'd swill their beer around and follow shadows for a while. They'd stop to wheeze and throw up a few quarts along the way, then an inevitable farting nap in the light rough by the green.

As he lost sight and sound of them, Salvador took off the other way. He skimmed the tree line to the twelfth tee, bypassing it and heading down a small path. He stopped and made sure they hadn't spotted him and stood still for moment.

Then he heard it, the clicking of the demon's cane. The chill returned. It was heading along this path into a small open space.

This little path and the space it opened into were covered in light sand from the bunkers. Little sunflower windmills lined the edges and a canvas covered toy boat with a mast and ropes and portholes listed in the middle of the arrangement.

He followed the clicking sounds further down the path. His heart was racing from a possible meeting with this demon. He didn't want that but, as before, the whole thing was out of his control. He had to follow. He ended up at an almost secret wooden outbuilding mostly hidden by trees. It smelt of two stroke, leather and grass cuttings.

The clicking had now stopped and Salvador stood outside the door. There were only the distant angry sounds of oafs and a few leaves changing position. This place had everything from mowers and chemical supplies, the caddy's changing rooms and someone had made an effort to apply a nautical sense to the area.

There were no lights on and no noises from inside. He pressed his ear against the door and felt the cool of it. He was sure someone or something was there, breathing and listening right back at him, right the other side of the door. He could almost hear the sound of the air inside being disturbed by the shape of something moving. A solid opening of this door would uncover this fucking demon, once and for all. He stepped back a couple of paces and put his shoulder into the door. It was locked and solid. He kicked it, called it a fucker but it kept its secret.

He moved further down the path, checking behind him

every three paces. Then he was out into the open space in front of the colonial style clubhouse. He took a moment to ease mind and body in a new breeze cooling his face.

He was interrupted by the sound of the blues from his pocket. Voicemail. He took his phone out. The origin of the call was 'Home.' Who's in his house? He played it back. He could feel someone there but they didn't say anything. He thought he could hear low breathing behind the occasional static crackle. He focussed on this static like he'd focused on that door and tried hard to extract some sense from it. Maybe there was the quietest whisper, a feeling of sadness the other end. It made him feel sad. He listened for about a minute and the caller hung up.

Someone was in the house. He had the feeling if he closed his eyes, he wouldn't open them in this same scene. He held off for as long as he could, he had to get home, but so it was.

He opened his eyes in his bedroom. It was calm, a welcome peace after ritual and fires, anger and fear. He checked his watch. If he'd just jumped from the club to here in an instant, there was someone else here.

He picked up a kiddies baseball bat and headed out into the hallway. There was a noise. It came from the end of the hallway by his office. The carpet allowed a silent and cosy approach to the office door and Salvador stood outside. There was the noise again and it was definitely from inside this office. Salvador gathered breaths and tightened his grip on the bat.

He caressed the door handle, focused on head height and smashed himself inside ready to swing at anything. But nothing presented itself to be swung at. There was the noise again, on the floor behind his desk in the corner. He crept over to it. The closer he got, the more he could make out its exact location and the sort of noise it was making. He knew this. It was his VR headset making it's 'fully charged' noise.

'You won't know till you open the jar,' he remembered.

He sat down in his chair and put the headset on, Jemma's session that day. This would probably be nothing, but where exactly did probability figure in all of this?

Sanctity

Yellow curtains, just hanging there, eternally closed, ignorant and lifeless, clothing the front of this little window. Nothing moved, the outside was yellow, the light was yellow.

It wasn't even a nice shade of yellow. The color belonged to a white eighties rapper that never made it but still clung to his bright yellow pants.

The curtains were made of a nasty stiff material, like a short pleated shower curtain. The front door cracked open angrily and dislodged the coat rack behind it, further annoying the shooter as he plundered inside. He smashed his gun down on the table, reached for a beer from the fridge and sat in a ripped old armchair facing the door.

Quietly, in the next room, she was on alert and fixed on the yellow curtains, her only color against the darkness in the house, the feeling of terror gripped her again, she knew it was a matter of minutes before he came in to see her.

She could hear him pacing heavily in the next room, which one was he talking to today? Sometimes his friends told him it was OK and sometimes they told him it wasn't and that made him angry, which friend would this be?

He was looking into the small mirror next to the door leading to the back of the house, which friend indeed? He pleaded with the mirror to stop what it was saying and put his head in his hands shouting 'no, stop, not again.' The mirror told him, 'Yes and yes again and again and you will never stop.' He twisted his head in his hands to pour this demon out of his ears but it was too late, it was deep in there, buried, spikes dug into his brain and it wasn't going away.

He announced to something outside the window that he had to tell her why she'd done wrong or she'd never learn, he hoped she'd listen and wouldn't do it again but he had to tell her, right?

The door creaked opened slowly, oozing him into view and she tightened her gaze on the yellow. In her little head she started singing her song, 'Follow the yellow brick road, follow the yellow brick road.' It was the only thing that stopped her shaking. She could feel his black sticky energy seeping in ahead of him, surveying the room, checking for strangeness and an indication it was safe to follow.

She offered herself a small internal sigh and hoped it wasn't as bad as before when she couldn't eat for three days.

The idea of tears came to her all the time but no longer welled up in her little eyes, she ran out of tears a long time ago. She felt very little. She was very little. She kept hold on the yellow and hoped her song wouldn't creep out and be heard. She didn't blink. She could sense him approaching, the lightest of creaks in the floorboards and his erratic breathing coming ever closer.

He bent down to her ear and lingered, taking in her traitorous smell, she couldn't help starting to shake even as 'because because because because because' tried to shore her up. She heard him draw a deep intake of breath and knew what was coming, she tweaked her ear to try and mask it but it was too late, he opened his throat and exploded violent noise into her ear.

'How could you do it?'

Normally she'd ask herself, *How could she do what?* He never told her what she's meant to have done, and she never had done anything, but today, she knew why, and before she could imagine the worst, a punch landed on the top of her forehead and sent her head back against the wall, only her ropes preventing her from falling beyond that.

She felt confused and dizzy and waited for her focus to return but before she did, another blow landed this time on her ear leaving her muffled in that ear and dizzy again, she didn't even feel the pain any more, only the dizziness that came afterwards. Sometimes she wished when she got dizzy she could just keep getting dizzier and fall asleep forever.

Another terrifying shout closed her eyes.

'See what happens? That's the last time you'll ever get a chance to run away. Now you can't move from here can you?' he said tugging on her ropes. 'How could you make me take you out into the world after what's happened?'

She shook her head ever so slightly.

'So will you do that again, my wife?'

'No my husband,' came her auto response, almost inconceivable to expect from the little soul after this beating. Here were two people quivering under different emotions, he was breathing noisily and wetly and she didn't know if there were more punches coming.

'Now tell me your mommy and daddy are dead,' he shouted.

'My mommy and daddy are dead, my husband.'

He'd insisted to her that he'd saved her, he was a hero, everyone else in town had died from some nonsense and he'd saved her and brought her way up here to salvation, and one day, when she was older, they'd start the world again, they were so blessed, he'd said.

He made her admit to the fictitious death of her parents all the time, the punches rained in, the kicking, the starving and the shouting but making her do this was from a darker place.

His tone softened as if the demon had suddenly departed, leaving him here alone and he didn't know why, he knelt beside her battered little body, her uniform filthy and torn and there was nothing of her, she was a tiny mouse on the floor, he lifted her up to seated again.

'Remember I love you,' he said. 'But a wife can't do those things to a husband.'

She remembered her wedding day, *that day*, he called it. She'd seen weddings on TV and in Mommy and Daddy's photos before she was even a lump in her mommy's tummy but this was her wedding, she didn't have a white dress but he washed her hair especially and made a daisy chain for her head.

One of his friends married them, she couldn't see which one, and they both said 'I do' and she was now married.

'No, my husband.'

He told her to look at him and she slowly turned her head round, of all the things that happened in this cold house, she feared this the most, meeting his eyes and seeing behind them, it terrified her, his head was on fire inside, at least when he hit her, she couldn't look at him.

Her daddy told her about God and the devil and she knew her husband was the devil.

He smiled and took her limp little hand.

'Do you want the surprise I got for you?'

The 's' and the 'p' in 'surprise' showered her with his messy spit spray, she could smell it on her face and lips but kept calm and pretended it wasn't there. She kept singing in her head, 'Because of the wonderful things he does.' If she shied away from him even for this, she'd suffer.

Her answers were well drilled, only what he wanted to hear and don't get it wrong.

'Yes please my husband.'

He clapped his hands in glee and shuffled off squeaking with joy into the main room.

She'd had surprises many times before, he kept bringing

her things because he thought she didn't love him anymore and wanted to go, some of the surprises were at least gifts of sorts but some of them just made her dizzy.

They played a game once when she first got here, just before they got married, he took her outside and said. 'Find me, find me, count to fifty,' and stumbled off clattering through the trees down the hill, panting with a puerile joy.

Still having in her the belief of escape and some memories of what to return to, she couldn't believe her luck and her little feet took her as fast as they could in the opposite direction, down a long dirt road past a big blue car, she had no idea where it led but distance from him was being generated.

Maybe there was a real road at the end of this track, maybe there'd be people she could run to, she'd crash into them, gripping on tight and wouldn't let go either, she didn't look back, just focused on the people she'd find and what car would take her home.

The track started to narrow and the trees started to close in, she found herself having to jump over things and knew she was getting slower, dry tears started to rise as the end was becoming less and less clear.

Eventually the woods closed in and she couldn't go any further, she crept into a thick redberry bush and sat shaking, trying to stop the noise of her whimpers. It felt like hours had passed and then she heard him, crackling loudly through the brush around her cover, her breathing dimmed and her eyes widened, he stopped at certain intervals, somehow sensing her, getting closer each time and then finally stopped right by her redberry, he was still for a few seconds and then looked through the bush right into her eyes, extracting a small squeak as his arm came through, took her by the hair and dragged her out, scratching her face and legs.

But even at this very point of capture, her defense was slick and instant, she said she thought it was her turn to hide and so she hid here, she managed to squash some of his fury for a short time but it was never long enough.

He crept up to her door and poked his head round and she smelt him there, whatever it was, she had to thank him.

'Close your eyes,' he said.

She did instantly but left a little gap in one eye to maintain her bright yellow.

'OK open them,' he said bouncing in anticipation.

She opened her eyes and looked down at the dead crow on the floor and beamed a broad vibrant smile, a small part of a range of skills that might have promised a bright career one day.

'Thank you, my husband, I love it.'

'Do you though, really, do you?'

'Yes, my husband'

He picked it up, carefully nestling it into his hands and placed it on the shelf with various other decorations, mostly rocks and dead animals and one human foot. She knew to keep looking at it and grinning with glee until he left.

'There, we have another friend.'

'Yes, my husband.'

He clasped his hands together and headed off into the main room slamming the door behind him.

She returned her gaze to the yellow, he said she was a pretty wife and he'd always deserved a pretty wife.

Sometimes the animals on the shelf spoke out of turn and he'd cook one of them for their dinner, once he told her he'd cook her if she was bad again.

She thought if he did cook her at least she could make him sick, and Mommy and Daddy weren't dead.

Salvador faded into a new space accompanied by beeps and vibrations. There was a sanitized clean and shiny smell but not like a hospital. He opened his eyes but he was fuzzy headed. He knew he was in a big room but he didn't seem fully teleported into it yet. He wondered if that's how time travel will eventually work, your molecules becoming aware of your new space before you actually re-form into it yourself.

He was staring at a giant display screen in front of him, spanning almost the full width of the room. It was more like a hologram than a screen. He knew where he was. This was Cygnus Five, a space journey VR game he and his team had produced for Net Nano. This was the flagship Neuronet programme, the one Yuki took to Japan that time.

He'd been here at this control panel many times before. This game, thanks to their Japanese distribution deal, would soon be revealed to the world as the most advanced VR game ever created.

But it wasn't quite as he knew it and this was supposed to be Jemma's session that day, not Cygnus Five. He felt his head for the headset but couldn't feel anything. There were no other visible means of controlling the programme. The game was designed so a player could flick his right index finger top right and a menu would pop up. Then he could pause, exit, jump to another scene and all that stuff.

But nothing happened when he made that move. When he looked down at his hands, they were just his hands. He was fully immersed in the game and there seemed to be no way to extract himself from it. He looked around this flight deck. It was all exactly as it should be apart from his jacket was hanging on the back or his chair.

What the fuck? That wasn't in the programme. That was his jacket for sure but how could it be in the game?

Something wanted him here and he was pretty sure it wanted him here for a reason. So be it. Play the game, find that reason.

The control panel was drooling with all manner of fizzes and blinks and a sense of great power, the screen was mostly black with little white dots and he had not one clue what was expected of him.

He knew the different places players could go in the game and they could decide if they wanted to go to war with aliens or any amount of adventures, even just pootle around studying the awesome environment, but where did he need to go?

He suddenly got the feeling something was here in this place with him, an aftertaste of the golf club and the demon leading him to something behind that door. Or maybe it wasn't, more like it was really here with him now, like some-thing was waiting to get him when his back was turned.

He looked around and there was no-one obviously here but him. Someone was whispering to him from among the tech noises in the room but he didn't know if it was inside or outside his head and he couldn't make it out anyway.

The room was the size of a tennis court, the floor was level but for a cross shaped raised ramp about three feet off the ground, leading to a circular central control area, the driver's seat and that's where he'd been put.

Everything was light grey and an inert soft mid blue, nice and shiny and calm but uninspiring, unworthy of its own ability, he'd always thought. It should be deep orange and purple and olive green with smooth curves and flashing moving lights and sounds, a very bohemian Star Trek, but now wasn't the time to change design on Yuki.

He had to spare a smile for one of the surprise elements they'd built into the game. The cleaner character. No-one would ever know his true purpose in the game. Anything could happen when he's around. He'd be vacuuming the bridge of the ship, whistling a little tune, touching things he shouldn't be touching, and generate a nasty and sticky evening for whoever was in two three two on deck five as they had oxygen replaced with nitrous.

The pilot's seat faced front and center and was surrounded by everything a player could want from a spaceship. A black glass control panel tilted towards him and a few buttons demanding he approach it and take it for a spin.

There were several doors off to the edges of the space and signs in ancient Sumerian, his idea. The control panel had no signs. You either knew how to fly the thing or you didn't.

Salvador did. He turned to face the screen again and wondered where in this screen full of stars he'd go, if he was going anywhere at all.

The universe in front of him remained as it was and a humming green light faded in over on the right side of the desk. He slid over to it and put his right palm on the screen. A warm orange glow grew under his palm and he started to address the controls. It felt like his hand was in a bowl of thick gel, he was massaging it into position to jump.

He looked down at the panel, smiled a bit at the obviousness of it and without hesitation banged his palm down on the big fat red button, put there for only this task. You only need the subtlest finger twitch in the gel to make this happen, or a voice command, but it did seem wrong to send a ship into super light speed so meekly. It was way more fun to actually slap the thing into hyperdrive with a big fat red button and the focus groups loved it. With no instruction otherwise, this was Salvador's hail Mary.

The stars undertook an immediate transition from points of light to long thin canes of light wrapping round this ship and guiding it through the middle of them. The engines hummed and vibrated through him, starting to make music. A surreal view of spaghettified stars, nebulae and changing colors and patterns powered him towards whatever target it would be.

Seconds later, another light flashed on the panel. He'd reached a point where this speed would have put him right through the middle of something large and hard. The ship emerged from hyperspace like it'd never been gone, suddenly back to a silent map of pinned stars and all was again quiet.

The magical calm of this place didn't release him from his pounding head. He remembered the bar and the monsters, odds on favorite where this pounding head came from. Maybe this place was here to turn his pain from a school marching band into a smokey haven of reggae on the beach, broaden the vessels, move blood and oxygen around and gradually release him from the punishment.

Then suddenly the ship was tugged off onto another course, passing a planet at speed over its left shoulder and out into open space. Salvador was now just a passenger although he probably always had been. He tried to use the gel to steer the thing but it had its own ideas. So he smashed the big fat red button again and he was stretched a million miles, dropped into a sinkhole and re-compressed the other side.

This time he found himself in sight of a small orangey red planet. There seemed to be only this planet, a few moons and their star. Beyond the system in any direction, there were no stars, only black, like this little private star system was the only one in the universe. This wasn't part of the Cygnus Five programme.

The star wasn't happy, toys were leaving prams. It was throwing coronal mass ejections out far and wide, one or two now reaching halfway to the planet. It would only be another day or so until that poor planet was done for and that's where the ship was headed. It looked like someone had added another module, a star's death spurt wrapped round that doomed planet, frying everything on it.

Closer the ship came to the planet. Eventually Salvador could see its three large moons, ready to go down fighting with their master. He started to get the feeling he knew this place.

A thin atmosphere gave way to a dramatic landscape and a place drenched in early evening light. The ship headed for a range of snow-capped mountains and stopped to hover over-head. The ship threw out a beacon, which hovered beside it and everything just waited.

He started to recognize the mountains and the moons and he definitely recognized the settlement nestled in the mouth of the valley. This was Nriza. The two lights, this ship and its beacon. The aurora was the precursor of the coronal mass ejection about to hit the planet. These poor people had no more than a day left of their existence. There was no escape from what was about to happen to them. The shamans of Nriza were right. It was their end.

Is he the visitor they were all waiting for, the sign of their enlightenment? How could any of this have anything to do with helping Jemma? Then more of his dream of Nriza came back to him. The first visitor. He knew who the first visitor was in his dream but didn't take that memory back to the real world with him when he woke up.

He'd seen the pictures on every wall of Nriza of the first visitor. It was now clear to him. The first visitor was Jemma.

She was even wearing her light green hospital gown. The first visitor had told the people two thousand years ago he'd be coming on this day and the people would have to guide him to his enlightenment before he could deliver theirs. Was the enlightenment they were to give Salvador the truth, the answer? Was Jemma telling them how to guide him to it the only way she could?

The beacon had been static long enough to get a smell of the place. It pinged off down to the mountain tops and seemed to signal to the ship it was safe to do the same. The tree lined mountainside caves lead through to the sandy space of the interior. Salvador's ship was coming in to land.

The ship slowly squatted on a small open space, once the crater of the mountain around it. It came to rest and powered down facing the mouth of a large cave. He could see a faint light from the other side of the mountain hiding within the cave.

The engine noise diminished and he heard the hiss of a door breaching an atmosphere. He turned behind him and a door at the back eased open. A breeze riding on a low orange light entered the craft, informing this alien being of itself.

Going outside wasn't in the programme but none of this was. Salvador put boots onto a fine orange sand, tufts of grass here and there. There was a fine beauty in this place. Up here, it was unlikely anything apart from birds could get in or out. There was no welcoming party to greet him, no banners and fires, drums or chanting, just him and the ship.

Unknown to Salvador, however, something was lurking about fifty meters away through the thick trees in the mouth of another cave opposite. Out of the corner of his eye he noticed a shadow that was once there was no longer there. He moved a little closer to the door of the ship and maintained his gaze.

A creature leaned against the wall and moved closer to

the mouth of its cave, fully aware that its prey couldn't see it. It was confident of prevailing. Its prey seemed awkward and slow.

Salvador felt safe enough to consider moving. The only logical place to go was into the cave. The ship would have landed somewhere else if not and instinct was all had right now.

In the mouth of the cave, the walls were a shining canvas of all types of crystal and color, shadows and moods. It seemed like the movement belonged to animate things, a horrifying battalion of spiders crawling all over the walls, but it was only the movement of light, interacting in a way he hadn't seen before, light would meet other light and wouldn't merge, it might negotiate passage and bend around the other light, like ants to and from something those ants fancied.

The musty smell, normally associated with bat guano and moldy things, was a beautiful overpowering aura in this cave. It drew him to it, wanted him to take part, take it in and feel it. It pulsed his attention towards the large stone in the middle of the cave floor. A giant stone dagger was set in the ground about thirty feet high, a lesson in natural balance. The tip sticking in the ground was only about two feet across. This monolith had been fashioned by its nature for millennia, gradually deciding on this impressive but precarious statement.

There was a small tunnel against the back wall of the cave and he could just see a chink of the weakest twilight pretending through it.

Quietly the creature slithered through the trees and along the mountain wall towards Salvador's cave, sensing its prey conveniently trapping itself.

Salvador hadn't yet sensed he was being watched, sized up for the best ways to separate and prepare bits of him, roasting or light griddling, horseradish or mint. Still in the shadows and now at the mouth of the cave, the creature approached. Salvador suddenly saw a changing shadow, the movement of one black shape against a slightly different black shape. He moved carefully around the wall of the cave, his hands glued to its warm security. The feeling of invasion remained although there was nothing there to define it.

There was another movement from the blackness. This time the creature emerged, like it was popped thru a membrane. It was now crawling across the floor towards him. It was like a massive spider and all he could feel was the demon staring into him in the old town. The creature got closer and closer.

Salvador moved over to the stone. He felt safer. It gave off a numb buzz, a magnetism, but still the creature followed. When it became more clearly visible, it's shape had changed from a spider to a tall humanoid about seven feet, black as space, almost reflecting no light at all. Its eyes were hollow and shone only with the light from the ship behind it outside the cave. Its arms and hands were long and thin and there was a light blur around its edges.

The creature edged towards him. It moved smoothly, without effort or sound. It's eyes bored into him and Salvador was now unable to move. He heard the dagger stone next to him start to hum louder.

The creature then slowed, perhaps not quite believing how easy this would be. It lifted its arms to unfurl feather-thin semi-transparent wings and Salvador could only close his eyes and hold out his own arms as it came at him. But whatever merged into him wasn't that creature. The evil in the air exploded and showered him with a euphoria, an infusion of pure love and calm, a baby wrapped up in its mother and the dagger stoned reduced its pulse to normal. The fear had gone.

It felt like this stone was protecting him and when he opened his eyes, Salvador saw an old man with long grey hair standing in front of him. The Luiseño shaman had stepped out of another dimension at the river and into the open ground of this cave. Salvador had met him before. It was now.

The energy in the air around the dagger stone was a radio dead space hum, sitting under a pylon, the stone was broadcasting, reacting to this shaman.

He looked into Salvador like he'd just seen his cigarette fizz into the San Rey river.

'Good to see you again, Salvador,' he said. 'Got a smoke?'

'No, sorry, don't normally.'

The shaman smiled.

'You know why you're here.'

'I think so.'

'Jemma went through her trial at the river and now it's your turn to go through your own trial here, to find the light. Your path has been long but it is almost at an end. Find the pattern and you will be shown what you need to find.'

'Find the pattern.'

'You will need faith,' continued the shaman. 'Do you have faith, Salvador?'

'I do,' said Salvador because, right here by this dagger stone, faith was being vibrated into him. Here he will get his answer. Here he will save his Jemma.

'Then you are ready,' said the shaman. 'Follow the light, Salvador.' In Salvador's next blink this shaman had gone from here. He saw something move over by the far wall and there he was, walking into the mouth of the tunnel. The dagger stone was still humming and pushed Salvador to follow him into the tunnel.

22 Monkey

The humming influence of the dagger stone slid away as he went deeper into the tunnel. The near perfect darkness robbed him of any signs of this shaman. Salvador followed the breeze that must have been coming from the open side of the mountain and had to feel his way along the wet cold walls.

There were loose rocks of all styles on the ground. He occasionally launched one against the wall or sent one clacking off along the tunnel floor like a hockey puck.

The light started to grow around him as the breeze led him on. He turned left then right then rounded the bend, and that initial chink of light now became a vista extravaganza as that final bend showed him the world outside the mountain. The aurora wrapped and danced around three large moons and a breathtaking expanse of planet opened up. He stopped in his tracks for this, the most stunning of nature's art. The incoming light and its shadows formed and glided over the cave walls of this beautifully crafted alien world.

It was only the sudden movement of air against his face that told him something had just glided silently over his left shoulder. The moonlight caught hold of it. This bird required only one smooth wing pump to get it out into the open, circling once and dropping sharply. Its death plunge transformed this creature into a javelin, sleek, noise-free speed. Its long sharp talons were probably primed to abduct some small fuzzy thing down below.

He got closer to the edge and the breeze picked up around him. It resonated over the mouth of the cave to create a low howl as it passed the mountain, calling the creatures in this tunnel to awaken. A colony of bats heading out from a nearby cave screeched past on its evening mission.

Then Salvador noticed a shape silhouetted in the moonlight, sitting still at the edge. It was a tiny little Monkey, just passing the time, chilling at the edge of a mountain hanging his little legs over the edge and rocking them back and forth like a schoolboy at assembly.

The little monkey looked up at him. Salvador smiled back and took a seat beside him. The mountainside was a sheer drop. He could just about make out the base of it gaining foliage and easing out onto the open plain. Salvador and Monkey exchanged nervous first glances and then Monkey did the right thing and introduced himself. Salvador shook his little hand and they looked out quietly into the open space.

Salvador wondered what this little monkey was doing here but figured Monkey probably wondered what he was doing here as well. Was Monkey waiting on his friends to come back from some monkey expedition in the tunnel? Was he lost, tired, might this have been a suicidal little monkey, about to take the final plunge when he was interrupted? How do you talk a monkey down from suicide, which little girl monkey had done this to him?

He wouldn't have been surprised to hear sage words from this little fellow, perhaps show him a sign, maybe he was the sign. But Monkey wasn't prone to unsubstantiated chatter. He absorbed Salvador while he maintained his gaze on the wider world.

The shaman had once again fucked off just when he got interesting. Salvador would need to take this on alone. He told this little monkey it was charming to meet him but he had stuff to do. Monkey blinked at him with eyes far larger than his head deserved. Then Salvador heard a whisper, maybe something on the breeze but he could have sworn it was words. He looked at Monkey and wondered if it had come from him but Monkey was non-committal, just stared at him.

Salvador took off along the tunnel to the left of the mouth of the cave and after a few paces, looked back at Monkey. Monkey was still staring. Salvador thought, 'Come on, let's go then,' and Monkey obliged. He scuttled over to him and executed a tasty little move off the wall onto his right shoulder. Salvador welcomed him aboard like an old friend. He had the feeling that friends were going to be useful here.

Salvador and Monkey drifted off down the tunnel and the light again started to surrender, forcing him to use the wall to navigate again. The slope took them steeper downwards.

Salvador stopped. He heard noises. First the quiet whispers of distant conversations and then the comings and goings of busy everyday life. As the voices grew and a low orange light started to break through the pitch blackness, he saw several people dressed in linen and color, most with the same native look as the shaman. They looked busy, hauling pots and rope, blankets, food and all sorts around what had become tiny lanes.

This was no longer the mountain. This was a thriving little town under an aurora sky. He'd been through these streets in his dream. He knew these people. He felt their expectation and hope. They were preparing for the arrival of the visitor.

'My arrival,' said Salvador.

Salvador and Monkey passed several of them and acknowledged them, thinking at least Monkey would be of interest, but he was ignored. If this was how these people treated their second coming then heaven may not await many. Were they aware of his apparent deity but dare not speak to him or was he invisible?

Monkey seemed relaxed about it all and hung onto his neck, unfazed by fame or anonymity. Having Monkey with him felt like it gave him Monkey's power, a sensing of things so much sooner than humans.

They approached an older woman sitting in a doorway weaving a basket and bent down to ask where he was. She looked up but not at him, past him over his shoulder, confused at the origin of his voice as though she too had heard a whisper but didn't know from whom, considering this briefly then returning to her basket.

Salvador noticed a small pathway off to the right just past her, leading to a dead end, a wall and a high red light. There was an old wooden door cut into the stone of this wall below the light.

Monkey watched him reach for the handle and pull the door open. At that moment, the sound of street life was replaced by the muffled sound of an old blues tune, sliding and wailing with 'What That Woman Gone Done' from the other side of an inner door. He could now hear conversation and the chink of glasses joining the music. He opened the inner door and found himself in a bar, but not just any bar. This was La Mesa bar in San Juan.

'Seriously, what the fuck?'

There were a few guys nursing beers at the bar and one or two others mulling around the place. One older man headed over his way and Salvador was forced to stand aside quick smart as he was about to walk straight through him. He was invisible to everyone in this place, either that or they all just thought he was a bonehead.

Avoiding the temptation to mull the bizarre, he looked around and even this scene was familiar, not just because it was his bar, because he suddenly remembered being here in this bar at this exact moment. That guy would get up and head up the stairs, the music would shift to something more country and then he heard her again, right on cue.

'Follow the yellow brick road, follow the yellow brick road,' sung out from over at the back of the bar. The little girl it belonged to looked right at him. She saw him. She skipped up to him.

'Are you OK mister?' she asked

'I am thanks. Where are you going?' said Salvador.

She looked down as if something had just diverted her attention. She was listening out for something and started to look a little more concerned, worried, in a hurry.

'I'm not allowed to say,' she said. She skipped off through the door and she was gone under a parasol of song.

Their interaction didn't seem to have affected the map of his time here that day. One of the old guys playing cards over in the corner banged his hand down on the green felt tabletop and shouted something akin to 'in your face' and the barman dropped the glass behind the bar. Everything was still as it had been. And then the obvious question came to him. If he was here that day, he'd be sitting at the bar right over... there.

And there he was. Even before he moved round and saw himself in full view, he knew that nose could only belong to him. Should he meet himself in this new dimension? He moved closer to the bar. Then a whisper asked him, 'Did you see yourself that night?' He looked at Monkey and Monkey looked right back at him. The whisper did seem to come from the little fuzzy fellow but anyway, no, he hadn't seen himself that night. He might be invisible to everyone else here but he wasn't invisible to the little girl so maybe not to himself either. He couldn't risk meeting himself if he hadn't already met himself that day. It was a paradox in the making. His journey from that day would change. He might no longer be here and here is closer that he'd been.

At that moment a black dog ran past him and he remembered the clicking cane of the invisible demon that day. He checked around the bar but, as it was then, there was no sign of him. The dog nosed it's way out through the front door and he saw himself leave to follow the demon up the road.

There was something different about the bar this time round. He couldn't put his finger on it, subtle differences, someone saying something before they did last time, maybe just a change in light.

He'd leave where he came in. He eased open the door, turned for a last look and everyone in the bar had stopped what they were doing and were looking at him, motionless, no facial expressions, lifeless statues. This wasn't that day anymore.

23   Nerosonic

The door closed behind him. This wasn't that little alley any more. There were no people busying themselves for the occasion. This was a vast open square covered with sand. It was flanked on each of its sides by large stepped pyramids, one of which had just thrown him and Monkey out into this space. He looked behind him at the doorway that should have been there but it was now stone.

The aurora was dancing with more fever and the breeze was swirling light sand into the air around him. In the distance, in the middle of the square, he saw a collection of people surrounding a fire. Apart from that fire, there seemed to be nothing. Nriza's moons were becoming imprisoned by haunting storm clouds and thunder was erupting over the mountains behind one of the pyramids.

A flash of lightning lit up the world as far as he could see. He heard the laugh of a child somewhere between him and the fire. In that middle distance, he saw the outline of something he couldn't quite make out.

The aurora and the fire helped him see random aspects of it and eventually Salvador had an idea of what was approaching, swaying from side to side about fifty yards away from him and the fear was back in him.

Another flash of lightning revealed the entity. It was standing up on its back legs, so many legs. It was facing him, now a fair bit closer than it was.

Salvador moved but it turned itself to track him. There was no going round this entity. It seemed to be able to react to any move he thought about before he made it.

He could see each new lightning flash bring the entity closer. It swayed more aggressively, now oscillating up and down, preparing for an attack.

The thunder was closer now and the rain started to fall. Salvador knew each spell of darkness between the lightning flashes brought this entity closer to him. Then again, there was a child's laughter closer to the fire. He needed to be over by that fire. The shaman would be there.

Monkey then sensed something. He hopped off Salvador's shoulder and headed off towards the entity. Salvador shouted after him but he'd already vanished into the middle of it.

The people by the fire accelerated their dancing and noise and another lightning strike showed this entity right on top of him.

He closed his eyes to what he should have achieved for Jemma and all the other things. The places they never went. The children they never had. The image of little Ashlen on that police flyer. That would be their little girl, just like that.

Suddenly there was a loud buzzing sound right in front of him, his door buzzer. But he was here. Was he about to wake up in his own bed again the day Camille and Jemma came round?

'Wake up,' he said.

The entity suddenly broke apart into a swarm of the blackest insects and formed a humming pulsating wall of themselves in front of him. It hung there, holding its ground, an energetic but silent curtain, watching him, sizing him up, occasionally separating and rejoining itself. Whenever the swarm separated, it allowed in the small light of the fire behind it. This time a low humming sound intensified, like something large was about to take off a short runway. Salvador had to cover his ears but it was too much. The swarm and the sound wrapped around him, pulling him all the way onto the ground. It set his natural vibration to match its own. He was helpless.

'Wake up!'

But he wasn't waking up. The strength and energy in this entity was endless, terrifying. He felt the air move around him as it surrounded him, studying him and pecking at him. It entered his ears and mouth and exploded into his mind, a mess of static, starting to rearrange his thoughts into its own.

Just when Salvador thought he was being taken over by this entity, taken over by the most evil of spirits, the demon in the old town and all his deepest fears, with another bolt of lightning, he was suddenly shown another way.

He saw this entity in a different way. He knew what this was. Nerosonic. This kid had come into Net Nano one day and bluffed his way in to see Yuki. He'd dressed up as an engineer from the phone company, overalls, ID, the whole nine. He'd and got pretty easy access to the server room. He took a photo of him in the main server room and asked someone to give it Yuki. Three minutes later he was in a room with Yuki.

He pitched this new way for characters to see things in virtual space. Instead of seeing colors and hearing sounds and smelling smells and the stuff we normally use to know what's going on, this nerosonic programme allowed the player to detect everything by minute changes in the air turbulence around them. You were aware of everything in your field of vision and every movement it makes. You can see your space from any angle. Yuki was IN with capital 'fuck yeah.' He said it was sensing in a purely logical way. It was hypnotic, better than human, exo-human he called it. The kid called it neurosonic but one of the guys set up the file wrong and it stuck.

· · ·

Salvador could now see the weight of this monster, how it moved. Everything could be anticipated. He was behind it, then on top of it, anywhere he wanted to be. He could even feel it.

He saw this evil in the clearest light. This malevolent swarm was rocking angrily back and forth, side to side. It was a thick liquid, pulsating. Matter vanished from one flank only to appear instantly on the other. It was playing with him, ready for its strike and Salvador knew when that strike would come. Then he heard the shaman and he knew how to beat it. Faith. Have no fear of it. Embrace it. Go to it.

At that moment the sound stopped, Salvador opened his eyes and Monkey appeared through the middle of the entity. The entity recoiled and dispersed its evil into the storm and the blackened creepers wrapped around Salvador were unwound. They were the moments before a death, the stairway, isolated from what was above and below. His knees hit the sand and took in some breaths and spat out the taste of the swarm.

Monkey stood in front of him and chuckled like he'd pulled a windshield wiper off a car. Salvador felt what he imagined the love of a parent would be for this little monkey. They embraced like Monkey was a recovered kidnap victim and Monkey jumped up on Salvador's shoulder.

They continued across the sand towards the fire. The storm clouds lifted, the rain pulled itself back up its nozzle and the three moons re-appeared, switched on like table lamps, still wrapped in an aurora that seemed to be humming like the dagger stone did. Salvador started to make out the colors and moving forms around the fire and a breeze cooled around them.

Monkey again hopped off his shoulder and headed off towards the fire but, as he did, Salvador sensed something else behind him. There was another shape in the distance, its back lit by the moons. It was a large bird, gliding, almost skimming the sand, piercing the air and destined for Monkey. It was so fast. Suddenly it passed over Salvador's left shoulder and was on its way towards Monkey.

Like a parent seeing their child contemplating traffic, Salvador reached down and picked up a stone. He launched it at the bird like skimming at the beach with Camille. It was close enough to divert the bird. There would be no licks from Mrs. Otto today. The bird missed Monkey and disappeared into the distance. He could see it skim the top of the fire, kicking off a few sparks to climb again. Monkey carried on towards the fire.

The chanting and dancing at the fire had got quicker, it was reaching some kind of conclusion. The shaman was there with them. It danced and skipped to the tune of a new breeze which tossed up the sand around him. Some of the sparks escaping this gyrating plasma were accompanied by a crackle and splutter, instances of their final cycle of life as they were blown away into the obscurity of the square.

The shaman saw Salvador and came over and Salvador was back by the San Rey river that night looking at Jemma by that fire.

'You have the faith, Salvador. Are you ready to see the light?'

At that moment, another flash of lightning shot over in the distance although there were no signs of a storm. Through the fire, slowly merging into focus, were the movement and sounds of what looked like a scene from a half hour afternoon drama show.

A woman was in the kitchen talking, arguing with someone. It was Jemma. He remembered the day. He remembered the argument. This partial scene had been isolated and transplanted to this bewitched place on this distant planet. She was talking to someone who wasn't there, stirring a sauce that had no pan.

There was his Jemma making that great pesto lemon sauce she always did with pasta. He wanted to walk into the fire and into her scene, get hold of her and never let her go.

What a stupid argument. Salvador was at a point in his career where he wasn't sure why he was doing it any more. The good things his work could do now, not rolled out in endless stages, now.

Jemma had known this for a while and it was time to give him a hard time, get stuck into doing something about it or stop breaking her balls about not doing it.

He didn't want to hear it but knew it was true and that made him mad. As the mood reached chilli hot, Jemma did what she always did. She stripped naked in that kitchen and leaned back with her arms crossed, closing his mouth and sending him a new direction. His inspiring wife fucked him right there against the worktop with the lemon pesto smell all around them.

The argument had just reached its insistent height with the familiar words that once more dived into him, standing here by this fire.

'You believe in it,' she said. 'You say it's possible so just do it Babe, never give up, follow the yellow brick road.'

Salvador remembered her saying it like he was there again with her in the kitchen. He could even smell the lemon pesto. Follow the yellow brick road. If your mission is good and true, pack your bags and see where it all takes you, go without fear, abandon the usual for the unknown.

Before Jemma and their kitchen vanished into the fire, she looked from within her scene directly out across the fire at Salvador and smiled. That's right, he remembered, that night after the argument, after the sex and after the lemon pesto, Jemma suddenly broke off from what she was saying. She looked up and out of the window and smiled at something out back. He thought at the time one of her friends had just turned up. He followed her gaze but there was no-one there. She was smiling at him here by this fire like he was in the backyard.

Jemma made a video the next day called Yellow Brick Road. She left it cued for him when he got home. He watched it back with the same tears he had running down his face now. It was an apology for being hard on him and she said she was really looking forward to the beach that weekend.

He got in his car and drove to San Juan elementary, straight into her classroom and gave her the biggest sloppiest huggy kiss and told her he loved her twelve times. All of this amused the assembled tiny people who chuckled them apart but Salvador left her there happy that day.

Yellow brick road. Was this little Ashlen trying to help Jemma from the other side? Jemma had to be trying to tell him something else in that movie.

Salvador wiped his eyes with his shirt sleeve and his focus returned to the fire which still blazed but now without the shaman or any of the others around it. Monkey was also no longer here. Salvador spared a moment to offer thanks to his little Monkey. He didn't think he'd be seeing him again. Till next time.

He looked around for a direction to be revealed to him. At that moment, God suddenly found the fuse box and another blinding flash of lightning surrounded him.

This time the light persisted. Salvador was freshly blind but then he heard breathing just in front of him, a familiar smell, then there came another whisper.

It said, 'Can you hear me? Can you hear me Baby?'

Awakening

Another 'Can you hear me?' brought Salvador from the light. It felt like he'd come from a deep sleep to the surface as he started to wake. He'd been dreaming of that girl on her phone at Coronado beach that day but again it came. 'Can you hear me?' this time closer.

With a third 'Can you hear me,' Salvador opened his eyes. Jemma was curled up next to him on the couch in the den, her mouth almost on his. She broke into a smile and very lightly licked the tip of his nose. He threw his arms around her and squeezed her so tight he drew a squished flat little noise out of her.

He buried his face deep in her shoulder. This great hypnosis, he was with her again. All he wanted to do was hold her and look at her so close he couldn't focus properly.

'Baby, I've got to go,' said Jemma. 'I love you.'

'Tell me this is before all this happened?' he said, but he knew it wasn't.

Jemma smiled again and kissed him on the head. His next blink woke him up with a start and sent her to another place. He was sweaty and trembling. He didn't need to look round the room. He knew she wasn't here, just him on this couch and his VR headset on the floor by the table.

He headed down to the den. He thought of coffee but that can wait. Then there was a noise in the kitchen. It sounded like the coffee machine starting to fizz and bubble its magic. Was Camille here? He went up the steps to the kitchen but there was no-one there and the coffee machine wasn't doing anything.

Since he was in the kitchen standing in front of the thing, it would be rude not to start the day with a coffee. The machine was instructed to deliver a flat white.

A few minutes later he got back down the steps and focused on the TV control. He sat on the couch and the TV came to life above him. As it did he had to look behind him. He had the feeling there was someone there but there wasn't. It was the same feeling as when he woke up next to Jemma just now, before he work up again alone. He felt her in this room.

'You there Baby?' he said, not surprised to hear nothing back.

He looked through the home movies menu and found Jemma's Yellow Brick road. There she was, suddenly looking right at him, sitting on the edge of the bed, centering the camera on her lap. His baby girl was staring into him. She started with a smile and followed with a message from the deepest part of her.

She was so sorry to be that hard on him, she just wanted him to be happy and he wasn't happy. Coronado at the weekend would give him the moments to consider all of this. He'd find what he was looking for, oh and he's making dinner, she fancied sea bass.

She planted a kiss on the camera lens, smiled through the blur and reached over to stop the movie. The next movie cued itself up. It was the movie of the day Jemma was talking about. The day at Coronado beach that weekend. Salvador sat back, smiled and closed his eyes. This Coronado movie did indeed follow the Yellow Brick Road.

The sun was almost directly overhead and there wasn't a breath of a breeze to relieve his skin from it. Here on this couch, he rubbed the heat off his arms as he felt it sting again. The sea was a flawed mirror dropping its edges onto the sand. Salvador had just completed his charge to that sea, finished tickling Jemma on the beach and retreated to the top of the beach for some quality filmmaking.

Another day, there might have been a line of camper vans up there on the ridge containing small strong rubber people waiting to throw their boards around in the surf. Today though, no surf and no rubber people.

Over there a few years ago, before he met Jemma, him and his friends had their own little spring break. They'd settled with a bunch of weed, a couple of guitars and a fire. Love was made and answers were wrestled from nature.

The hum of the surrounding humanity grew onto him from this TV screen. It was a vibrant happy day here on this pretty stretch of sand.

'That's not my dog,' shouted some freckled ruffian as he ran down the beach, teeth dropping weekly, all mischief and wrongdoings.

This boy had been collared by some old geezer, charged without evidence, possession of an errant black dog, the one that almost foiled Salvador's race to the waves just now.

This dog had seen a fine moving target in Salvador. A dog cannot be happier than this. He hammered off after Salvador, he'd mapped his trajectory and speed, he knew the perfect interception point and was odds on to nail it. Focused on avoiding the humiliation of a poor splashdown, Salvador managed to spot the fuzzy fool just in time. The dog offered a frustrated single *woof* as Salvador put on a bit extra and regained his plan.

The dog had displeased several of the ladies having coffee. His tail had caught on a tablecloth and dragged much cake onto the deck amid squawks and bluster.

The geezer insisted, as our lad vanished across the sand, that he was lying and by Christ he'd get a belt across his back if he didn't come back. The lad offered a solitary finger and was gone.

Salvador pointed the camera at Jemma sitting on the beach. They'd planted themselves on that spot of beach and prepared for rare moments of doing nothing. They'd brought along two bottles of white wine, some ice and a couple of glasses and they may well drift over to the seafood place for some octopus a little later.

The camera suddenly pointed straight up in the air and the sun whited it out. Salvador had to stretch in this sunshine. He imagined Jemma sitting behind him. 'Quality work there, Spielberg.' The stretch wound down and the camera started aiming again. It caught a yellow frisbee flying past him about ten yards away on the beach. The catcher picked it up and slung it back low and hard on the run, leaving him one option, surrender to trajectory and hit the water.

Soon they'd be packing up and heading off. Then Salvador remembered the car that looked like his dad's old car. It'd been on the small dirt track in front of the shops. It's a few seconds on. The camera strayed to the sea and to the top of the palm trees. It shot Salvador's feet and tracked the sleek black dog across the sand. Then the car was in shot. Pretty soon an angry dad will emerge and give his daughter a proper shouting.

As he walked past the little shacks and shops alongside the track, Dock of the Bay was playing from one of the shops. His favorite shop on the beach was next to the cafe, the Pepsi shop. Well, it used to be his favorite before that day with Tony.

He knew some of the things it sold were at the golf club that night down near the outbuilding and the sun picture was definitely in the school hallway. They had a fan or two in San Juan.

He scanned around the beach to shoot more palm leaves swaying and ants making their way somewhere and turned back to the scene along this little slip road in front of the shops and his dad's old car.

The Pepsi shop was dark inside and it reminded him of that day here with Tony, those demon eyes tracking him. Just to the right of the front window hatch was a beaded door and a flickering light.

The beach side door of the car slowly opened and a small girl slid out and wandered to the edge of the dirt track to a low fence. She climbed over the fence onto the sand.

A man in a floppy hat emerged from the beaded door. He was already annoyed by the beaded strips lingering on him.

Salvador knew this guy. This guy was at the school after he saw Iris, stacking up tables and stuff over by the trees.

He had a length of rope draped over his shoulder. He looked happy with his purchase of a small toy boat and stroked some dust off the deck. This soon changed. His eyes popped and the little boat started shaking. He looked like someone who's just been tied up naked on the bar at a school reunion. The car no longer contained who he'd left there. He would have tried 'Do not get out of the damn car,' but what happens when you say 'Don't get out of the damn car?' People get out of the damn car.

He dumped the little toy boat where he stood and headed off across the track to retrieve his daughter. He hopped over the fence and took her by the top of the arm. She hadn't gone nearly far enough or fast enough. She was hauled back in her tracks, his grip made her arm go white. Salvador didn't hear his exact words to her on the day but now he did.

'Why will you never learn? I'll make sure you never do that again,' he said and his mouth was in her ear with volume all the way back to the car. She welcomed the car if only to shut him out for a time.

She planted her little face in the back window, resting her arms on the shelf and looked straight out at Salvador. She started blowing mist onto the back window. Salvador glanced down at the cop's flyer on the table. This little girl was Ashlen. Maybe if her dad had known what was was going to happen, he might have liked her more today.

Her dad picked up his boat, dusted it off, checked it survived and put it in the trunk. He turned to the beach, slipping another lingering look through the back window to her as a reminder. Ashlen was still focused on Salvador though. She started to draw in her window mist. She drew a love heart and then rested her head back on her arms on the shelf and smiled.

Her dad let out a two fingered wolf whistle and the little black face of a dog on the beach turned briefly, only to establish if this noise meant food or not. If not, he was perfectly fine doing this thanks.

After the second whistle failed, with a look of *an asshole's work is never done*, he made his way over the fence to manually recover the mut. With a noise only dog owners understand, 'Getinereyafucker' echoed across the beach, drawing attention from the ladies in the cafe.

The door was closed with prejudice and her dad got hooked up to exit. You could hear the yelling from him inside the car even with all the windows closed. The dog was paying attention but Ashlen was stuck in the back window. The only things she saw were Salvador and his camera.

Salvador paused the movie. When was this day at Coronado? The movie's date tag said June fourteenth. Salvador checked the cop's flyer again. It said Ashlen was last seen... June fourth. He was filming this ten days after she disappeared.

This wasn't a day out with her dad and the pooch. This was no dad. This was the fucker that took Ashlen. He worked at the school. Jesus, he had access to all of them.

Why would someone kidnap a little girl and then bring

them on a road trip? Was it an emergency mission to buy that little boat. Had the current little boat come to grief in some horrific way? Which category would Morres put him into? The arrogance of hiding in plain sight.

Salvador continued the movie. The brake lights on the car came on. Soon it'd reverse to the end of the track. Ashlen was still in the backseat and still looking out the back window but now she was looking down. Salvador tracked her gaze. The license plate. 954 NRA. He looked down a little further to the time stamp on the movie. It was 6pm.

'It's all about Ashlen,' he said, standing up to focus closer on the license plate. He'd been so certain there was a link between Jemma and Ashlen and there was a link, but it wasn't to tell him that. It was to tell him this. He picked up the cop's flyer on the table. All the signs had been pointing to this, the beach, his dad's old car, the song, yellow brick road. It all led right here.

It should have been so obvious but only now was he dragged kicking and screaming into the reality of it. This was his pattern formed. He imagined Jemma still there behind him, grading bizarre pictures drawn by nine-year-olds. 'Finally,' she'd say. 'Better late than never, Boogie' but she'd be smiling a big happy smile.

He remembered the shaman's words at the San Rey river. 'The goodness of the human soul will go to great lengths to save itself but it'll go to far greater lengths to save another.'

Salvador wasn't surprised at Jemma's ability to do this but what of her? Would little Ashlen's salvation let her forgive herself, bring her out of it, reconnect her reason to live?

Salvador felt Ashlen's eyes on him as the car continued towards the road. She gave him a new smile from the back of that old car, this time with hope in it. She knew she was no longer alone.

If she's still alive, this saves her.

His mind strayed again to the parents. They would help each other stumble exhausted down off the porch as the back door of a squad car opened. Two small feet would dangle to the floor behind it and gain their balance. They'd see their little girl emerge from behind the car door in a police blanket. Her eyes would open wide and recognize her parents. She'd run over to them and disappear entirely into them like a stone into water. As far as all three of them were concerned, that wouldn't change any time soon.

At that moment, all the pictures and plates, anything that came to hand, things that had been hurled across the room at the wall would be healed, glued back together, the deepest curses retracted. Memories of the countless sobbing hours would be gone with the return of their baby. Penances promised to gods would now be due.

Salvador pulled himself back into this den. He was tingling, that last lottery number had just popped out and a nine year old girl will now make ten.

He didn't need to check if Jemma was still grading pictures, the feeling of her was gone. He'd like her to feel this moment. Maybe she did.

Salvador picked up the phone and found the number he had for Detective Morres.

25

The rain was tipping down onto this hillside. It bounced off the cops assembled here and down the track past the old blue car the other side of the cabin.

One or two cops had already lost their footing and got muddy knees. As they climbed through the trees to the top of the ridge they started to see the roof of the cabin and held their position for orders.

There were two other cops, snipers up in the trees. They'd secured a line of sight to the little house. Everything sat still, dripping for about half a minute and Morres finally waved the signal to those on the ground. This needed to happen before someone in the house saw the steam coming off his guys.

They spread out and kept low, skimming up to a clump of trees about fifty yards from the front door. The snipers had said there was no movement through the one open window on the left and the other window had its curtains drawn.

Any crack in the wall could be an eye. They had to assume they'd been seen. They also had to assume high powered weapons and very few words from their intel.

Morres joined another cop in the clump of trees and two others took up position at either end of the cabin. On the other side of the cabin, a cop checked a stack of cut logs. They were still sappy. They'd been cut yesterday or the day before.

Morres had got hold of a motion detector so they can get touch close to the cabin and see what's inside.

He gave the signal to deploy it. The cop approached the

cabin, held it to the wall and pressed the button. A few seconds passed before he signaled *One* back to Morres and that one was right here against the wall he had his machine on. This person was alone in the cabin and they weren't moving.

Morres signaled another cop to the right and one more to the left sides of the cabin. Everyone else converged quickly on the front and back away from the windows and flattened against the wooden walls ready to breach.

Suddenly a loud crunching sound exploded shards of wood out of the wall a few feet from Morres's left shoulder, quickly followed by a crisp gunshot from behind them over the stream. They took cover round the other side of the cabin avoiding two more shots on the way. Radio silence was aborted and Morres asked the snipers, 'What the fuck?'

The shooter had to be in the trees behind his snipers to get this angle. He must have seen their every move to get to where they were now. He could have opened up on them at any time. He would definitely have known they were cops due to the giant POLICE written on them. He knew he was shooting at cops, didn't give two shits. This gives a cop a cold feeling and a quicker step.

One of the snipers had turned on his branch, trying to uncover this shooter. A shot came whistling through the trees, skimmed another branch and caught him high on the left leg, knocking him out of the tree some fifteen feet to the ground below. He landed in a crumple but propped himself up against the tree. The other sniper dropped from his tree and headed over to check he was OK. He'd live but this one had hit thigh bone.

The cop at the right of the cabin held his machine against the wall again, still the single stationary reading.

Morres trusted in superior force and plenty of ammo. He preferred peppering the area and see if anything dropped out of the trees. He cleared the sniper's positions and it was quickly a chattering chaos. It created carnage in the trees beyond the police snipers as leaves and branches fell to the ground.

The smoke gradually cleared from the cabin and drifted off over across the treeline and into the thick woods. They didn't notice anything human drop from the trees and had to assume he was still there. There was only one thing to do, get in that cabin and see who was inside.

There were no windows at the back of the cabin. They moved to the small single door. Then the cop with the machine gestured to stop. A second signal was now in the house. This second entity had emerged from the floor midway between them and front door and joined the other person. So what, this guys come up through the floor from some tunnel somewhere? Or was this a second guy?

Both people inside now moved to the far right wall and stopped. They needed to breach the cabin right on top of this guy and that was the front door. If the sniper was still in the trees it would all start again. Morres told them to breach the back door in five seconds and took off round the front counting 5... 4... 3... At 2, he waited for shots to splinter all around him but he'd gained his angle for the door and just as his shoulder made contact, the back door fell like the third comeback fight and the rest of them were down the little hallway and in the kitchen to greet him.

They all laid eyes and weapons on their man over by the stove holding a knife to the throat of a little girl. A rifle was propped against the cabinets, slowly dripping onto the floor.

Morres knew this was her. She was alive.

Morres lifted his hands, unpointed his weapon and begged the man take it easy, nothing needs to happen here. The man was in tears. He was muttering and spitting complaints of this unwarranted attack on him and his wife. If there was anything you could say to these wet, fired up cops to further inflate their war against you, that was it.

Morres moved himself out of the doorway to stay clear of the sniper. The man's blood pressure rose. His eyes dotted all over the cabin, analyzing the cops' faces, analyzing his total lack of escape route, and there he held this little girl's life in his hands.

For a brief moment six wet men and one dry child stood silent, dripping in the steam and adrenalin of this little wooden cabin. Morres asked the man please look at him. No-one was going to hurt him. No-one was going to shoot him. Just take it easy with the knife and have a chat.

This reminded the man, indeed he did have a knife. He tightened his grip on it and the girl's throat. He shouted at Morres that he'd saved her, they were in love and now they were married. One day when the world was safe again they'd begin the world again, leave them alone.

The dull light from the kitchen window fell through the rain onto the man in front of the stove with the little girl. The man again looked around the room at the cops in turn and then looked up to the ceiling, put his hand on the girl's head and closed his eyes.

Morres moved two fingers on his left hand and the man's head exploded. The sound of a single shot from a resurrected sniper over in the trees followed and the guy was cold before he hit the floor.

Morres ordered time to freeze for long enough to focus on the rain hitting the roof. He took a breath and took time to walk around the room, in between his guys and over to the man on the floor. This wasn't just the removal of this sicko. At last, he could now enjoy the removal from this world of another, Hector Valdez.

A DEA colleague had put about seven rounds into Valdez some time ago. Him and two other guys took time to come and show Morres the photos and describe the way of Hector's passing. At the time Morres was heroin level out of it. He didn't care about anything so he filed away those photos in the part of his mind he never wanted access again.

Now they revisited him in joyous flashes and just some of the awful weight lifted off him. He restarted the timeline and shut the front door. They searched the house, finding the room he kept the girl, with its ropes and manacles and the menagerie of death displayed so proudly. They found a hatch in the floor leading to a tunnel under the forest and this was shut and guarded. Two cops attended to the girl. She definitely didn't want to see what remained of the man behind her. They took her off into another room in the back.

The girl didn't look into any faces, just moved where she was told. She said nothing from this moment, all the way back to the ambulance at the end of the track and all the way to the hospital. There was nothing to be said and the people around her let it be. There would be specialists back at the hospital ready to start the process of bringing her back and journalists with the promise of a national spot.

Radios crackled as the business in the house was concluded. Forensics and clean up teams were about to share in the dripping end of horror. After a few minutes the support team said the perimeter was secure and they could move.

Morres moved over to the dead man and didn't need to check a pulse.

Salvador was in a car park. It was dark. He wasn't naked, bonus. There was an unholy smell of chemicals, like he was standing in a bucket of it, and something was making a noise over at the far end of the car park from under the trees, like a high whining sound. The noise got louder. It some kind of a bell, maybe an alarm. Then there was a blinding flash right in front of his eyes and he woke up naked in his backyard.

It was so bright, he could barely keep his eyes open. The phone was ringing, louder and louder. Only one thought came to Salvador's mind. The hospital. Jemma had come round, it's a miracle, come get her. He ran to the phone.

The static on the phone in his hand gave way to a female voice. He confirmed his identity and the next thing he knew, he was waking up on the floor with the phone receiver still swinging above his head. It took him a few moments to digest where he was and then all the demons that lived in him started ripping their way out of him.

The phone call was Mission Hospital but they weren't telling him to come get his recovered wife. In the early hours of this morning Jemma had passed away.

Salvador felt nothing but he would. That cut you get, takes a while for the white to turn red and then it keeps coming. Then it started.

Something had sucked all the air out of the room. He couldn't breathe. He headed back outside, it was so bright. He didn't know where to look so he looked at all the things they got for this house together, the purple plant pots, the stone lizard on the wall, pointless things now. He found a patch of grass and looked at it until he collapsed onto it.

The sound of the phone's bell stayed a little longer and faded as his memory let it go. His head was buzzing like he'd just been caught right on the sweet spot. The phone bell was replaced with the phone static before she spoke.

He closed his eyes and saw Jemma there on the beach again. He took in the smell of the sea, the smell of her hair, the cool breeze across them. He kissed her there on the sand. And then came the sting. Suddenly he was bent double. His demons had ripped their way out of him, taken oxygen and were now circling him. As one, they saw their chance. They circled closer and closer and from every conceivable angle they sank their teeth and claws into his body.

They ripped and scratched and bit him until he was without form, without reason and without purpose, a pointless entity existing only to consume oxygen. He was of no consequence to the universe without her and the universe was of no interest to him. He didn't care for the race for fucking president or the color of the new fucking iPhone, not for the sunset on a warm evening or the warmth of fucking friendship.

Three months of dreading this moment, denying its possibility, now here it was. He was being drowned, given just enough air then drowned again over and over. Salvador just wanted it to end, a trap door to open up in his backyard and suck him away from here to the hell he deserved for his failure. Walking through the old town on a warm sunny afternoon, she'd tap him on the shoulder and show him something in a shop or slip her hand into his when she felt at peace, when they lay back on the sand and looked at each other.

They'll never walk across that Irish field to a little pub again, settle in by the fire, open a bottle or three over lunch, maybe with a little one in tow. They won't curl up and watch terrible television or do stuff to the house together. No more pissing themselves laughing trying to keep the car on the road, arguing who takes which bag or which side of the bed when they get there, Pinot or Chablis, this spot or that spot on the beach. These memories were echoed in the blackest mirror here.

'She's not here. She'll never be here. That will never happen again.'

Salvador's throat dried and he coughed out whatever was lingering in his mouth onto the turf. He found a spot that might be able to absorb some of his seeping grief, a cool damp patch of grass. He rolled over to sink his face into it. No-one would ever wrap him up safe from the world again.

Then he heard the quietest whisper. He couldn't tell where it came from but it was Jemma's voice, using the warm breeze to speak to him. She reminded him Ashlen is alive. One day they'll meet that little girl, long after she's stopped being little, in the afterlife, see how she liked her time in the sun.

Of her countless fine moments, here was her finest. She'd saved Ashlen. It was all about little Ashlen. It was all she wanted to do. He heard the breeze tell him she loves him and goodbye isn't final. He wanted just one thing. To find his own end and see Jemma again in the next place.

Then he heard the familiar sound of a metal tipped cane on a stone floor and he opened his eyes. But it wasn't the grass that faded into view, it was Camille lying next to him on the bed, almost touching noses. She smiled at him and in the next blink he was on Coronado beach sitting next to her. They were thirteen again.

There wasn't another person here on this beach, no dogs, no cars, no ladies in the cafe, just them. He looked at Camille next to him, little Scrunchie, there she was, just looking out across the beach to the sea, hair tickling her face in the breeze.

'S'up Scrunchie?' he said, keen to hold back the sadness he'd brought with him, focusing on her. After ten seconds, he knew he had her. He'd stared her into submission, breaking out that smile of hers and taking an elbow in the ribs.

'I know why I've been here in this ridiculous dimension,' he said.

'Jemma.'

'Ashlen. Jemma was here to save Ashlen and we saved Ashlen. Jemma is gone.'

Camille didn't need a second to take his hand and watch him focus on a boat in the distance.

'I had a dream this morning,' he said. 'Sometime I'd managed to wake up in my car naked in some parking lot. I was back in a parking lot but it was dark and I wasn't naked. I've been there before and now I remember there was a van parked there. Then I was awake and the phone was ringing'

'I've been seeing more too,' said Camille. 'All the little scenes and all the little stories and all the places I go, its all been getting clearer. I think I know now. You do as well don't you?'

Salvador suddenly did.

'It wasn't Tony and his horseshit or you vanishing in the old town. I believed you were here, I believed you were real. I so wanted to. It was the man and the car you were seeing. Ashlen was taken by this guy driving a 49 coupe de ville in sky blue, just like my dad's old car. You said you'd been in that same car with that guy, locked in some room, scared. You remember the woods. The guy that took Ashlen lived in the woods, same car, same woods, same idea, same guy. You were taken as well weren't you?'

'I remember,' she said. 'I know you were sad when I went

away and I don't blame you for being angry. The thing is I didn't just go away.'

'You were taken.'

'Yes.' A few seconds passed to guide her into it. 'Remember when we were here that time, you tried to sneak a couple of beers from out back of that cafe?'

'Good times, Scrunchie.'

'That guy chased you all down the beach and you ran past me laughing and shouting something. That night, we got the bus back to San Juan. We took off on our bikes, like we always did. I was only about a mile from home and this car pulled up. This guy asked if I wanted a ride. I said no I'm almost home and the guy just said 'Fine' and drove off.'

'The light blue coupe de ville. What did the guy look like?'

'Just normal really, old, about forty, weird floppy hat. There was a song on the radio. 'Sitting in the morning sun...' she sang. 'Nice song. The car smelled of popcorn. Anyway, he drove off and I carried on round the bend. I could even see the lights from the Jariwalla's house two doors down from mine. They had all these security lights and stuff.'

'I remember.'

'Just as I got round the bend that car was pulled over at the side of the road. He was waving at me to stop. First thought was go faster but he was right in the middle of the road. I couldn't get past so I stopped'

'Oh my God, you retard, what did we always say?'

'I know, I know. I asked him what's up and he came up to me. He smelled like what was in the car, like popcorn but it was like old popcorn. He didn't say anything. He grabbed me and put this cloth over my face. That really smelled like old popcorn. It's all I remember. After that all I remembered was seeing the trees through the windows and being locked in this wooden room with yellow curtains. I was there a couple of days then he brought me some soup. It tasted like almonds but it wasn't nice soup. The next thing I know, I'm getting groceries at the store in San Juan and I see you. Jesus I missed you soft boy'

'Me too, Scrunchie.'

'And fuck, I've been some places since I saw you,' said Camille. 'My signs all started to add up and then I knew. I wasn't even sad, just glad to know finally. The long line of cars I kept seeing was a funeral. The people standing around were in a cemetery. They were gathered around a gravestone. I'd seen flashes of this gravestone but never saw it clearly till I did. It was my gravestone. Camille Van der Bilt, 1990-2003. It was beautiful.'

'Marble or alabaster?'

'Got to be alabaster, don't you think?'

'Always.'

'My parents didn't ignore me because I did something wrong. I wasn't there. I was a ghost.'

Salvador squeezed her hand and sand squeezed through her fingers.

'I don't live in New York do I? I'm not a lecturer at NYU.'

'I don't think so, Scrunchie.'

'When you tried to snag the beers that time, it's what you shouted as you ran past. "All I gotta do is jump, Scrunchie, take off. I bet I can fly". The last dream I had before seeing you here, I was that bird again but this time I did take off and I did fly. It was beautiful, looking down at everything all busy down there, so peaceful up here, just the wind around me, totally in control. Then I was here on the beach with you. Ever since I got here I've still been feeling like I'm flying. It's wonderful.'

Camille looked over at Salvador.

'I always knew I was here for a reason,' she said. 'Just didn't know what it was. But it was you, to help you.'

'You did Scrunchie, you did,' said Salvador. 'You helped me get that asshole, the asshole who took you. You led me to Jemma in the old town, we figured out our signs and I got where I needed to get. You gave me the love I needed to finish. You helped me save little Ashlen.'

'You were here for me too,' she said. 'When I'm with you I feel like I'll never be alone. I don't know how, just you being here told me I'd never be alone, you'd never leave me. Because of you, I know I never will.'

'I love you, Scrunchie.'

'I love you too. Don't be frightened, Salvador. I love you. Is this the last moment of my existence?' And with that, Camille was gone from this beach, her hand print still in the sand underneath Salvador's. He looked back out to sea. That boat had vanished round the point. His tears were silent at first. He felt his demons stir again but before they could birth themselves from him and start their attack, he noticed something else.

Over to the right behind him, there was the familiar sound of a metal tipped cane on a stone floor. This time, the sound merged with the sounds of the beach and became people talking and then there was a flash, a lightning strike out to sea. He was blind to anything on this beach. He could still hear people talking near him but he couldn't see them.

The sounds changed and his vision started to clear. Together, they clarified themselves to be a hospital room. The sanitized smell came late but come it did. It was still mostly a blur but Salvador realized he was floating high up near the ceiling in this room.

There was a bed by the window. Had he been jumped to one final destination, the cruelest of all destinations? Was he looking at Jemma's aftermath in that bed in the early hours of this morning?

His eyes finally rebooted but brought him a vision of horror unlike anything he could imagine.

He remembered Camille on the beach. 'Don't be frightened,' she said.

She knew. She meant this.

It wasn't Jemma in this hospital bed. It was Salvador.

Jemma was there in the room with her hand over her mouth. She was crying. Dr. Ramirez and Angel the nurse were there as well. Salvador couldn't pick up what they were saying but he knew what this moment was.

This was the moment he dreaded when Jemma was lying there, whispers, glances, soothing hands on shoulders and movement towards the machines. This was the moment to be switched off, the moment it all stops, commit your memory to the rest of humanity and hope it's been of some worth.

Ramirez looked up at the clock on the wall.

'Six o'clock. It's time.'

Then Salvador heard the clicking cane of the man coming down the corridor outside. He saw the demon enter the room. No-one else saw him. He approached to stand beside Salvador's bed.

Angel brought Jemma over to the other side of the bed and held her as she looked down on him. She was drawn, exhausted, unable to summon the energy to surface what was inside her. That would emerge later. She leaned down and kissed him on the forehead and wrapped her arms around him.

As soon as she did, Salvador was on the bed and felt Jemma's touch for the last time. He couldn't open his eyes and he couldn't move. She whispered 'Can you hear me? Can you hear me, Baby? I love you so much. I'm sorry. Good bye Baby,' in his ear and kissed him on the neck. Salvador just wanted to tell her 'I'm OK, Baby, here I am,' but he couldn't.

Salvador could also feel the demon standing over him on the other side, taking all his light, but Salvador saw a different figure than before. The demon's eyes weren't the burnt orange evil of the old town or the hollow lasers of the Pepsi shop.

Every time he'd experienced this demon he'd been terrified but drawn to him, he couldn't help it. He felt the same now. He wanted to go to him again here but this time he knew why. He didn't feel fear. He felt pure love, for Jemma, for Camille, for Ashlen, for all the people he'd ever loved. This demon wasn't a demon anymore. All he wanted was to become part of him, a drowning man touching the surface, taking that hand. He was welcoming Salvador to become part of him as his wings unwrapped themselves.

There was no time to feel the fear of seeing himself die, the panic of struggling for what happens next, that didn't have time to materialize. His mind was filled with the greatest love. This was the moment he was here for. It's the only moment any of us are here for, a euphoric finality. Would he simply cease to be as instantly as the machine's power or would his soul take a while to finally check out?

Ramirez put his finger on the button and turned to Jemma for the final authority. Jemma obliged. Salvador's breathing stopped, a machine flatlined and Angel quickly turned the sound off, leaving a quiet in the room apart from the rub of Angel's hand on Jemma's back.

Salvador was gathered up off the bed into his wings. They felt warm and safe, cocooned in fur blankets and the sweet smells of Jemma. Salvador was back on the beach that day with his Jemma. He turned to her and took her warm hand for the last time and looked at her. She was happy. She'd saved her little Ashlen.

The angel looked up and closed his eyes.

Salvador hit the wall hard from the rooftop, too much

bounce, he scraped and scrambled for substance but it was too late. He lost his grip on the edge. As he fell, he saw a couple of them looking down on him and Salvador smiled right back.

Ever so gradually the angel and Salvador became the light green color of the wall behind them and they were gone.

About three months ago, Salvador pulled his car up at this hotel about twenty miles away for a meeting. Yuki wanted him to meet his investors. They wanted bona fide horse's mouth testament to what they were doing. Salvador hated meetings. He hated getting dressed properly and trying to equate dollars to the adrenalin of creating stuff. He understood there was that equation and he knew what they were doing worked. Yuki said, just make everybody feel warm and fuzzy. Fine, he can cuddle.

Morres charged back into his office to pick up the call that's been making noise for many seconds. Rachel confirmed that was the hospital, the headshot had died, 6pm last night.

Morres just got his lifer the chair. Pelican Bay prison needs to mention to the idiot locked up that attempted murder had become murder at 6pm last night. He's now going to see the inside of a chamber.

The idiot in that cell in Pelican Bay had shot someone under the gaze of at least four security cameras and then escaped in his own van. It was difficult to remember a quicker route to trial or a quicker trial.

This idiot had spied Salvador's mustang and waited for its owner to show up. It was to be a murder for a matter of sixty three bucks and a phone.

The meeting had all gone well but took a few hours and it was dark when Salvador hit the car park. Yuki and he would meet in La Mesa for a bottle or two to celebrate whatever just happened. Salvador's car was the only one left in the car park apart from this van, which had parked in the spot right next to his. By the time he got to the car, there was enough room to squeeze down the drivers side and get in without smashing the door up but he did mention in dispatches that the van's owner was a dick.

He was wedged between his open door and the side of the van and then the van's side door slid open and revealed a man in a ninja mask who was soon holding a sawn off shotgun to his head.

One security camera had a perfect line of sight to it and showed this moment quickly followed by an unexpected blast from the gun, Salvador falling onto the floor between car and van and the guy looking very surprised. This idiot had misfired, the police thought, although they hadn't got a word out of him at Pelican Bay.

The next thing Salvador remembered was being in a battle somewhere.

Rachel came in with a couple of coffees. Morres had known from the moment Salvador walked into this office that day that he was a ghost. He knew all about him. Morres was first to attend the scene, escorted him to hospital. The day he saw him, as far as he knew, he was still long term coma, yet there he stood in front of him. This ghost had given him something. He'll never forget it but he'll also never reveal it.

The idiot who murdered Salvador was a closed file, to be opened soon only to update his sentence. The file on Ashlen was definitely not closed. That would stay open till they found her. In three days they'll hopefully get hold of this sprayer guy at the school and who knows maybe even find Ashlen. Nothing else occupied him.

The door opened slowly and Jemma oozed through it. She hovered at the threshold for a moment, scanning around her and finally settling on the hallway floor and its steps. She might just have managed a subconscious smile but her mind didn't yet know why. She gave the door a gentle shove and it clicked shut without fuss.

She wanted the door closed to the world, she never wanted to be out there again. She'd have a coffee with lots of brandy in it and sit alone. The logistics of the funeral and which sandwiches to provide at the wake were yet to be registered.

Instead she was filled up with all the things her and Salvador had said and done here. Every step, every glance, every time he used to trip up that step. She was waiting for whatever was to be the central player in her mind next to show itself. She knew it would be lurking somewhere, ready to jump out and stick its claws into her. She'd already surrendered to the inevitability of losing it, she just didn't know when it would start.

Her and Salvador found this house together. Their emails crossed with the link to it. They knew it was the place. The paint fight in bedroom two, when they were so sure they'd have at least one squeaking occupant for it. They'd agreed on the color, this shade of light green and the room was set for its makeover.

It was stripped back to its floorboards, cracks had been filled. It was a simple task of applying paint. But the room found it was dealing with the Salvador and Jemma from the sixth grade. Jemma may have mentioned to Salvador in passing that he might like to apply some actual paint to the roller or did he just prefer painting the wall with air and roller fluff?

He did apply more paint to his roller and then he rolled that roller up the bridge of her nose and created primal native warrior woman. He said afterwards, her standing there in her overalls, striped with green paint, that was one of those bomb moments, he called them. He always told her when he had a bomb moment. It was when he realized he loved her even more than the moment before it.

The room found it got painted far quicker than it had imagined. There was a paint fight the likes of which only a game show called Paint Fight' could match. They'd masked off the windows with old newspapers but every other surface available was now green including the ceiling, floors and both painters.

Once they'd finished cracking up laughing and got to their feet, they saw the truth of it. Any part of the room that wasn't already covered in this sunny green soon was.

It was a gorgeous green haven. The shared shower that followed made it the perfect job. Salvador would apply a hard clear varnish to the floor another day but here they'd created a new green womb for a tiny person that would alas never be in it.

Jemma knew she couldn't stay here. Through no fault of its own, this house had provided wonderful memories and, in so doing, had alienated her.

After the funeral arrangements, it would be the machinery of real estate and Escrow. She didn't want to be here without her Salvador, without her Boogie. The laws of healing demanded some dedicated change to the norm in sync with the change that was forced on her.

She was alone and he was gone. She knew at this moment she'd pack a bag and leave for her mom's place before nightfall. Iris at the school had insisted, 'As much time as you need, darling,' long before today played its final hand. The thought of returning to a world of smiles and chinking glasses made Jemma nauseous.

She needed to clear her head completely. With little more sentience that the coffee machine, she made her coffee, reached for the brandy, she made sure her hand skimmed Salvador's bottle of bourbon, and made herself what she hoped would start to put her brain to sleep.

She took her brandy coffee through to the den and lay back on the big couch opposite the fire. She was unable to sense any relief in the room but she knew no room could offer her that. Even her mom's house would have memories but her mom would play her part and the hugs would start her release. She wished her dad was still around.

She did sense Salvador in this room though and almost said, 'Baby are you there?' but pulled herself back. She wondered if she should start stimulating her own torture quite yet, bring in the horror, get the bad joojoo over and done with so healing can begin. She knew that horror would come soon enough on its own so why wait for it to jump out from behind a curtain at her? Take the lead and ruin its fun?

The dried tears carried from the hospital still covered her cheeks. She didn't want to wash them off. She saw Salvador's cellphone on the little table in the corner. She'd kept it charged all this time and she took it to the hospital every day so she could give it to him when he wakes up.

She dialed a number she knew so well and, over on that little table, Salvador's cell phone rang. She needed to do this, a deliberate blackening of her grief, a tactic to lessen it, a stomach pump to remove the poison. She knew he wouldn't physically answer but his voicemail would and she'd hear his voice again. If by the most remote chance her last few months had been just a horrible dream, maybe he'd just pick up and say, 'Hey Wiggle, what's up?'

She just needed to hear his voice and engage in an organized emotional disintegration. It would start here and now under her own control. She dialed and folded her hair around her ear as she held her phone up against it. As Salvador's voicemail started to play, in came her demons.

She collapsed her head into her hands, allowing the hollow silence after Salvador's message to persist until it stopped. She dropped the phone to the floor and, for the first time since the shooting, she surrendered her strength and let herself feel the twisting.

She didn't remember at which point she'd succumbed to sleep but she had. It was dark outside and the brandy coffee sat cold and lifeless on the table in front of her.

She felt different. Had she released some part of this poison or was she yet to fully arrive from sleep? She looked around the room as if she was looking for something but she had no idea what. Then finally she did. Her dream.

Her dream was filled with him. It was a succession of micro dreams, dreams that released her into the world of the man she loved more than life. As she sat quietly here on this couch recalling the dreams, she knew her unraveling had begun but she told that to fuck off. She would take every last sense of her time with her Salvador until she finally succumbed.

First she remembered being in a hospital bed. There he was. She felt like she was there. It was so real. She could almost reach out and touch his silly nose but for some reason she couldn't move. Salvador was chatting to her about the strangest things. He was looking for clues to something. He was saying he was trying to save her. She knew that look, he was in pain but trying to smile through it. He was wrapping her up there on that bed. He felt so warm, she could feel his arms around her, feel his breath on her neck. Why was he trying to save her, from what?

Then suddenly the two of them were in the old town. That wonderful sunny day when they bought her favorite dress. God, that dress, he couldn't keep his hands off it, the filthy little urchin.

She opened the curtain to show him the dress and there he was, sitting there looking at her. She could smell the shop and hear the conversation die down around them. The way he'd looked at her.

When he wrapped her up and kissed her, the world around them came to a stop and she never ever wanted to move from that moment. Another smile came over her when she remembered their adolescent middle finger medley outside Triskell and a warmth joined the smile when she felt the passion bubbling up, the need to get home and get naked. She could feel her hand stroke through Salvador's hair as she went inside.

She could feel him inside her. It was beautiful.

Then she saw Salvador standing over her in front of a big fire. There were other people there and they were all looking at her. She tried to reach out and take his hand but again she couldn't move. He was saying something to her. 'Be brave, come back to me,' he said. 'Come back from where, Baby, I'm right here?' she said, but he couldn't hear. Then she was wet and there was a little monkey jumping around in a tree, a little Marmoset monkey, Salvador when he was pleased with himself.

Next, she was watching her baby sleep, just looking at him. He looked so peaceful, like a child with his eyebrows and silly nose. She wanted to wake him up. She asked him 'Can you hear me?' a few times till he opened his eyes and smiled like he always did at her, first thing. She needed to say goodbye to him but she didn't know where she was going.

That argument they had one night in the kitchen. That time she told him to stop whining and do something. The Yellow Brick Road movie. She felt the guilt all over again on this couch. How could she have done that to him, his little monkey face all sad she'd shouted at him.

Her next dream installment came into focus. She was sitting on the table at the back of the den, reading. Salvador was watching home movies for some reason, this one was that day they spent at Coronado beach. She'd never seen this movie but the day was still fresh in her mind.

She felt like she was there, smelling the sea, laughing and clapping as Salvador bombed into the sea like a teenager, lying on the sand with wine and tickles.

She got the strangest feeling the ghost of Salvador she felt in this room was even closer now. Maybe he was actually sitting on this couch next to her. She ran her hand over the cushion.

The way Salvador filmed things. He always tried to insert abstract stuff right in the middle of filming something, like a palm tree on its side or a close up of two lizards chatting would be some kind of creative masterpiece.

Then it was that big old blue car and that asshole dad shouting at his daughter just before she and Salvador left the beach. She didn't see who it was on the day, just a glance, but now she did. It was little Ashlen from school. Jemma's tears rose up when she saw her little Ashlen. But that wasn't Ashlen's dad. She knew Ashlen's dad.

Jemma sat up. She didn't need her dream any more. She

looked over at the TV remote control on top of the speaker, took it and cued up Coronado.

Detective Morres sat quietly at his desk, trying to turn three days into none and then his phone rang.

"The average human mind, in times of great danger, can perform incredible feats to ensure self preservation. A great human mind can perform incredible feats for the preservation of others"

Anon

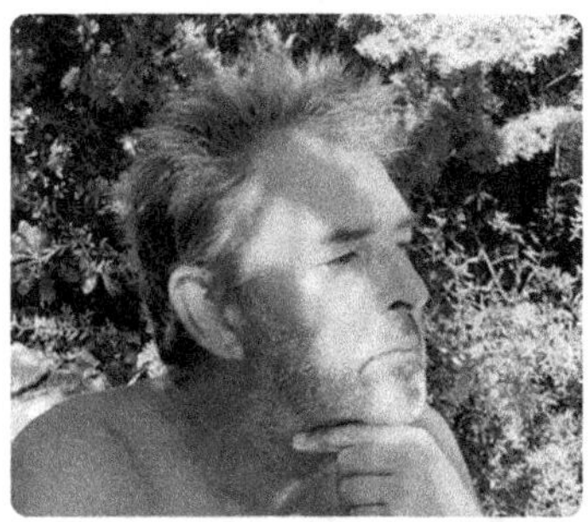

Dominic Schunker was born in London and currently lives up a mountain in Javea, Spain. He has a very small German Shepherd puppy called Poppy.

Dominic's fiction encompasses ghosts, time travel, aliens, demons, nasty fat corporations, conspiracies and God, and is based on the right of every human being to become randomly haunted and taken to the limit of their sanity.

An Unfortunate Dimension is his debut novel and bears a close resemblance to a testing period in his life, a period that changed his perception of our world.

One day, good will prevail over evil.

Machine Sense is the second novel by author, Dominic Schunker, and is due for release in Spring 2019.

Zak sees things change that no-one else does. His best buddy suddenly became someone he'd never met, president Garfield is now president Valdez. Something is screwing up the timeline. To everybody else though its always been as it is. He's been alone with this since he was a teenager but then he meets Allie, someone else who sees the same changes. Her mum does as well and it seems his daughter, Izzy is showing signs of seeing the changes too.

There follows a tale of nazis, reverse engineered alien spacecraft, Auschwitz experiments and alien/human hybrids with eyes that change from green to blue for no apparent reason. They discover this is not a random universal glitch, someone is changing the timeline to benefit themselves and what's worse, they're targeting people whose eyes change like Izzy. Things just got very real for Zak.

www.offworldpublishing.com

Don't miss out.

You can sign up to receive emails whenever Dominic Schunker publishes a new book.

Visit www.offworldpublishing.com to subscribe.

There's no charge and no obligation.

Offworld Publishing does not distribute subscriber contact details to any third party.